ESSENCE OF RUIN

VOLUME ONE

BY

ALEC LOWNES

Essence of Ruin
Volume One

ISBN (print): 979-8-88993-063-1
ISBN (e-book): 979-8-88993-062-4

Edited by Kirsten Lund
Cover by Huu Ha
Interior Design by Tangcu LLC

Published 2025 by MoonQuill®
Arlington, VA

www.moonquill.com

Table of Contents

Chapter 1

The caravan's wheels clacked against the rough stones of the seldom used path as Willow watched her town, her home, and everyone she knew recede into the distance. While sitting on her wooden bench, she gripped an iron cane tightly between her hands, hard enough that her muscles began to ache. She willed herself not to cry. Not now. Maybe later, but not now.

There were others in the covered wagon—two elderly men, a middle-aged woman, and a young man around her age. He sat on the other side of the cart, surreptitiously glancing at her every few seconds. She tugged her sleeves down to cover her wrists where they'd ridden up and tried to ignore him as the caravan trundled on.

The small village of Bridgewater was almost lost in the dust haze on the horizon, and Willow became painfully aware that this was the farthest she'd ever been from home. The wilds were dangerous, and she'd never been well enough to venture outside of town.

The young man glanced again. He looked away when they were all jostled as the wagon went over a particularly large stone. Willow groaned at the impact and tried to find a more comfortable position on her folded cloak. Her muscles ached as they always did, but now her back joined the symphony of pain, courtesy of the caravan's incessant rumbling. And she was bone-tired from all the packing—physical activity like that sapped her completely. How many more miles would it be until they stopped to rest?

"Hey, um. Excuse me," the young man from across the wagon said.

Willow's grip tightened on the iron cane, her thoughts immediately going to the bag at her feet and the small fortune it contained. He'd already been in the caravan when it stopped in Bridgewater—she didn't know anything about him.

"Yes?" Willow asked. She reluctantly met his gaze as she shuffled her heels so they came in contact with the heavy bag.

It had battered her spine something terrible as she carried it into the wagon, even with the gold coins padded within layers upon layers of clothing. It was all the money she'd have for tuition and lodgings for two years. As for food, well, she'd need to find some other gainful employment once she reached the city, although who'd want to hire her, she had no idea. But she'd find something. She had to.

"I don't mean to be rude, but I noticed we're of the same age," he said, adjusting his glasses.

He had short, sandy blonde hair and a slightly round face, which spoke of a comfortable, pampered life. Hers would be round like that, too, if it weren't for her condition. If his clothing was any indication—a fine leather vest over a white linen shirt and light canvas pants—they probably had more in common than not. Her family had been one of the few in her village who had been able to afford clothing like that from the traveling caravans.

While it had been a tall order to tailor her travel wear to hide the strangest aspects of her physique, the cut of *his* clothes actually made him look good. Her eyes lingered as she considered the fact that he was the first man she'd met in years who didn't already know enough about her to look on her with pity and revulsion. It had been impossible, *impossible*, in Bridgewater to make friends with a story like that—not to mention making anything more than friends.

Shit, how long had she been staring at him?

"And?" Willow asked, unsure of where the conversation was leading.

"Well, I was wondering if you were also seeking entrance at the Arcanum."

She looked more closely. There was a large bag tucked under his bench seat, wedged between his feet. A cloak was also stuffed under his backside, as hers was, to cushion the rough ride. It was a fine cloak, too.

Like hers.

"I am," she said, her usual caution overcome by a brief flash of excitement. He'd said *also*, hadn't he?

His face cracked with a smile, and he leaned forwards, hand outstretched. "Leopold."

"Willow," she said, and he grasped her hand. She winced as his handshake pressed her swollen knuckles together, and his face transformed from excitement to shock as he released her.

"Oh no, I'm sorry," he said.

Willow withdrew her hand and lightly massaged the fascia between the knuckles.

"No, it's no problem." His gaze flashed to her hands, and she quickly folded her arms, tucking her hands into her armpits to hide them from view. "You're going to the Arcanum?" she asked, desperate to get his mind off of what he might have seen. The pain in her hand had almost faded. She knew he hadn't left a bruise—there wasn't much of her *to* bruise.

"Um, yeah. Yeah, I am. Hoping to," he said and smiled shyly.

"Well, I hope we both have luck," she said, returning the smile. Then she quickly turned towards the back of the wagon before he caught her eye. Was she flirting? By the gods, why? Hadn't she learned enough of humiliation and embarrassment back home?

"But you've been practicing for the entrance exams, haven't you?" He leaned forwards, excitement saturating his voice. "If you're going to the Arcanum?"

Willow dodged. "It would be foolish to attempt entry if you hadn't."

"Can I see? I've never seen anyone else work real Arcanum spells. All anyone does in my town are the farming ones."

Willow's mouth dropped slightly. "Um, I..." She searched for an excuse. "I just got on. I'm a bit tired from the—"

"Just a simple magelight then," he said, nearly jumping with energy.

Willow glanced back and saw the other passengers in the wagon, all watching them. Whether she liked it or not, she had an audience.

Oh, what the hell. Simple magelight, indeed.

Willow sighed and nervously brought her hands up in the spellform: an open bowl, fingers pointed inwards. All eyes went to her strangely shaped hands. She closed her eyes and tried to forget the stares, exhaling a long breath to get her mind right for the casting. She started in on the spell.

"Blazing light," she intoned like a mantra, over and over.

She could feel the essence in her body respond sluggishly to her visualizations, creeping through her arms and down her hands. As the essence emerged from her fingertips, she concentrated on influencing its concept to that of blazing light. The structure she made with her cupped hands provided the scaffold for the essence's behavior: condensing inwards, releasing its blazing light.

As she repeated the intoned concept over and over, between her cupped palms appeared a pale spark. It grew slowly until it hovered at just over the size of a copper and emitted a faint but discernible light.

Then she passed some interior threshold, and the exertion was just too much. With a gasp, she dropped her hands, and the ball of essence boiled away in an instant. The exertion had left her weak and shaky like she'd been wrung out. Willow leaned her head back against the clattering wood of the wagon arch and let out a breath.

"Ah," she said. "There, magelight."

There was silence in the cart. She opened her eyes to find everyone looking away, suddenly engrossed in their own business. Even Leopold was looking at his feet. He almost seemed embarrassed.

"Well, let's see yours," Willow prodded, suddenly annoyed as heat burned her ears.

He'd had the gall to ask her to demonstrate magic and wouldn't even meet her eye! They were both going to the same place, trying to get into the same school. He wasn't any better than her.

Except, as the twisting sense of dread in her gut whispered, he would be.

"Maybe I'll make a flame," Leopold suggested, and Willow shook her head.

"Let's see your magelight," she persisted, knowing full well the catastrophe she was walking into. But she couldn't stand his pity. That was worse than what she feared—what she knew—was about to happen.

He sighed. She watched as he assumed the same spell-form with his hands and repeated the words.

"Blazing light."

With each repetition, the sphere of essence between his palms grew in size and intensity. It lit up the covered wagon brighter than the sun outside within seconds. A few moments more made it nearly impossible to look at.

He aborted the spell, and the sphere of essence boiled away. He wasn't watching Willow—in fact, he was looking out of the back of the wagon again and away from her. For a moment, Willow felt a surge of anger and humiliation.

"Impressive," she forced out, biting off a more colorful epithet. He didn't deserve that. It wasn't his fault she was a freak. "You should do well at the Arcanum. How long have you been practicing?"

Leopold shook his head, then closed his eyes. "A couple weeks. It was my first spell."

Willow had been working on the same spell for the last five years.

Chapter 2

Willow spent the rest of the ride that first day in abject misery and humiliation. She'd known that she wasn't very good at spellwork, that it came harder to her than it should. The spellbooks her father had procured from his merchant contacts in far-off cities had spoken of advanced spells and concepts. But after years of effort, she was still stuck on the very first practice spell. Yes, it was initially supposed to be hard to get your essence to move in response to your will, to imbue it with a concept for the first time—but it wasn't supposed to be this hard.

Her spellwork primer hadn't said how long it should take to learn the first spell. Willow had naively assumed, no hoped, that even if she was a little behind, she'd be able to catch up with proper instruction at the Arcanum.

She should have known how desperately behind she was. She'd ignored the signs, and now... Well, she could always work harder, if such a thing was possible. The sun approached the horizon, and the caravan rolled to a stop in a large meadow. Waist-high grass caught the caravan's shadow like stripes of night in a golden thicket. The guard, who she learned was named Bryan, came around and told them to unload for the night.

They'd be sleeping under the stars.

After a whispered conversation between Bryan and Leopold, she heard the young man recite the spell concept again. The circled wagons were soon illuminated with a blazing ball of essence. He lifted it high into the air, incanted a concept of steadfastness, and lowered his hands. The ball stayed hovering above them, casting bright yellow light on the still grass.

He wasn't even at the Arcanum, and he could already do concept addition. Willow was so fucked.

She laid out the provided bedroll in silence, smoothing it on the springy grass. Then, to her surprise, Leopold laid his roll down nearby and walked over.

"Hey," he said.

"Nice work," she said, trying to affect a cheery tone but finding it about as hard as casting her own magelight.

"T-Thanks," he said, and she finally looked up at his face.

He was nervous. No, not nervous. Embarrassed.

"I can feel sorry all by myself, you know. You don't need to join in."

"Ah, um." He glanced around, then sat down next to her bedroll on the trampled wild grass. The crushed, sticky shoots gave off the tangy smell of juniper.

And now Willow felt like an ass.

"Sorry, that's not fair. It's not your fault that I'm…"

"What?" he asked, leaning forwards.

"So… bad at magic. Just so bad."

"You'll get better with time. I bet you can get your spell brighter by the end of the trip if you practice. How long have you been at it? A couple days?"

"No," she said and left it at that, the finality ringing like a bell.

They sat in silence for a moment, both looking at the hovering magelight before he turned back to her again.

"What happened to you?" he blurted out, and she almost blushed. Then she laughed nervously.

"I've never had someone ask. Everyone just knew back home. I got sick as a baby, I almost died. Afterwards, well..." Feigning nonchalance, she held out her arm and pushed the gathering cloth up to her elbow as she held her breath, waiting for his response.

Leopold gasped, and she winced.

"You're starving?"

"It's not about how much I eat," she said, lowering the sleeve over her nearly skeletal arm. "I have a healthy appetite, as I'm sure you'll see, but it doesn't matter. No matter how much I eat, I waste away. And... I hurt."

"A lot?" he asked.

She shrugged. "All the time."

Heavy footfalls announced the guard, Bryan, making his way over for his rounds. Willow was relieved as he approached, blotting out the bright magelight. She'd spoken many times about her condition with her mother, but there was something terribly different about discussing it with Leopold. Embarrassing, maybe. She didn't want him to think she was a freak.

"I heard we've got two mages in this wagon," Bryan said with a smile. He still had his armor on, and from the way the metal plates moved, Willow could tell he was heavily muscled underneath. What little hair he had was dark and clipped short above his strong brow.

"Prospective mages," Leopold corrected and gestured up at the magelight. "I can only impart two concepts at the moment."

"Well, don't worry. I won't ask you to defend the caravan. I've got that all taken care of." Bryan patted the sword at his hip with obvious glee.

Leopold shifted nervously. "What about when we get closer to Durum? I heard there's a warbeast…"

"We'll be using the warded tunnels," Bryan said. "They start way out beyond the warbeast's territory and keep us shielded and cloaked the whole way through. If not for them, the whole city would starve. You don't have anything to worry about."

Bryan looked down at Willow, and she felt his eyes rake along her body. Her clothes were well-tailored, but there was only so much you could do to hide the effects of wasting. Hurt and shame colored her cheeks. She looked away.

"And how are you holding up? Have you found the wagon comfortable?"

"Comfortable enough," Willow bit off.

"And sleeping on the ground, will that be alright for you? Or do you need to sleep in the wagon?"

"The ground is fine," she said, even as she began to bristle. She had to remind herself that he didn't know her—no one outside of Bridgewater did. They wouldn't know that, despite appearances, she wasn't entirely decrepit.

"Alright, well…" He glanced around, then saw her cane propped up against the side of the wagon. Striding over, he picked it up and hesitated. "What the hell?" he exclaimed as he hefted it.

Despite her discomfort, Willow couldn't help but laugh. "It's just my cane."

"It must weigh almost ten pounds." He swung it experimentally through the air, splitting the gathering mist. "Solid iron," he said, almost in awe as he handed it to Willow. "Why would you have a cane made out of solid iron?"

"My father thought it would help to strengthen my arms." She shrugged, smugly, as if hauling the weighted cane were nothing. "Didn't really work, but it seemed like a waste to get a new one."

"Right," he said with a note of doubt in his voice, then he glanced further along the circle. "Well, you two stay in the circle of wagons during the night. No telling what's out there in the grass. We'll get the fire started in a jiffy, and it'll keep most things away until morning. And holler if you need anything."

They thanked Bryan, and he went on to converse with the next reclined passenger. Leopold glanced at Willow's cane.

"May I?"

She handed it over and he hefted it as Bryan had.

"Shit, it really is solid iron."

CHAPTER 3

Days in the wagon train blended together as they crossed from waving grassland to thick deciduous forest. Wide tracks had been worn in the forest floor by wagon trains that roamed between villages, tamping down saplings and keeping the ground bare. The trees made Willow feel claustrophobic in a way she'd never experienced in Bridgewater.

It was the first time she'd seen a forest.

The routine of the journey asserted itself aggressively and became aggressively boring by the third day. By the fifth, she felt as if she were in a waking stupor as she stared through the back of the wagon at the endless trees receding along the worn ruts. Sometimes she'd see a squirrel in the brush, or more rarely a deer. Once she saw a flash of flame from beside a creek.

"Did you see that?" she asked Leopold, but of course he hadn't.

As usual, he was nose-deep in an introductory magic text. He didn't seem affected by the nausea which afflicted Willow the moment she opened her own books on the rocking caravan.

"What? No," he said, tilting his head back and pushing his glasses up his nose.

Willow pointed into the foliage, but the flame didn't appear again. "I thought I saw a salamander," she said.

"Really?" And just like that, she had his attention.

Magical creatures were rare around human habitations, and most of those that got too close were the dangerous variety. Willow had never seen a wild magical creature alive before.

"Fire, near the stream. I can't think of what else it could've been."

"I wonder if they'd stop the caravan, let us try to catch it. I heard they give you a boost in essence if you eat them."

Willow knew an offer of help when she heard one. There was no pity in it, which she appreciated—he was trying to be thoughtful, though she became uncomfortable at this reminder of their gap in ability. When he wasn't reading up on magic theory, he practiced his spells, but Willow just didn't have that kind of energy to spare. Not with how strenuous keeping herself upright in the wobbling wagon proved to be. She barely had enough in her by the end of the day to practice her waning magelight a couple of times before she went to sleep. And even then, the effort did more to exhaust her into unconsciousness than it did to enhance her casting ability.

"Stop the whole caravan for one salamander? I doubt it. Can you imagine Bryan pacing while you hunted in the brush?"

"No, I suppose not," he smiled.

Despite their rocky start, they had become, if not friends, then close acquaintances during the journey. There wasn't a lot they had in common with any of the other passengers, but they both had an interest in magic.

Later that day, the wagon train broke through the edge of the deciduous forest to a wide-open plain. The raggedy perimeter of trees seemed almost lonely as the plains grass swallowed the world; the horizon expanding until its furthest features were lost in a haze of distance.

"We must be getting close," Willow said, rubbing her thumb along the metal of her cane. "Durum is supposed to be located on a vast scarred plain. The warbeast tears anything up within a mile of the city, apparently."

Leopold looked up from his book again and leaned out the back of the wagon to survey the countryside. "You don't think it's out here, do you?"

"Bryan said it wasn't." Willow suppressed a smirk.

Leopold was strangely afraid of the warbeasts. Willow herself found the idea of them so inconceivable as to render fear moot. Creatures created in war whose size and destructive ability challenged even the defensive might of the walled cities. Those left alive after the war they were birthed for usually proved to be the prowling type, seldom attacking the walls themselves. They were created to keep up a never-ending siege against an enemy that had long since become their masters' friend.

Constructing and maintaining the warded tunnels was cheaper than attacking and destroying the beasts directly by using the city's offensive measures.

When the caravan stopped near dusk, Willow and Leopold disembarked and finally took in the surrounding countryside as they set up camp.

"You see there?" Bryan pointed off into the distance.

He'd just gotten the wagons circled, and Leopold was casting the sustained magelight that would last them partway through the night—allowing the caravan to conserve its store of firewood.

Willow didn't have the best eyesight in the world, but she thought she could just make out something dark on the horizon near the tip of Bryan's finger.

"That's Durum. You'll be able to see it better in the dark. There are lights atop the walls brighter than stars."

"Can you see the warbeast from here?" Willow asked, thinking of Leopold.

"No, you needn't worry about that. Chances are we won't even catch a glimpse of it. Its territory is so vast that it probably won't even be in sight line while we're within the tunnel. I've seen it once, though. It's not an experience I'd like to repeat."

"What did it look like?" Willow asked.

Bryan had taken on a strangely paternal role towards herself and Leopold during the journey, and she wondered if he had a child back at home he was missing.

"Like a dog, I suppose. A dead dog. You could see its skull, and it had these things coming off its body. Like tendrils or snakes. They writhed on the ground, slipping this way and that. Slid right over the tunnel while we were going through—I think it was looking for us. I think it knows the tunnel is there, but it can't get in. I wonder... I wonder how it feels about that."

From its description, Willow wondered if it felt anything at all. Magical beasts were much like any other kind of animal, but warbeasts were usually driven insane by their creators to better harry their targets. Over time, that insanity abated, resulting in the prowling warbeasts.

Willow was still trying to make out the shape of Durum in the distance when a flicker of movement closer at hand caught her eye. She pointed.

"What's that?"

Bryan narrowed his eyes. The setting sun cast the world in a golden hue, but soon enough it would be too dark to see anything outside their circle of wagons.

"Huh, looks like a deathworm."

"Deathworm? Is it dangerous?"

Bryan shook his head. "No, not dangerous. I've never heard of one approaching a caravan. They're pretty rare, it's the first time I've seen one. But they're cowards. Big, soft tubes of meat, they wouldn't attack a caravan. Too dangerous. They go after smaller magical creatures, things that wouldn't have any defenses against them. You don't have to worry."

"Right," Willow said but found it difficult to turn away from the undulating speck in the distance. It felt like a threat to her, no matter how cowardly it was supposed to be.

Willow woke suddenly in the darkness, thrust out of a dreamless sleep. The bonfire at the center of the wagon train was still crackling merrily. In the circled wagons, she couldn't tell what had woken her. She shifted her weight around—a root of some kind was digging into her spine—and turned her head towards the flames.

Leopold was sleeping a few paces away, his mouth slightly open. He was strangely endearing, and she briefly entertained a fantasy of what might happen if they both got into the Arcanum. He could be someone who saw her, not as an invalid, but as a fellow student. They could be equals. Friends.

If she was admitted at all. The familiar worry began to gnaw at her stomach, and she thought that it had probably been what disturbed her sleep. The endlessly circling worries about what would happen when she finally arrived at the Arcanum, and they tested her for admission. Why had she thought she could do this? What other choice had she had? It was impossible to imagine life as a mundane invalid back at home. It was also impossible to imagine it as a mage.

A clanking came from the darkness, and Willow turned her head to see Bryan pass within the circle of wagons. He scanned the sleepers, found her watching eyes, and smiled.

"Just a tremor, go back to sleep," he said.

"A what?"

The earth buckled under her body and threw her a good three feet towards the fire. Willow screamed and she heard Bryan shout from what seemed like far away. The metallic clank of an impact cut short his yell.

"Ugh! Wha—"

Leopold startled awake, tangled in his bedroll. Willow glanced around and saw the most disturbing thing she'd ever laid eyes upon.

The ground was *moving*. It heaved upwards like the surface of a lake in a storm, then sucked back down again as if there was something burrowing just under the surface. The roiling earth made no sound, but as the wave slid through the circle of wagons, other sleepers were awoken by the jostling and began to scream.

"What the hell? What the hell," Leopold stammered as Willow crawled along the upturned earth towards him and began ripping at his bedroll. She ached all over from being rolled on the ground, and her hands were bruised from the quick jerking she was giving the blanket, but she managed to disentangle Leopold.

"I don't know," she said. "Bryan—"

She turned and saw their guard slumped against a wagon wheel. Was he dead? Had he been killed by whatever the thing was that had moved under the camp?

"We have to get Bryan," she said. Then the strained wooden creaking of a wagon across the circle caught her attention and made her turn.

Sure enough, the line of wagons on the other side of the fire was rising as whatever it was came back at them. Leopold pulled her up and they reached Bryan just as the central fire was scattered by the thing underground.

"Bryan? Bryan!" Willow shouted, shaking him by the breastplate. It was light steel, barely thicker than paper, and probably meant only to deflect claws and teeth. There was no way it could hold up against whatever it was that was coming.

"Bryan!"

"He's breathing," Leopold said, his ear in front of Bryan's mouth. "He's alive."

Suddenly, the splitting, snapping sound of rending earth filled the air. Willow and Leopold turned towards the fire to see a rent forming in the ground between them and the scattered coals—a chasm ten feet long and widening by the second. The sounds of tearing roots filled the darkening night like a roar.

Then, as if things couldn't get any worse, from the cracked earth rose a tubular *thing*. It was at least six feet wide, no telling how long, and its head ended abruptly at a puckered star which looked almost like an anus.

"His sword. Where's his sword?" Willow turned back to Bryan and scrambled at his side, but the sword was gone. Thrown, probably as Bryan was incapacitated. On the ground though, beside his unconscious body, was Willow's cane.

"Blazing inferno, blazing inferno, blazing inferno!"

Willow turned, cane in her hands, to see Leopold shaping his body in a spell-form. From the motion she could see the spell was meant to explode. She almost stopped him before he began the second layer.

"Directed motion, directed motion."

The containing layer of essence poured over the sphere of yellow light which had formed between Leopold's hands. He was staring hard at the creature—which could only be the deathworm Bryan had so flippantly dismissed earlier in the night—as he weaved his body into the complicated spell-form of shooting forwards and dissipating upon contact.

Leopold grew still, the spell's concept and form complete, and lowered his hands. The ball of yellow light, now encased in a glowing white sphere, shot towards the deathworm.

Willow watched in awe as it crossed the distance between them almost instantaneously and smashed into the worm. The ball erupted in a burning flurry of fire, engulfing the entire right side of the worm in yellow flame.

Which then guttered out entirely. Save for the sound of the *whoosh* of fire, the entire process had been completely silent. She had expected the worm to scream in pain or start writhing in its death throes, but it did no such thing.

Instead, it opened its mouth.

The puckered orifice at the front of the worm expanded sickeningly into an empty hole, and it faced towards Leopold and began to *suck*. It wasn't that it was sucking air, as there was no roaring like from a tornado. But it was sucking *something*, because she could feel the pressure too.

She realized all at once it was sucking essence. It was a magical creature, and its innate ability was probably to consume essence like a worm consumes soil. It was trying to suck the essence right out of Leopold. Why? To neutralize him? Would it eat him? Would it eat all of them?

Leopold fell to his knees and grasped feebly at the air as his essence deserted him. He attempted to start a concept, but the words were little more than blubbering as his arms dropped to his sides. The worm was a mere six feet away, sucking, coiling as if it would lurch forwards and gobble him up.

Willow got to her feet and gripped the iron cane like a club. She wouldn't be able to kill this thing. She wouldn't even be able to stun it. Magical creatures were famously resilient, and even something as boneless as the deathworm would be able to fend off a strike from one as weak as her. But she wouldn't watch as it killed someone she knew. And besides, she couldn't run anyway. She'd rather go down fighting, like Leopold.

Gods! She wished Bryan was awake. Or that she'd been able to find his sword. She lurched a step at a time, the cane burning her hands with the pressure of her grip. The worm slithered forwards—it was only a foot away from the kneeling Leopold, whose eyes were half-closed in exhaustion. It opened its maw even wider and poised itself above his head.

"No!"

She swung the cane around in an arc towards the vertical portion of the worm, just below its "head."

Her hands burned. Then went beyond burning. She opened her mouth in shock even before the cane hit the deathworm... and then passed effortlessly through it. The metal bar shot from her hands, and she barely heard the vibrating *thunk* as it lodged itself in the ground to her side.

Something was wrong—she was going to vomit. In the moment before the pain, that eternal moment, the pause tells how bad it will be. And this pause... just kept going... and going... and going.

The deathworm's upper half fell to the ground with a wet thud. Her eyes followed it down until she saw that her hands were covered in its blood.

No, not its blood. Not hands—white, shining bone. Her blood, her bones.

Supper came rushing up her throat, and she screamed and vomited at the same moment. The world swam and she tried to catch her balance, but there was so much pain. Her hands weren't going to hurt, not ever again. They were done, gone. Only skeletal bone left and ragged hanging flesh.

The night closed in around her, and she was unconscious before she even hit the ground.

Chapter 4

Willow slowly came to in the back of the rolling wagon. It must have been daytime outside, because she could see Leopold's drawn face above her, looking out through the closed canvas backing. She tried to turn her head to see what he was watching, and he started at her movement.

She realized her head was propped against his leg, nearly in his lap.

"Willow," he said as if he were surprised she was awake. "Don't move."

She blinked twice, then tried to roll her eyes. They were foggy at first, like she'd been asleep for a long time.

"What—" She tried to sit up.

"No, stay down. You have to stay down, at least for now," he said, then leaned his head out of the back of the wagon.

"Bryan!"

The wagons slowed as Willow was still trying to sort through her jumbled memories. The last thing she recalled was going to sleep in the wagon circle. Then Bryan. He said it was just a tremor...

The clanking of thin metal plate announced their guard's arrival at the back of the wagon. He leaned in and looked down at her.

"Aren't I special?" she croaked. "Stopping the whole train for little old me."

The way Bryan looked at her, the concern on his face, brought back another memory—of him slack-jawed against the wagon wheel. The deathworm reared up over Leopold.

Willow gasped and tried to pull her arms up, but they were tied down and pain exploded from her wrists as she pulled at the restraints. She screamed.

"Stop moving," Bryan ordered, jumping into the wagon and leaning over her. He rummaged in a pack at his side and passed a little black nugget over to Leopold. "Mix this with water. Quickly! The pain will soon overwhelm her."

"Oh gods," Willow moaned.

The pain in her wrists was excruciating, far beyond the pain of the restraints against her arms. They had tied her to the bench of the wagon—she realized it was to keep her from rolling off during transit.

"Shh, it'll be alright soon," Bryan said, and inspected where she only imagined her hands would be beyond her vision. The memory of gore and bone came back to her, and she moaned again.

"My hands," she cried. "My hands!"

Then a thought came to her, and it was so small in the enormity of what was happening that she couldn't help but fixate on it.

"I'll never do magic now," she said and couldn't stop the sob that bubbled up. "I didn't even get a chance to fail. Now I'm just a cripple."

"Not yet you aren't," Bryan said, accepting a wooden mug from Leopold. He held the mug to Willow's lips. It smelled strongly floral, the scent horrifyingly familiar. She'd only smelled it when her mother mixed the concoction to give patients on their deathbeds.

"No! I'm not going to die," she struggled against the bonds again. But the pain flared and made her light-headed. It was getting worse.

"It's for the pain," Bryan said, his voice smooth and even. Willow stopped, looked into his eyes, and saw that same thing she'd sensed before. It was as if he was a father comforting a child.

"I'm afraid," she whispered. He nodded.

"We're almost to Durum now. We're already in the warded tunnel. Once we get there, you're going to the best mage I can buy. You're going to get your hands back. Thank the gods everything stayed together, or I don't know what we would've done. This is to help you sleep, to keep the pain away."

She looked mistrustfully at the mug, then at Leopold. There was fear in his eyes, and he worked his jaw a couple times before sound came out.

"I saw the warbeast," he stammered, pushing his bent glasses onto the bridge of his nose. "But it wasn't nearly as scary as the deathworm."

Somehow that admission loosened something within her, and Willow let out a held breath. She accepted the foul drink and shut her eyes as sleep overtook her.

*   *   *

When she next awoke, Willow found herself in a soft white bed. Things were fuzzy at first, and her body hurt in the way that she associated with sleeping late through long winter mornings. She wondered how long she'd been out.

There was a quiet bustling going on around her—soft footsteps on stone—and she blinked to clear the fog from her eyes. She almost raised her hand to rub her face but felt a thick padding covering the end of her arm and the memory of what she saw right after the deathworm attack asserted itself again.

Where was she? What had Bryan said? Taking her to a mage?

She looked left and saw another bed; to her right, there was another bed too. The place reminded her of her mother's small resting chamber where she let patients lie if they needed to recuperate overnight. Except that this was much cleaner and larger than her mother's chamber, which had only held four beds—plenty for their small village.

Someone padded by, dressed all in white, and Willow fought to catch sight of the person's face, but she had trouble focusing. Looking up, she saw a great vaulted ceiling. Daylight streamed in through arched windows at her back, which gave the place a heavenly sort of glow. She supposed that if she were in actual heaven, her hands would be fixed.

Her hands. She looked down and saw two bulbous wrappings where her hands should be, easily four or five times the size of the normal appendages. They'd done something to her hands and wrapped them afterwards. She'd have to wait until she flagged down one of the scurrying nurses before she found out what.

Just as her eyesight was resolving, a familiar face walked out of the misty aisle in front of her.

"Leopold?" she asked, laying back down on the pillow. "What are you doing here?"

"You're awake," he said, smiling as he pushed up his crooked glasses. "Bryan told me to stay with you until you awoke. I got hungry though. It looks like I failed at my duty."

Willow grunted and tried to scoot up against her headboard. Leopold quickly set down his wooden tray on the chair beside the bed and waved his arms around her hands, as if thinking to help her. He realized too late that there was no good place to grab on. It was almost amusing.

"I can get it," Willow said, trying to feign normalcy. She shimmied back until her head was propped up against the hard wooden board. Leopold seemed to decide that she had it and replaced himself in the chair with the food.

"Here, I suppose I should share," he said.

He held out a sliced roll stuffed with meat, which smelled absolutely delicious. Willow realized then that she was ravenous, but she sighed and waggled her wrapped hands in the air, helpless to accept the gift.

"Thanks, but if you want to share, you're going to have to feed me."

"Um, uh," Leopold stammered. "Do you... are you okay with that?"

What a loaded question. Was she okay with Leopold feeding her like an invalid?

The word *no* didn't even come close to how not okay she was. She didn't want him to see her this way, to think of her like this—helpless. But besides her parents, she'd never known anyone willing to stick around to such a degree. Unless she'd imagined it, he even cradled her head on the trip from the attack to the city. Was it insane that she didn't want him to stop?

Willow shrugged to cover her roiling confusion with nonchalance. "I've been fed before. This isn't the first time I've been bedridden."

Leopold scooted closer and held the roll as she took animal-like bites out of it, chewing quickly before stomaching each and going in for another. In less than a minute, the entire roll was gone, and she was looking for seconds.

"You wouldn't happen to have another—"

"By the seventh lord, what did you just feed her?" a woman's voice cut Willow off.

She turned to see one of the white-clad nurses standing at the foot of the bed. The woman was wearing a headdress with white fabric wings extending to either side and a white full-length gown. Her own mother had only worn a white apron while attending to her patients.

"J-Just a roll. Some meat—"

"She's to be on liquid exclusively," the nurse admonished, and Leopold paled. He shrank back in the chair as the nurse moved up the side of the bed to stand over Willow. "Up already, I see."

"I'm so hungry," Willow said, hoping she could ameliorate some of Leopold's guilt.

"I'll have a bowl of broth sent over straight away."

Willow doubted if broth alone would fill the sucking void of her stomach. She hoped that Leopold would secret her another stacked roll, but didn't dare voice the thought. There was such a thing as asking too much of a new acquaintance.

"Now." The woman's voice took on the much softer tone that Willow recognized as what her mother called *bedside manner*. "How are you feeling, dear?"

"Fine. I feel fine, I guess," she said. "My head's a little fuzzy, and my vision is blurry."

"That'll be the aftereffects of the anesthesia," the nurse said. "You were under for quite some time while the surgeons rebuilt your hands. Magically suspending consciousness for that long takes a while to come back from."

Willow sighed in amazement. Bryan hadn't been lying. How in the hell he could afford to get her treated by mages, she couldn't imagine. And if this place was any indication—

"Miss, where am I?" she asked.

"You are at the Sisters of Mercy hospital, sidebound to the Arcanum."

So it was true. They'd really made it. She was in Durum.

"My pain," she said and flexed her elbow. "It's gone, too."

"Pain?"

"I have chronic pain in my muscles," she said. "I can't feel it anymore."

"If it's chronic, then I'm afraid it will eventually return," the nurse said. "Many of my colleagues thought you were severely malnourished when you arrived, and several wanted to start you on emergency supplementation straight away. But your guard talked them out of it. I couldn't wholly believe him myself, but he was quite... insistent."

Willow felt her face flush with the heat of embarrassment and swallowed hard. "I've always been this way. Wasted." The nurse nodded back. "My hands. What about... my hands?"

"Well, the operation was a complete success. All of the missing skin, muscles, and tendons were successfully regrown and grafted onto your bones. Honestly, I've never seen such an injury before in my life. One of the surgeons said they'd seen something similar once on a dead body after fighting a manticore, but never on a living person. How did it happen, if I may ask?"

A sucking hole, the tooth-ringed maw. The image came to her without warning and her eyes went wide as her skin broke out in a sweat. She tried to breathe, but it felt like the deathworm was there again, sucking the life out of her.

Something touched her shoulder. She turned her head to see Leopold there, his hand outstretched, eyes round with concern. That was right—she saved him. The deathworm was gone.

"I, um... the caravan was attacked. A deathworm," she said. "I think I... I hit it. With my cane."

The nurse nodded, as if expecting her to continue.

"That's it." Willow swallowed thickly. "I don't remember anything else. I hit it, and when I looked, my hands were ruined. I passed out after that."

A flicker of distrust flashed across the nurse's face, but she quickly regained her neutral manner.

"Well, however it happened—"

"My cane!" Willow turned back to Leopold. "Did you get my cane?"

Leopold shook his head. "By the time I remembered it, we were already in the warded tunnel. It's probably still back there with the carcass."

"Ugh," Willow groaned, pushing back into the pillows which engulfed her shoulders and head. "Fuck!"

"Language," the nurse said.

"Sorry," Willow apologized but still smarted at the loss.

Her father had that cane commissioned especially for her. Now here she was, so far away from home and all alone for the first time in her life. Certainly, Leopold had attended to what he probably considered his duty after her impossible stunt, but how much longer could she hope he'd stick around?

"You better rest now," the nurse said. "The broth will be here soon, and then later today we'll take off the bandages. I expect you'll be discharged tonight."

"Great," Willow said. Suddenly, she realized she had nowhere to stay in the city and little chance of finding a place before night fell. "Great."

* * *

True to his word, Leopold had stayed with her. Bryan visited later that day and surprised her by going down on one knee and gently touching her bandaged hand.

"Willow," he said. "You saved us. Everyone in that caravan owes their life to you."

"I wouldn't call it saving so much," Willow said, highly uncomfortable with the level of reverence Bryan was showing her. "I smacked that thing with a stick. And then I threw up, then passed out. Not so heroic."

"Even so," he said. "Whatever you need, anything you need, don't hesitate to call on me. Because of you, I was able to see my wife and son again. That is a debt not easily repaid."

So he did have children. She was right all along.

"I don't have any place to stay tonight," she said, hating to ask for help but not knowing any other way out of the situation. "And they're not letting me out until it'll be too late to find anything. You wouldn't happen to know—"

"You'll stay with us, at my house," Bryan said.

Her eyes went wide. "Oh no, that's too much," Willow said, embarrassed.

"I insist." Bryan's tone said that was the end of the matter. As grateful as he seemed, he also seemed to be the kind of person who was used to getting his way. She supposed that was a useful trait to have in a caravan guard.

"Alright, well..." She trailed off, and Bryan smiled as he rose to leave.

"I have some other business to attend to, but we'll have dinner ready for you to eat whenever you arrive. I'll give good Leopold here the directions."

"Wait!" Willow exclaimed as a sudden thought sent adrenaline flooding through her system. "Wait."

He turned back and regarded her with an amused little smile on his face. As if he'd already solved everything by his mere presence and was only waiting for her to catch up.

"I don't have enough money for this, not nearly enough. I don't know how much it cost to get my hands back, but I saw them before... I don't have nearly enough. Will they keep me here until I repay the debt?"

She knew she was rambling, and that ridiculous smile on his face kept widening until she felt heat creep up her neck. But lashing out at her insistent host would be bad form in the extreme.

"No," he said. "It's already taken care of."

"Taken care of?"

Bryan nodded. "Being a caravan guard, especially to young mages going to the city for the first time, has its benefits. I have quite a few favors to call in, and I was happy to call them in for you. Rest now, Willow, and arrive hungry. We'll have a feast you'll not soon forget."

CHAPTER 5

Hours later, the same woman with the white-winged hat came back and began to unfurl the bandages around Willow's hands. She had the most terrible premonition of blood and bone, muscle and tendon, and almost looked away in fear.

What was revealed wasn't her hands as she'd last seen them, but as they had been days before—albeit cleaner and her nails painfully short.

"We had to reconstruct the entire surface," the woman said.

She inspected the smooth skin of Willow's knuckles, skin that should've had creases in it from everyday use.

"Even the backs of the hands, there wasn't much left," she tutted. "But it looks like you're all healed up. Everything joined to the bone well enough, and I daresay the muscle tone is better than anywhere else on your body. Whatever you were doing that got you so grievously injured, try not to do it again."

"Trust me, I don't imagine I'll be in that position anytime soon," Willow answered with a shudder.

The rest of her possessions were returned to her in a bundle, and she was left behind a curtain to dress. As she fastened her clothes, she discovered that her hands didn't ache like the rest of her body—the muscles in her fingers didn't burn and throb. She could get dressed twice as fast as she normally would.

She supposed that wouldn't last long.

To her relief, Leopold was waiting on a bench at the entrance of the great cathedral-like building. He looked up from his book when she limped into the hall.

"All ready to go?" he asked, shutting the book. She noticed it was the introductory text on spellcasting and a startling thought came to her.

"How many days until the examination?" she asked. It wasn't possible that she'd slept through the entire examination, was it?

"It's tomorrow, lucky for you," he smiled. "Still have your book?"

Willow gave a sigh of relief. Then she patted the bundle held awkwardly at her side with hands now strong enough to carry the weight.

"Well, study up. I don't know what the effect of having brand new hands will have on the exam..."

"I'll be ready," she said, and at the same moment, her empty stomach twisted. How *would* her new hands affect her casting? Might they hamper her meager abilities even more?

Leopold pushed up his glasses—which had been bent back into shape sometime in the last few hours—and studied her briefly. Willow had the disturbing sensation that he'd seen right through her.

"Alright," Leopold said and stood from the bench. "To Bryan's place."

As they left the hospital, Willow looked back and found herself shocked at the sheer size of the facade. It looked like the pictures of cathedrals in her books—ancient ruins from civilizations long past.

The streets were paved with close-fitting flagstones, and each had a curb that was suspiciously clean. Buildings rose on either side of the city street that were just as impressive, each containing a second story and built of pale-yellow stone blocks, roofs studded with dark wooden beams. She couldn't keep herself from staring.

"Incredible, isn't it?" Leopold grinned.

Willow jerked her head back down and bristled. The last thing she wanted was to seem like a backwoods hillbilly. "I never asked where you're from," she deflected. "Was it a city like this?"

Leopold shook his head. "Barrowhaven. It's a little bigger than what I saw of your town. We have a few two-story buildings in the center, but nothing like this."

"Just the mayor's mansion for us," Willow said. "And even that... well, they think they'll have to rebuild soon enough. The beams are beginning to crack."

Leopold grunted at the uninteresting trivia from Bridgewater, but speaking of it brought Willow a reverie of home. Would her parents even know that she'd been injured on the journey out? Probably not, since nobody was killed on the wagon. They might not even receive word of the attack when the next caravan came around. All said, her almost-lethal adventure was ultimately an uneventful waylay for the caravanner's guild.

She couldn't even imagine what her parents were doing now that she was gone. Did they enjoy not having to take care of her day in and day out? Did they miss her as much as she missed them? She'd sworn she wouldn't return to Bridgewater until she could take care of herself, and what's more, be an actual boon to her hometown. And she had no intention of reneging on that promise now.

After two turns, during which Willow was mostly caught up in her reverie, Leopold stopped in front of a wooden-linteled doorway, and she pulled up short behind him. He gestured to the door.

"This is it," he said, then pointed to the number carved into the lintel. "Twenty-Three Grave Street."

"I wonder why it's called that," Willow said.

Leopold gestured down the lane. "Because of the graveyard down there."

"Right," she responded.

"Well, I've got to go. Exams start an hour after first light. I'll be here at dawn to take you." He blinked, as if just realizing how what he'd said sounded. "What I mean is... Bryan twisted my arm. I didn't mean to suggest—"

"Thanks, Leopold," Willow smiled.

He hesitated for a moment, then looked down at her hands, which almost seemed to glow with the paleness of her new skin.

"You really... did do it, you know," he said, then swallowed. "I was even less than useless. It just shrugged off my attack. I couldn't do anything. You saved us... saved me."

"Oh, I don't know—" Willow said, but he shook his head and cut her off.

"Thank you, Willow. Thank you for getting me here. I've wanted it for so long, I never thought I might not even arrive."

Willow swallowed hard and nodded. "I know what you mean."

Leopold nodded and turned, walking down the street towards the graveyard and leaving her to knock at the door all on her own.

* * *

Far away in another part of the city, a caravan guard approached a wide-set building, its shingle hanging above the door and depicting an anvil radiating sparks. He tripped the latch and swept inside, holding a tightly wrapped bundle close to his body.

A corpulent man behind the wide counter at the other end of the room looked up. He squinted his eyes in the magelight, then a smile broke over his face.

"Bryan, I see you're back from the caravan. How was the job?"

Bryan didn't answer until he was across the shop, sweeping past tables with mounted magical objects, each worth at least a solid week's pay on the road. The real expensive stuff, he knew, Geoff kept in an iron safe in the back of the store.

Geoff's expression grew puzzled at Bryan's silence until the guard reached the counter and put the canvas-wrapped bundle down. From the way it clanked against the hard wood, it had to be heavy.

"It was bad, Geoff. Real bad. I almost lost the caravan. And my life."

Geoff looked taken aback. "What happened?"

"Deathworm attack."

"Deathworm? But aren't they—"

"They never attack," Bryan interrupted. "Yes. Not one has been recorded to attack a caravan. Until now. I don't know why it did, why it thought it could take on the caravan. They only go for small magical creatures. But it burrowed up in the night and caught me off-guard. I got knocked out, helpless. I should've died. No one there should've been able to face it down without a weapon. But... well..."

Bryan looked at the parcel and pulled back the canvas wrapping. Within was a twisted bar of metal covered with a viscous jelly. A small block of wood was screwed onto the end.

"One of your passengers held it off?" Geoff asked, pulling a cloth from his belt and wiping the red deathworm ooze off the iron. "I don't suppose you told them you kept the artifact?"

Bryan stiffened with guilt for a moment, then shook his head. "I can't imagine it would work anymore, but it might make the base for a powerful weapon," he said hopefully. "Something like that would mean... Well, it would mean I'd never be in that kind of danger again. Margaret and Benny..."

"Might do, might do," Geoff muttered, lost in thought, and set an articulated metal stand on the counter. He turned a ring at the top and a beam of magelight shone down on the twisted metal.

"What was this? Not a sword. A club?"

"A cane," Bryan said, and Geoff inspected the broken-off handle.

"Strange material to make a cane out of, must have weighed at least ten pounds."

"It did," Bryan confirmed. "Right away I suspected it might be an artifact, but after the deathworm..."

"Right, of course." Geoff went into the back of the store for a moment, returning with a bucket of sudsy water.

They both worked at the metal together, Geoff guiding Bryan to ensure he didn't damage any inscriptions that might still exist on the twisted bar. After a quarter of an hour, they had gotten it mostly clean. Geoff then procured a magnifying loupe and began to go over the twisted item.

"Can you tell what it might have done?" Bryan asked after a few minutes. Geoff was still bent over the bar, scrutinizing every inch of it. "I could really use something like it for a sword. Hell, I'd train on a mace if I could whip it around like—"

Geoff straightened, and Bryan stopped at the look on his face.

"What?"

"You're not having me on for a jape, are you?" Geoff asked. Bryan could see the vague lines of anger in the other man's face. He'd seen Geoff furious before, usually at being swindled in a trade, and he didn't want to antagonize his friend.

"No, no, of course not. I wouldn't lie about this."

Geoff pocketed the loupe and pushed the twisted bar back across the counter to Bryan.

"What? What's wrong?"

"There's no inscription on this," Geoff said. "Not a single etched line."

"But the damage—"

Geoff held up his hand. "Wouldn't be enough to wear every trace of an inscription away. I can still see the working marks on it, a craftsman in Raly forged it. I recognize the stamp."

"Does he do hidden inscriptions? Maybe something within the bar..."

Geoff shook his head. "Not him. Straight iron-worker. Mundane blacksmith. Whoever used this to kill a deathworm did it with pure strength."

"That's not possible," Bryan said. "She's just... just a child. She can barely walk."

Geoff narrowed his eyes at Bryan and leaned across the counter. "Are you certain you know what wielded this weapon?" he asked in a deadly whisper.

CHAPTER 6

Margaret, Bryan's wife, quietly woke Willow early the next morning. The sun hadn't even touched the horizon and already Willow smelled the savory notes of pork and eggs. By the time Willow washed with the small basin beside her bed and left the room, the house was already in commotion.

Little Benny was practicing rhyming games with his father, Bryan, who had gotten home late the previous night. At the sound of Willow's door opening off the dining room, Bryan startled a bit and looked over his shoulder at her. Something had changed in the way he looked at her. She wondered what it could have been that made him act so skittish now, especially when he'd seen her at her worst on the caravan. Did he regret offering her his home?

"Did you sleep soundly?" Margaret asked as Willow slowly made her way into the small room. She tried to dodge the many pieces of scattered furniture but nonetheless suffered a hit to the knee that made her wince as pain shot up to her hip.

"I did," Willow gasped, limping to the table. "And thank you… for hosting me. After the examinations, I'm sure I'll be assigned a dormitory to stay in, so I shouldn't be taking up the room for very long."

"You're welcome to it for as long as you need," Bryan said, and when she looked back, the mistrustful glance from earlier was gone. It was like it had never happened. Had she imagined it?

"Need, steed... bleed," Benny tried, but wasn't quite satisfied with his rhyme.

"Weed," Margaret corrected, setting a plate down before Willow as she gingerly lowered herself into the wooden chair. "We don't need any talk of blood now, not while your father's back. Leave that dark business out there, that's what I say."

Bryan raised his mug to his wife, and she leaned in for a kiss. Willow began to inhale her porkchop and eggs—much faster now that her hands were free of the usual aches and pains they suffered—and finished just before there came a knock at the door.

"That'll be Leopold," Willow said, and eased herself back from the table.

Bryan crossed the small room and opened the door. He greeted Leopold with a firm handshake and offered him a bit of breakfast, but Leopold turned the offer down.

"We've got to get going, and soon," he said, peering around the door to find Willow, who was just getting her sack cinched around her shoulders. "Examination starts an hour after sunrise and the sky's already pale."

"Is it that far away?" Margaret asked from the rubbish bin where she was scraping Benny's crust of bread.

"The Arcanum's at the center of the city," Bryan said. "Next to the hospital."

"It'll be quite a walk then," Margaret said, and looked at Willow. "Would you like to take a lunch?"

"Actually, yes," Willow said. "I wouldn't mind more of that pork, if you could spare it."

"Of course, my dear, please, take another steak," she said, laying a slice down into a waxed cloth bundle. "Maybe a bit of bread as well."

She sealed the bundle with the warmth of her hands and handed it across to Willow, who stood at the door with Leopold.

"Thank you very much, Margaret, Bryan," Willow said, then nodded at the small boy. "Benny."

"Many, penny," Benny said with a smile.

"Whinny. You'd better be off," Margaret said. "You're a might ways off from the Arcanum. Hustle and you'll get there in time."

Willow and Leopold walked from the house on Grave Street into the wan light of morning. For the first time, Willow saw just how close it was to the massive wall which encircled the city. The sky was split neatly in half between morning light and pitch darkness from the seamless stone of the defensive wall. From where they were on the street, Willow thought she saw an irregularity up on the wall—perhaps one of the ancient cannons which were used in ages past to smite attacking warbeasts.

Leopold led them with a surety that Willow—at that early hour, in a city she'd never traversed—would have been unable to manage. She was intensely grateful that he'd fulfilled his promise of the previous night, though why he'd done so was just as confusing as it had been in the dark. Was she right in questioning his explanation that Bryan had roped him into guiding her?

"I procured a map at the inn," Leopold explained as they went on. "I spent all night studying it while I practiced."

"I should have practiced," Willow admitted. "I was just so damn tired by the time we got out of the hospital."

"Well, you've been through a lot," Leopold said. "And besides, it's not like you can fail the exam. It's more of a formality anyway."

"Yeah, well," Willow said, unsure if that would prove true for her.

The deathworm incident seemed to have given Leopold an inflated sense of her physical prowess. Only the nurses would know the extent of her disability, and how, even after everything, it might prevent her admission to the Arcanum.

True to Bryan's word, it took almost an hour of trekking through the winding alleys of Durum before they came within eyesight of the Arcanum. Its polished stone caught the morning light and blazed like bars of liquid gold against the lightening sky. A singular tower at the center of campus rose higher than the others, upthrust to the heavens. The pinnacle blazed like a jewel in the sun.

"There's the observation tower," Leopold pointed to the shining summit. "Although it's got a funny name on the map. It's meant to keep track of the warbeast and any incoming attack."

The doors to the Arcanum were fully twenty feet tall and wide enough for three people to pass abreast. By the time they arrived, Willow's feet and legs were killing her, especially without her cane, the loss of which she'd have to rectify sooner rather than later. There was a small trickle of young adults her and Leopold's age making their way through the great stone lintel.

The doors were wooden and painted red, studded with what she could only assume was iron banding. As she passed, she saw that shining carvings adorned every inch of the banding, and she realized the doors were magically protected with swirls of copper inscriptions as well as being physically imposing. She'd heard that in the long-ago past the Arcana were the only things that kept those in the city alive from the lethal wilds. She supposed it made sense for the buildings to be set up as a last bastion against invasion.

Past the double doors was a soaring stone hall with vaulted ceilings fully thirty feet high, shining with some strange internal light. Whether through inscription or cast magic, the expense of illuminating this hall must have been enormous. A thin trickle of bewildered young adults about her age were making their way towards a severe woman sitting behind a heavy wooden desk. Willow and Leopold folded themselves into the line. It wasn't long before it was Willow's turn. She could feel Leopold positively vibrating with energy behind her. If only she could share his anticipation.

The severe woman, whose gray hair was tied up tight in a bun behind her head, looked Willow up and down when she approached.

"Name," she said. It was barely a question.

"Willow Tremont," she responded and laboriously slipped the straps of her pack from her shoulders.

"Hometown."

"Bridgewater."

"Admission fee."

Willow reached into her pack and brought out a tightly wrapped bundle of gold coins. They represented a full half of all the money she had for the next two years at the Arcanum, and the other half was already earmarked for next year's tuition. If she wanted to eat, she'd have to find some way to make money in the city before next year's was due. It was all her parents could afford to send her with. Unless she'd wanted to wait another year.

She hadn't.

The woman took the tightly wrapped bundle and quickly counted forty gold pieces before making a note in a ledger next to Willow's name. Then she consulted a ruled sheet beside the book.

"You'll go to examination room fifteen," the woman said without looking up. Willow got the distinct feeling she'd been dismissed and stepped to the side for Leopold to advance.

"I guess I'll see you on the other side," she said and tried to smile.

"See you there," he agreed, just as the woman looked up again with a scowl.

By the time Willow hobbled to examination room fifteen—one of the many small doorways on that first floor of the Arcanum—she'd already finished eating the wrapped parcel of pork and bread. The examination room was closed with a heavy wooden door. With not a little nervous anxiety, Willow knocked on the oaken surface.

"Come in," she barely heard a woman's voice say from the other side.

Willow tripped the iron latch and walked through into what was clearly a repurposed classroom. Instead of desks, it was set up with all sorts of measurement equipment, both arcane and mundane.

"Hello? I was told to come to examination room fifteen?" Willow asked into the room.

"This is fifteen. Come around the curtain," the woman's voice said from the other side of a freestanding white curtain. Willow couldn't see any frame around it or rings in the ceiling. It must have been standing by magic alone.

Excellent. At this lone example of casual magic, Willow's heart throbbed with anticipation. That, and dread.

When Willow rounded the corner, she saw a middle-aged woman in a white frock sitting in a chair beside a long tabletop—what would normally be the lecturer's desk.

"I'm Mary. You can have a seat there," she said before pointing to the chair opposite her on the same side of the table.

"I'm Willow," Willow said, then took her seat.

Mary's eyes glanced over her as she bent to sit, lingering on the folds in the fabric around her arms and legs. Willow felt a knot of anxiety tighten in her stomach, but she pushed through it.

"Last name?"

"Tremont."

Mary took up a pen and, without dipping it in an inkwell, began to write on a fresh, lined piece of paper. In fact, there was no inkwell in sight. Was this magic too? How backwards had she been living out in Bridgewater?

"Alright, Willow, I'm a nurse-in-training with the hospital, and I'll be doing your physical examination. Afterwards I'll try to figure out these instruments to get some of your essence readings. This is just for intake statistics, you understand."

"Uh huh," Willow said, powering through a surge of panic. "Any chance it would affect my admission?"

"Only if you were completely unable to do magic. But you are, right?"

Willow nodded. She wasn't sure what it meant that the nurse hadn't included the consequences of the results of the physical examination in her response. Maybe nothing—or maybe she was about to stretch the limits of admission criteria.

"Yeah, the complete lack of magical ability is incredibly rare. Even the simplest farmhand can weave a knot-loosening spell in a few seconds. I can't imagine how they get along though, those who can't do it at all."

"I suppose they just find mundane solutions to their problems," Willow pretended to guess, feeling a sheen of sweat stand out on her back.

Mary shrugged. "Alright. I hate to tell you to get up again so soon, but..." She looked at Willow's elbows again through the fabric of her blouse. "You'll have to disrobe. Down to your smallclothes."

And this was it: the moment she'd dreaded. She thought this might happen sooner or later, but until a few moments before, she hadn't expected it to be part of the intake examination. Perhaps the result of nosy students and professors wondering why she moved like an elderly lady, but not before she'd actually gained admission. She wanted to refuse, to tell the nurse to mind her own damn business, but she *had* to get into the Arcanum. She'd do anything to gain admission, even this.

Willow began to undo the buttons on her stiff outer jacket.

She tried not to watch Mary's face as each article of clothing came off until she was left standing in just a thin shift. But as the other woman's eyes grew as large as saucers, it became more and more difficult to ignore what was happening.

And how it made her feel.

Shame. Shame like she'd never felt at home because everyone in Bridgewater knew about her. The doctor's daughter. The waif. Everyone knew what had happened, how she'd been left looking so sickly. Expert tailoring helped, but invariably, a shirt would cling where it wasn't supposed to, and for a moment she'd look more dead than alive. Everyone at home pretended not to notice. But not here.

Mary's mouth opened and closed silently a couple of times, like a stranded fish, as her eyes roamed the wasteland of Willow's body. Her limbs were only a few finger-widths thick, skin stretched tight between swollen joints. Each rib stood out like an anatomical drawing, the same with her spine. Her waist was wasp-thin, and the skin on her hips sucked into the deep depressions of her pelvis. Willow tried not to blush with shame, but it was mostly a useless exercise.

"What..." Mary finally got out but seemed unable to grasp a second word.

"I was sick," Willow pronounced, face hard with bottled anger, the only antidote she'd found for her bouts of terminal shame. "As an infant. I got the Wasting, now I'm like this."

"You look—" Mary, not noticing Willow's hard expression, paused and appeared to reword something in her head. "You look as though you're starving to death. I've seen corpses with more flesh on their bones."

Willow shrugged her shoulders and barely kept from grimacing. Mary winced.

"I've always looked like this."

"How are you even standing?" Mary whispered, then shook her head. "When was the last time you ate?" she asked in a stronger voice.

"Just before I came through the door."

"And what... uh... was it?"

"Porkchop on bread," Willow said, trying to distract and calm herself with the memory. "It was supposed to be lunch, but I have a strong appetite."

"You... do?"

"Always have. Maybe the Wasting did something to my gut."

"Something... but it wasn't the Wasting. No one's ever survived it."

This was news to Willow. Other infants had died in Bridgewater of the Wasting before and after she made it, but she'd never heard that she had been the only one to survive.

"You're wrong. My mother's a doctor, and she was certain—"

Mary shook her head slowly as she interrupted. "No one survives. It attacks the nerves at the base of the skull, cutting off all control over the body. The infected invariably suffocate as they lose control over their diaphragms. Their fate has been prolonged in some using magic, but the disease waits to rip apart all the healing work no matter how long the process is undertaken. Whatever it was you had, it wasn't the Wasting."

Confused, Willow stood there silently while Mary got up with a ruled tape and began taking measurements. Should she believe this nurse? She *was* trained at the Sisters of Mercy, but Willow had no idea where that put her in relation to her mother's own training. If it hadn't been the Wasting, then maybe that meant it was curable? Whether it was or wasn't, that had no effect on her immediate future or her current condition. She *would* become a mage, which was the most certain way forwards. Afterwards, she'd explore the possibility of unlikely cures.

"I don't think I can even do a skin-pinch test," Mary said to herself and prodded Willow's upper arm. Willow winced at the poke.

"Did that hurt?"

"A bit. It's tender."

"Are... all of your muscles tender?"

Willow nodded, grateful for Mary's refocus on clinical observations rather than wide-eyed shock. "Everything except my hands. I just had them redone. They were torn apart on the caravan over."

At that, Mary's attention switched to Willow's hands, which looked strangely proportioned to the rest of her body, almost oversized. She could even see impressions of muscle under the skin, which hadn't been present before the journey.

"Torn apart?"

"There was an attack," Willow said, glad to have something to distract her during the examination. "Our caravan guard paid for the reconstruction at the hospital."

Mary turned Willow's hands over. "I cannot deny that your hands are different. Can you move your fingers for me?" Mary had taken Willow's left hand firmly between her own, fingertips probing.

Willow wiggled her fingers and Mary's eyebrows quirked up into an even more curious expression.

"What's wrong?"

"It's just... I can barely feel your muscles. They hardly contract at all. Squeeze."

Willow squeezed, expecting pain to bloom against the inside of her palm as it always did when she tried to grasp something too tightly, but it didn't come. Only the smooth feel of pressure mounting against her skin.

Mary's expression faltered.

"Ow, ow," she said, and Willow quickly released her.

"Oh, I'm sorry. I'm just not used to being able to grab anything. Usually the pain—"

"No, I understand," Mary said as she shook her hand out. She never looked away from Willow's hands. "You're stronger than you look."

Willow sighed. "I suppose they'll go back to the way they were after a while."

Mary picked up the tape and measured Willow from the crown of her head to her bony heels.

"Five foot ten. And how much do you weigh?"

She was expecting this, and Willow almost didn't cringe when she said the answer.

"Eighty pounds."

Mary nodded and wrote down the figure. Willow appreciated how quick she was to feign indifference to her temporary patient's disability.

"Alright, that's all the physical measurements done. They've taught me how to use this set of essence meters, but don't be surprised if it takes me a bit to get them up and running."

Willow knew what it was like to be out of her depth. "No, absolutely. No problem."

"You can get dressed again. I'll be on the other side of the curtain."

Relieved, Willow dressed slowly, gingerly sliding each layer of fabric into place over the sharp angles of her body. She heard Mary muttering to herself and clanking on the other side of the curtain. Willow's curiosity finally overcame her embarrassment, driving her to do up the last few buttons and step out into the larger room.

Mary was sitting at a small desk and tapping on something that looked a lot like a crystal point of black obsidian. Willow could see illuminated symbols on the side that faced Mary, but she couldn't read them.

"Blasted thing," Mary grumped. Then she noticed Willow standing beside the curtain. "You might as well sit down here. I think I've almost got it working."

Willow saw her reflection in the crystal's depths as she sat down across from Mary. For a moment in the dark mirror world, she saw anew all of the things Mary must have seen, things that she had long ago learned to ignore. The way her neck was too thin. The way it seemed to swim in her stiff overcoat.

She looked away from the reflection, down at her hands, and prodded the muscles on their backs. They didn't hurt yet, but she could already feel a tingling in the fibers. Soon enough, she was sure, they would flare with pain at the slightest touch.

It didn't matter. Nothing mattered but this examination, here and now.

"Alright, I think I've got it. You haven't done any magic this morning, have you?"

"No. The instructions said not to," Willow said.

Mary nodded. "That's right. This thing is going to measure your essence capacity and regeneration rate. I'm told all you have to do is grab the crystal at the top, and we can get started."

Willow nodded, a little excited at the prospect of knowing more about herself. Back home, no one knew their essential attributes. Such measurements were only written about in books, like the introductory text to spellcraft she'd brought on the caravan from Bridgewater. You only needed to know them if you were going to be a mage.

Willow laid her palm against a facet of the device, wrapping her fingers around the rest of the gem.

"You're supposed to push essence into the device now. It'll store it and calculate the value."

"How much should I push?"

"It says *a trivial amount*. I'll let you know when you've reached it."

"Okay," Willow said and focused her will.

She could feel the essence flowing in her body and visualized it as lines that ran up along her veins and circulated in her organs. At this time of the morning, she still had a good amount of the flowing energy left. But as experience told her, that would change as the day wore on and she got more and more tired.

She grabbed hold of the essence with her mind and attempted to direct its flow—as usual, it resisted her. Once she had complained to her father that channeling essence was like spitting molasses through a reed. Her father had told her that nothing worth having in life came easy.

A slow trickle of essence began to flow through her palm and into the crystal. Strangely, she could feel the crystal absorbing the essence, whereas with any other object it would just splash ineffectually against the surface.

Willow felt beads of sweat stand out against her forehead, and her stomach gave a traitorous rumble. Mary looked up from the device.

"Are you... pushing yet?"

"Yes," Willow grunted and redoubled her effort. Her essence responded fractionally.

"Oh, we've got it," Mary said. "You can stop now."

Willow let out a breath she didn't realize she'd been holding and leaned back into her chair. She tried to steady her breath to keep from gasping and was only partially successful. She could feel Mary's eyes on her as she regained her strength.

"What now?" Willow asked, afraid that the device would come back immediately with some kind of disqualifying mark. Although what that would mean, given that she'd already paid tuition, was beyond her. Surely she'd put out enough essence to qualify for classes?

"Now we just have to wait," Mary said.

"Wait?"

Mary nodded. "It needs us to wait a certain amount of time, then it'll return the essence to you. Apparently it's supposed to feel pretty weird to have your own essence injected into your body. The directions said I should warn you."

"Warn me, got it," Willow said, her breathing finally under control again.

"You... can do magic, can't you?" Mary asked.

"Of course I can do magic," Willow snapped. "Do you think I'd come all this way if I couldn't?" Despite her reaction, the niggling doubt wormed its way back into her head.

Mary shook her head, as if lost for words. "No, I suppose not. Ah, it's all done waiting now. If you'd put your hand back on top?"

Willow assumed the same grip she'd had before and nodded, relishing the smooth feel of the device against her palm without the bruised tenderness of her wasted muscles.

"Alright, here it goes."

Mary had been right, it did feel weird. Like someone was blowing hard against her palm. She could visualize the essence building up against her hand, the pressure mounting, but before more than an iota had trickled back, the pressure released completely.

"Oh shit." Mary looked down at the written instructions she'd been following. "I don't know what that means."

"What? What is it?"

"It seems like the device malfunctioned. I'm going to have to call metrology to fix it."

CHAPTER 7

"Metrology?" Willow asked as Mary wove a spell-form in the air, whispering the concept under her breath. The spell manifested as a shining green star, hardly larger than the head of a pin.

"Metrology assistance requested in room fifteen," she intoned, then broke the spell-form.

The star moved quickly away, disappearing as it passed through the thick wooden door as if it were nothing. Of course, Willow realized, the nurses would have some way to communicate with each other through the vast hospital building.

They sat awkwardly across the table from each other. Willow kept looking at the device, then searching the instructions upside-down as if she could find something that might explain what had happened.

"Should we... continue with the rest of the examination?" Willow asked as Mary began to tap her foot.

"Honestly? I have no idea. The next part is asking you to demonstrate magic, but I'm afraid of messing up this measurement if we have you do any magic."

"Right," Willow said. At that moment a knock came at the wooden door.

"Enter," Mary called out.

The door swung open to reveal a young man who couldn't have been much older than Willow. He was dressed in a loose-fitting shirt and pants cinched with a thin leather belt at the waist. He had some kind of device in his hands—flat and almost crystalline.

"You requested metrology assistance?" the young man inquired, and Mary waved him in. He quickly crossed the room and placed the device, which looked like a small plate, beside the obsidian crystal and began tapping on the surface.

"You look harried," Mary said with the hint of a smile in her voice.

"Been running around all morning. No one knows how to use the new devices; they keep getting errors."

"Well, same here," Mary said. "Sorry to inconvenience you."

He waved the apology off. "I'm getting paid, aren't I? Came back early from break, I suppose I should have expected to do some work."

"Do you specialize in... metrology?" Willow asked, and the young man nodded. "You don't want to be a mage?"

"Oh, you're a mage if you graduate no matter what you specialize in, but if what you're talking about is throwing fire and raising the earth, then no. I'm much more comfortable with inscribing and metrology, thank you very much. Leave that other stuff to the daredevils."

His face relaxed, and he let out a short laugh. "Happy day. It saved your essence. That means you won't have to come back tomorrow to repeat the test. You don't know how many times I've been yelled at for making people come back.

"Alright," he continued, then gestured at Willow's hand. "I'll do the test this time, your nurse will take over once we don't need the device anymore. Put your..."

He was staring at her hand—no, at her wrist. Willow shrugged, and her shirtsleeve fell down another inch to cover her skeletal arm.

"I um..." He seemed to have lost his train of thought. "Sorry. What I meant to say was, put your hand back on the device and we'll restart the test."

Willow placed her hand without comment. She supposed she'd have to get used to people gawking, but she wasn't used to it yet, so she tensed.

"Alright," he said and tapped on the small plate instead of the device. "Here it goes. You'll feel a bit strange when it injects your essence."

And again, she felt it. The pressure against her palm, the almost imperceptible trickle of her own essence back into her body. His eyebrows drew together in confusion.

"Huh, resistance is super high. This must have been what happened earlier, the device just crapped out. I'll increase it."

"What does that—" Willow flinched. Where before there had been a gentle push against her palm, now it felt as though she were balancing the haft of a spear on her hand. Her face twisted in discomfort, and she grunted.

"Different people have different amounts of resistance," he said and shook his head. "But this is like pushing essence into a rock. You don't have anything on your hand?"

"No." Willow grimaced.

"Glove or metal of any kind? Did you put any kind of balm on before coming in?"

"Want to check?" Willow snapped, and the assistant started.

"Um, no. I don't think I need to," he muttered, tapping the plate again.

This time when the pressure increased, it was like trying to hold back a dam with just her hand. But she did feel the essence slowly work its way back into her body, rejoining the flowing mass.

"Ah, we've got flow," he said.

Then they waited for an incredibly uncomfortable amount of

time. Willow held onto the device with all her newfound strength, willing herself not to let go and mess up the test.

If this was what it took to get her into the Arcanum, then she'd do it.

Suddenly the pressure cut off all at once, and she gasped in relief. Mary looked from Willow to the young man, but he looked anything but relieved.

"And?" Mary poised her pen above the sheet she'd been tracking Willow's measurements on.

He gritted his teeth. "You messed up the test. You shouldn't have done the spell demonstration while you were waiting for me."

"Spell demonstration? We didn't do the spell demonstration," Mary said and looked at Willow.

Willow shook her head. She felt like she'd been wrung out, and her right arm ached something fierce from all the essence that had been pumped back into it.

"You did. Or, what, did you think you'd get some practice in before the demo?" He turned to look at Willow.

"I did no such thing," Willow growled as she disengaged her fingers from the crystal. They came away tacky with sweat, and her new joints creaked.

"Well, you did *something* because I'm getting zero here, and the only way that happens is if you do magic before the test. If you're not topped all the way up before we begin."

"I assure you, I haven't done any magic this morning," Willow said between clenched teeth.

He waved her off and turned to Mary. "Record *undetermined* for the regeneration rate. Keep the volume calculation blank. We'll have to retest sometime in the future."

"Retest?" Willow's heart sank, not quite believing what she was hearing. "What does that mean? Do I not get into the Arcanum until you retest?"

"What? No, we just have to retest later for your specific measurements. You should still be given admittance assuming you're able to produce a spell, which, obviously, you are able to do."

From the way Willow's arm thrummed from the passage of her own essence, she wasn't sure.

"Fine."

"Alright, well," he said and got up from the table, his little circular crystal plate in hand. He glanced down at the surface, then moved his finger across the glass in a few downward strokes. "Have to reset the push force," he said and looked uneasy for a moment. As he turned to leave, she could just hear him mutter, "—super high."

It was just Willow and Mary in the room then, and Mary cleared her throat as if to dispel the ghost of the young metrologist's passing.

"Well, he was a bit of an asshole, wasn't he?" she said. The unexpected brashness of the statement made Willow laugh. Mary joined in and Willow found that once she'd dried her eyes, she did feel much better.

"It's almost over," Mary said, looking at her sheet. "Just the spell demonstration. There are a few different effects you can elect to produce—"

"They're limited?" Willow blurted out, anxiety twisting her stomach again.

Mary looked up briefly. "It's quite a long list," she said, returning to the sheet. "Psychokinesis, fireball, condense water, incorporealize, magelight—"

"Magelight," Willow said.

Mary took the interruption in stride. She made a mark on the sheet, then leaned back in her chair. "Alright, whenever you're ready."

Willow let out a long breath. This was it. She could still feel the extra essence thrumming in her arm, making her hand twitch and jump every few seconds, although the pressure from it was lessening as time went on. She targeted the essence mentally, visualizing it as an arm the shape of her own but blown up to twice its size, and moved her hands in the spell-form.

"Blazing light."

She felt the extra essence transform within her own body. It seemed to take on the concept much easier than normal, and she wondered for a moment if storing and then injecting herself with essence might help her become more effective at casting.

"Blazing light," she said a second time. The essence flowed outwards through her fingertips into her cupped hands. It was flowing freer too, as if it wasn't subject to the same sluggishness her essence normally behaved with.

This could really be the answer!

"Blazing light," she said with confidence.

The essence condensed within her hands to a pinprick of shining light brighter than any she'd ever made before. She smiled, beholding this most successful spell.

"Alright, now the steadfast layer," Mary said.

Willow jerked her gaze up. "What?"

Just like that, the small spell evaporated, boiling off into the ether. She tried to assert control over it, but the injected essence slipped through her fingers. It was much less bound to her will than her normal essence was, which made it useless for spellcasting.

"Oh, I'm sorry," Mary said. "I just meant that you need the steadfast layer to complete the magelight spell. Don't worry, you can try again."

Willow let out a sigh of despair. "No," she said, barely able to keep herself from crying at her own failure.

She'd only ever mastered the first half of the most introductory spell in the book.

CHAPTER 8

It took two days of terrible waiting for the decision to come from the Arcanum, and even then, she didn't have the luxury of opening the envelope alone. Leopold arrived at Twenty-Three Grave Street a bare hour after the decision had been delivered, and she still hadn't opened it yet.

"We can open them together," he said. His eyes spoke his confidence that there was no way she wouldn't get into the Arcanum.

She'd paid the money, after all. She would've thought so too, except for the fact that she had an undetermined essence capacity and was unable to even pass the spell demonstration test. She'd checked the mail each day, waiting for a letter inviting her back to redo her test with the crystal, but it hadn't come.

"Come on," Leopold said and took out his pocketknife. He slit first his own envelope, then hers. "No use putting it off."

"You first," she urged, sure of what her own would say.

He hesitated a moment, then slid the sheaf of paper out from within the brown envelope and unfolded it. A quiet click from the kitchen told Willow that Margaret was listening in.

"I'm approved to start classes tomorrow," Leopold said with a smile. Lucky him. "Okay, now yours."

Willow took a deep breath and fumbled in the envelope for her sheaf. Her hands were already beginning to waste, and the pain of the muscles eating themselves was even greater than the pain of her old, wasted hands. She gingerly grasped the sheaf and spread it open using her forearm.

"Well?" Leopold asked after she'd taken quite a bit of time to read the close-set text.

"I'm admitted," she said, and Leopold smiled.

"See, I told you—"

"Probationally," Willow continued, still reading the text.

There was quite a lot of it. It set out the conditions and stages that would lead to her dismissal from the Arcanum, no refund given. Was this better than being rejected outright? Willow wasn't sure. She'd be able to attend classes at the Arcanum—something she'd wanted for as long as she'd known she wouldn't be able to do any other worthwhile work—but with a sword hanging above her head.

"What... what does that mean?"

"It means that if I can't produce a satisfactory introductory spell within the next two weeks, I'm gone," she said. "It means that if the metrology department can't get a lock on my measurements, I'm gone. It means that I don't even have housing."

"Don't have housing?"

"Maybe they—" She tried to swallow past the lump in her throat. "Maybe they don't think I'll be around long enough to move in."

"What in the seven hells?" Leopold growled, snatching the sheaf from her fingers. It wasn't difficult, since she was barely holding on anyway.

She turned away as Leopold began to peruse the regulations that spelled her doom. For five years she'd been working on just the first half of the magelight spell, and now they expected her to master layering within two weeks. It was a joke. She didn't blame them for not giving her housing. Not with those impossible conditions.

"Willow."

Margaret's soft voice came from the door to her tiny room, which was still mostly the storage room it had been before Bryan had so selflessly given it to her. Willow tried to dry her eyes before she turned to look at the woman.

Apparently she didn't do a very good job, because Margaret descended on her and wrapped her in the soft embrace you'd save for hugging the terminally ill. It was just the same kind of hug her parents gave her. She rested her cheek on Margaret's shoulder and felt the tears fall hot and fast into the older woman's hair.

"You'll always have a place with us," Margaret said, whispering into her ear. "For as long as you want to stay in the city, you can live here."

"No, I can't," Willow said, shaking her head and trying to disengage, but Margaret was unyielding. "You've already given me so much. I can't—"

"Yes you can. Have you forgotten so easily what you did for me? For us? This is the least of what I can offer."

The deathworm. She saw it rear up now, as she did in her dreams, and felt the iron of the cane in her hands. She swung and the cane bounced off the gelatinous hide of the worm. The worm turned to her and began to suck. She felt her essence draw out through her skin before falling into darkness and death.

"N-No," Willow wheezed and began to struggle. The worm was on her, wrapped around her. Then, it wasn't. It was just Margaret. Willow felt clammy with sweat and her heart was beating terribly fast.

She remembered that Leopold was still in the room with them and looked at him. He was watching her, face pale. A sheen of sweat dotted his brow. He swallowed hard.

"You still see it, too," he whispered, and she nodded. "I can hardly sleep—"

Margaret interrupted. "Come into the kitchen. Let me fix you two something. You've both gone through it today in your own ways and you need to eat."

They followed her through the door to the kitchen like children, though Willow's thoughts weren't entirely present. She'd find a way to pay Bryan and Margaret back for what they'd done for her, even if it took her crying advertisements on the street corner. She swore to herself that she wouldn't take advantage of their hospitality for that one intense, dreadful night.

Another letter came that day for Willow in the bundle of mail, also addressed from the Arcanum, but she didn't discover it until later that night after she'd nearly eaten Margaret out of house and home. That letter was from the metrology department, specifying the date and time when she should arrive to be tested again. It was right after her first class, which may or may not mean that she'd already cast a spell that day. Well, if that was how they wanted it, she wouldn't correct them, the bastards.

After assurances from Leopold that he would do anything he could to help her stay in the school with him, he eventually returned to his inn to prepare to move into a dormitory. Bryan came home later that night. Willow couldn't help but hear a quick and whispered conversation between him and Margaret, where she warned him not to ask about Willow's admission.

That was fine by her.

The next day, her first day of schooling started when Margaret woke her at dawn. In the kitchen, she found Bryan suiting up in a set of light leather armor.

"Are you going out on another caravan?" Willow asked around the lard-fried eggs Margaret had set in front of her.

"Not a caravan, but while I'm in the city, I pull down some extra income as a wall guard. The pay isn't as high, but it's easy, safe work, and I get back home by dinner every night. What's not to love?"

After another pork chop and a slice of bread loaded with gravy, Willow was finally ready to set out for the school. It was a tortuously long walk, but she thought she'd make it before the first bells rang before her class.

As it turned out, she barely made it at that. The walk was so much more tiring without Leopold there to keep the pace, and even when she reached the vast castle-like arrangement of buildings, she wasn't sure where to go. Helpfully, there were aids at the entrance to each building. They quickly directed her to a small hall off the side of the main building she'd entered the day before.

Quite apart from the gorgeous reliefs and intricate carvings of the main hall, this building looked more utilitarian than not, although still constructed of the same light stone as the rest of the school. Its door didn't soar high into the sky but was normally proportioned. It didn't even have iron banding or intricate locks, which probably meant it had been built after the city walls were established.

A few other students were making their way through the small front door, and Willow slipped as gracefully as she could into the stream—which wasn't very gracefully at all. She'd have to get a new cane, and soon. People were already starting to stare, and she pulled her cowl up over her neck to cover her reedy collarbone.

There were only a couple of rooms past the door in the small hallway lit by magelight. She recognized the room number of the one on the left and followed a few straggling students in.

The room looked much like the schoolroom in Bridgewater, where she'd received her elementary education. It had a dozen chairs set behind long tables with a large blackboard set up at the front of the room. There was no teacher's desk to head the class, and Willow assumed that the professor would be standing nearly the entire time.

"Hey," Willow heard a familiar voice call. She saw Leopold sitting at the front of the room waving towards her.

There weren't that many students in the front row, and he had a seat on either side of him. Willow made her way past the other chairs, careful not to bang into any wooden backs, until she lowered herself into the seat beside Leopold.

"You're almost late."

"Bryan's house is so far," Willow huffed as she fished the textbook from her bag.

This first day, she only had two classes separated by her time at the metrology lab, so the load hadn't been that terrible. However, she could imagine a time in the future when she might need more help or somewhere to store her things closer to the Arcanum. She briefly wondered if Leopold would consider helping. And if she could bring herself to ask him, which was another matter entirely.

"Did you get moved in alright?" she asked as a portly man walked into the room and shut the door.

"It's small. I have a roommate, but it does the job." Leopold shrugged. "Honestly, your lodgings at Bryan's are bigger than mine."

The man at the front of the class harrumphed, which got the room's attention. Willow sat forwards and, even after everything that had happened with admissions the day before, she couldn't help but feel excitement bubbling in her veins. This was it! She was in school to learn magic!

At least for today.

"I am Professor Brandeweiss," he said. "And you are currently in Introduction to Theory of Essence-Crafting. If this is not the class you were expecting, you'd do well to leave now."

No one got up to rush out the door. After a moment he smiled to himself.

"Always a couple every year. Maybe they're getting smarter," he said, just loud enough for the entire class to hear. Then he picked up a piece of chalk.

"Essence," he said and wrote the word out on the board. "It's been known by many names across the years. Mana, juice, ectoplasm. All refer to the same thing." For each of these he wrote the name, followed by two that Willow didn't even think were words, as they were made up of lines and slashes.

"For all of recorded history, humanity and magical creatures have been able to harness and direct this substance within our bodies to create effects magical on the world around us. Magical creatures do this action innately, unconsciously, whereas humans are required to make use of spell-forms and concepts to enact our will. But when a mage masters the spell-form and concept, they can move mountains, melt glaciers, open rifts in space."

Yes, this was what Willow wanted.

All her years of practice, all her years of fantasizing about this moment, and it wasn't disappointing. These were the things she wanted to do; to gain mastery over the world around her. With her body the way it was, magic was the only way she could have any effect on the world at all. A mage didn't have to be strong or nimble. They just had to know the secrets of magic, and that magic would do their bidding.

"Essence is one of the five essential humors of the body and the only one we can control by sheer force of will. While imbalances in the other humors bring sickness and death, usage of essence does not appear to affect overall health except when bent to that specific purpose.

"The concept that we impart upon our essence is all-important to the final effect of the spell. The form directs the essence and tells it what to do as it leaves our body, but the concept will determine the outcome. It is most important for a mage to understand how to produce the essence of a certain concept and their own ability with each type of concept.

"You might have been told in your introductory texts that all one has to do is recite the mantra to impart a concept, but this is a lie. The concepts in question are inextricably tied to the mage's own understanding of those concepts.

"For a mage who speaks a different language, the words *blazing light* would mean nothing at all. Even for those of us who have grown up speaking different dialects, you may be forced to use differing words than the others when concept selection becomes all important. You there, boy in the front row."

Willow was startled when the professor's finger landed so close to her seat, but it was Leopold at which it was pointing.

"Yes, professor?"

"Cast a magelight for me, if you will."

Leopold shook his head as if disentangling himself from the professor's lecture. He cupped his hands and Willow watched as he intoned his concept, shaped it, and layered a second on top.

The professor whispered a spell to himself and enacted a spell-form—that of slipping on a glove—then reached out and literally plucked the magelight from Leopold's hands.

"As you can see, young..." He looked down and it was a moment before Leopold responded.

"Leopold," he said.

"Leopold here has produced a magelight which shines with a yellow brilliance. If you look up to the corners of the room, the magelights there have a slight yellow tint but are much closer to the sun's rays. Why is that?"

Willow tentatively raised her hand.

"Yes, Miss…"

"Willow," she said. "His own individual understanding of *blazing* has colored the final concept. When we think of *blazing*, we usually think of a fire or a torch, which both produce yellow light."

"Correct, exactly correct," the professor said, which bolstered her confidence.

If she couldn't cast spells correctly, then at least she could read her texts and know what she *should* be able to do.

"And to illustrate the individuality of concepts, we'll have Miss Willow here cast her own magelight to highlight the difference in hue."

Willow's mouth dropped in shock. She felt sweat prickle her body. Cast magelight, here? She couldn't even cast it under the best of circumstances. She could barely get the first concept out, never mind the steadfast layer.

"Whenever you are ready."

"S-Sir," she stammered.

"Go on," he said.

There was no malice in his look—he really thought she could just do it on command. Somehow that expectation was worse than if she'd thought he was intentionally making fun of her after seeing her evaluation.

"Using the same words, if you will," he said, and Willow cupped her hands into the spell-form.

"Blazing light," she said, willing her essence not to fail her this time.

It moved sluggishly, like water in a reed-choked marsh. Apparently the effect of the essence injection had worn off as her body replenished its essence during the night.

"Blazing light," she grunted, trying to force the essence to move from her core, through her arms, out of her hands. It was like pushing against a boulder or wading upstream. There was no sense of momentum, just resistance. Maybe that metrologist was right. Maybe she did have more resistance than everyone else.

"Blazing light," she gasped.

A wisp of essence spilled from her fingers to coalesce into a sphere the size of a pin's head between her hands. It shone with a yellow light as well, but even in her distress, Willow could see that it was of a subtly different hue from Leopold's—a tallow candle to his pitch torch.

Willow took a breath, preparing to attempt a layer, when the professor stepped forwards.

"I think you have demonstrated the difference in hue quite acceptably, Miss Willow," he said. When she glanced up, she saw concern on his face. He'd noticed how hard it was for her and wanted to save her from embarrassment. In that moment, she felt infinitely grateful to him.

"Now, if we compare these two magelights side by side," he said, reaching for the essence core between Willow's hands.

She gasped as the strangest thing happened.

Her hands spasmed like they used to do when she was younger, at the end of the day when she'd run out of energy. Her palm flopped down, hinging unnaturally on her wrist, and her fingers went limp and numb. The professor noticed something too. His eyes went wide and he attempted to draw the magelight out from between her fingers, only to have it boil away in his hand.

Willow hissed to herself. Her hands felt as though they were studded with pins and needles, prickling all over as waves of hot and cold washed over them. It was as if every sensation it was possible to feel was buffeting her flesh at the same moment. She squeezed her hands under her armpits in an attempt to keep them from exploding. Were they going to explode? She didn't know.

"I'm—I'm sorry," she stammered up at the professor.

He was looking with great fascination at his own hand, the one he'd sheathed in a spell. He rubbed his fingers together.

"I didn't finish the spell," she gasped.

That seemed to bring him back to himself. He leaned forwards and spoke in a low voice that only she could hear. "Are you alright, Miss Willow?"

"Yes, I think so," she said. And it was true. Her hands were settling down, and she could feel her fingers again as they flexed against her sides. The burning sensation was retreating as she regained control.

"Do you need to go and see the nurse?"

"No, no. I'm alright," she said, pushing through the lingering pain.

He stayed there for a second longer, looking into her eyes before rising to face the class again.

"Miss Willow here has just unintentionally demonstrated one of the properties of essence, in that spells will cause disruption in their surrounding essence flow. I attempted, foolishly I might add, to retrieve her magelight before she'd layered it with steadfastness and completed the spell. Thus, subjecting my ethereal gauntlet to unregulated essence and canceling both it and her uncompleted spell."

A hand went up in the back of the class. "You said that spells cause disruption to essence flow, but your spell also was canceled. Does it work the other way around as well?"

A muscle in Professor Brandeweiss' jaw jumped, and his eyes flickered down to Willow for an instant before he responded.

"Not usually."

CHAPTER 9

It wasn't hard to find the metrology lab, as they were off in their own little building right on the edge of the Arcanum. No classes were held here, so no other students were rushing to get into lecture halls before the bell sounded. This was a working laboratory where real research was done every day. It was the kind of place in which she'd be sequestered in her second year, once she decided on a specialty. She had a strong intimation that her specialty wouldn't involve metrology.

The walls were stone, but the roof was single-story and flat, as if someone had sheared the top of the building without accounting for rainfall or snow. It appeared from the outside to be the cheapest possible building to construct out of cut stone, and it probably was. The size alone was more comparable to a large house than what she expected of an academic laboratory.

Willow knocked twice on the thin wooden door, but when no one answered, she tripped the latch and let herself in.

The interior of the small building was surprisingly bright—inscripted magelights dotted the ceiling like a grid of stars. There were less than a dozen graduate students huddled over workbenches, and a group of three towards the back of the room talked amongst themselves. She had no idea where to go. One of the students at the back of the room turned around, and she saw it was the young man from her evaluation. He waved her over.

"Hi. I assume this is the right place for my test?"

"It's the best place to be tested," another young man said and held out his hand. "Daniel."

"Willow," she said and shook. There was a woman in the group too, about Willow's age, who also held out her hand.

"Steph," she said. "I heard you killed the emmeter."

"Emmeter?" Willow asked as she looked towards the student she'd already seen before.

"Burket," he said and shook her hand too, which was at this point becoming quite tender. "The device you were being tested with is called an emmeter, or essence meter, and it *is* broken now."

"Oh," Willow said. A twist in her gut warned her of the possibility that she'd have to pay for it.

"It's no problem, we've got loads of them." Steph waved it away. "I'm curious how in the seven hells you did it though. That was one of mine."

"I told you already, she overloaded the injector," Burket said, motioning towards a small door in the back wall. He led the group and opened the door to a smaller room, which was similarly lit with those shadowless magelights.

"Yeah, but that shouldn't be—" Daniel began, but Burket shot him a look.

"That's what we're here to find out. How? And also what your real measurements are. You appear to be a bit of an anomaly. Very useful for debugging our instruments."

"Oh great, it's not like I didn't feel weird enough," Willow muttered as she stepped into the room. She hadn't missed the other two's glances at her neck and arms and tugged her sleeves down to cover her wrists. Burket must have told them about her. About the way she looked.

"Don't worry," Steph said softly behind her. "Once we get you measured up, your probation will disappear."

"Uh huh," Willow said, unsure if Steph also knew about the stipulation that she had to produce an introductory spell. Or did the woman not even consider such a task worth mentioning?

"We've only got an hour and a half," Burket said as he clapped his hands together. "Let's get started, shall we? Willow, you can sit there. We'll get the first test all set up."

The seat he motioned to was padded on the bottom and back, and she wondered for a moment which of the three had seen fit to modify the plain wooden chair for her comfort. It made her feel vaguely confused as to her feelings about the graduate students. Did she trust them? Could she?

"We're going to start with the emmeter again," Daniel said as he brought out the familiar crystal spike. "But we're going to place a rummeter between you and the device to measure the force it's putting out to inject you with essence."

"I thought you saw that on the first test," Willow said to Burket as he tapped on another crystal plate.

"I saw that the system was straining, but…" he trailed off.

"What?"

"It stopped displaying before it was able to inject," he said. She noticed he wouldn't meet her eyes. What did that mean?

"Alright, the test's all set up," Burket said. Daniel had strapped a thin metal strip to the side of the crystal point. "Just place your palm on that strip. And then try to push only through the palm, if you can."

"And that's all? Just the same as the test before?"

Daniel nodded. "Just the same."

Willow placed her hand against the metal strip and wrapped her fingers around the cool crystal. The strip had been inlaid with a tight packing of engraved characters, which she recognized from her introductory textbook on inscriptions. They would have essence flowing through them to produce an effect—in this case, measuring the essence flowing between her and the emmeter.

"I'm reading a lot of chatter," Daniel said, staring down at his own crystal plate.

Steph leaned forwards and adjusted Willow's fingers against the crystal, placing her palm more firmly against the metal strip. "Now?" she asked.

"A little better, but the readings are still fuzzy," Daniel said with a shrug. "Should be good enough for a first go-around."

"Alright, Willow, you can push now."

Willow closed her eyes and visualized her body's essence as she had earlier that morning. It was diminished to her sight, partially from her failed spell, partially from the late hour. She suspected that her waning mental energy had something to do with her inability to access the essence that must still be there. She knew in theory that as long as she wasn't casting, her body should be replenishing her essence. It never felt like that though.

She already felt exhausted somewhere inside, like she'd strained a muscle earlier that day from working so hard to not embarrass herself in class. So she pushed as if she were coddling an injured limb. Her essence responded sluggishly, like a viscous mucous rather than a flowing torrent. Others had described their essence flow like water—what she wouldn't give to have that experience.

From her solar plexus down her arms to her hands. Out through the palms, she felt her essence flow then disappear, sucked greedily into the emmeter.

"You can start anytime," Daniel said.

"I am," Willow ground out between her teeth. Sweat began to bead on her forehead.

"Registering em," Burket said. "One milliem."

"Just one milliem?"

From Steph's tone Willow felt a wave of embarrassment crash down upon her. She nearly lost focus on her essence. The metrologists were amazed, but she didn't feel like it was something good.

"Just keep pushing," Burket said.

"I am!" Willow repeated.

"I'm still not getting anything above the noise," Daniel said to Burket.

"That's fine. We'll get enough to move on to the second phase. That's what we're looking for anyway."

Willow groaned, trying to tune out their voices and focus on moving her essence.

For five agonizing minutes she pushed, until Burket called a halt to that phase of the test. Willow had been pacing her breathing like a long-distance runner, and finally, she let herself gasp and lean back into the padded seat. She felt the silence in the room like a thick woolen blanket. She knew they were staring at her.

"I never got a—" Daniel said.

"That's fine," Burket interrupted. "Are you ready to start the injection?"

Willow opened her eyes, hand still on the emmeter. She felt grimy with sweat from her two big expenditures of the morning and wanted nothing more than a bath, but she nodded nonetheless.

"Let's get it over with."

A knock came at the door. Burket's eyebrows quirked up in puzzlement as Steph stepped across the small room. Strangely enough, Professor Brandeweiss was standing in the doorway when she opened it.

"Professor?" Willow asked.

"Ah, it appears as if I've found you. I had the hardest time tracking you down after class."

"Oh. I had to come here, to metrology, for some additional testing."

"Yes, I read all about it. Probation, a most unpleasant situation to find oneself in. Although I must say, many of my students find themselves there only after some form of shenanigans or mischief."

It took an effort for Willow not to dip her head in shame as the professor stepped into the small room. It was then she realized that five was quite too many people for the stuffy room.

"I wanted to come down to the lab to observe your testing after what happened in class."

"Why?" Willow asked.

"Oh, just to slake my own curiosity. It's not often that one of my demonstrations goes so awry."

"I'm sorry." This time, Willow *did* bow her head in embarrassment.

"No matter," Brandeweiss waved the comment away. "You were in the middle of testing, correct?"

"Yes, professor," Burket said. "We were just about to start the injection phase of the emmeter test."

"Well, inject away," the professor said as he leaned against the door, which freed up a few bare inches of space in the room. "I shall not interfere again."

"Right," Burket said, then cleared his throat. "Alright, I'm starting the injection now."

Again, Willow felt a sensation akin to a light breeze against her hand, almost too little to notice. Steph moved to look over Daniel's shoulder, but Burket was still focused on his own tablet. Brandeweiss was leaning against the door, looking at all four of them.

"I'm increasing the pressure," Burket said, and she felt the light breeze turn into a gust. "Let me know if you become uncomfortable."

"Okay," she said, as if she needed this test to stay in school and to keep from being expelled before her life as a mage even began. She'd sit there until it became unbearable.

The flow of essence became a push, then a prod, then a strong pressure. Steph's eyes were wide as saucers and only growing as she watched Daniel's plate. Daniel managed to keep a straight face, but the blood had fled his skin, leaving his lips ashy and pale. Burket, perhaps because he had seen this once before, was focused entirely on his own plate. Brandeweiss continued to lean against the door as if in relaxation.

The pressure reached a crescendo, and then Willow felt her old essence squirt back into her arm. That same feeling of inflation occurred, like her arm was being filled with water. She gritted her teeth through the discomfort and held on tight.

"And we're... done. Done," Burket said and looked up at Daniel and Steph. Steph's mouth was open, and even Daniel hadn't been able to hide his shock at what he'd seen.

"That's not..." Daniel whispered.

Burket wedged his way between the other two to look at the plate, then wrote something down on a sheet.

Willow's arm hummed with trapped power, unable to move, unable to return to her body. Her fingers twitched with the thrum, and she finally unstuck her hand from the crystal to rub her knuckles. They were becoming tender again.

"What did it say?" Willow asked.

"One hundred and fifty runs," Burket said. "So, we've finally got a number on you. And we broke another emmeter as well."

"That's not her attribute. And the device wasn't designed for—" Steph began, but the professor interrupted her.

"I think after her morning demonstration and this little test, Miss Willow has been quite worn out. And it appears as if she's in no small amount of discomfort."

For the first time, the three students looked at Willow again, who was sitting and rubbing her hand.

"How—" Steph began, then swallowed the question and shook her head.

"I'll escort Miss Willow out. Unless you have any other tests you need to run today?"

"N-No," Burket said. "No, we have to... I think we have to get some different equipment."

"Right. Then follow me, Miss Willow, and let's see if we can't find your next classroom."

By the time Willow realized she didn't know where her next class was, and the professor probably wouldn't either, they were already back in the main building. The injected power was also finally fading to a mere tick-y rumble in her arm.

"Um, Professor," she said as she tried to keep pace with him. It was hard with her hobble. She really needed a cane. "I'm not quite sure where Introduction to Inscription is."

"Probably over in the southeast quadrant," he said. They turned down a hall with what seemed like a hundred little doors along its sides.

"Oh, is that where we're going?"

"No," Professor Brandeweiss said, and stopped in front of a door, which had his name painted on a small placard. He produced a metal key, turned the bolt, and then ushered her in.

"After you."

The professor's office was small, much smaller than her own bedroom. It was just big enough for a chair and a desk built into the wall. Every surface was covered in yellow-tinted papers, some bound in twine, others loose piles. There was no window in the far wall of the room. Only a tiny flickering magelight towards the ceiling provided illumination.

"Pardon me." The professor extended his hand upwards towards the light. The sphere flickered once more, then grew brighter and steadier until it had the same intensity as Leopold's in class.

"There, that should do it," he said as he moved a pile of papers off of what turned out to be a second chair and motioned to it. Willow gratefully took the seat. "We don't have inscripted lights in our offices, so we're forced to make do with magelight. It may seem quaint to you, but the Arcanum can't really afford to send people around to every office shunting essence."

"No, not quaint at all," Willow said. "Where I come from, we still use oil lamps. There are a few in town who know enough to produce a small magelight, but most of the spellwork there has to do with stripping fungus from crops or mending furniture."

"Bridgewater, I think your file said." The Professor tapped a sheaf of papers on his desk. Willow nodded. "I've never been to your small town, but if it's like many of the others around Durum, it's primarily agricultural?"

"Yes, that's right, Professor."

"Please, call me Carl. And I can see how you're twitching. No, we won't be going to your next class."

"But..." Her objection trailed off. She hadn't really been that interested in inscriptions anyway. They took a steady source of essence to function, and she could barely put out a halting trickle as it was.

"You're wondering why we're in my office. The simple answer is that after our little mishap in class this morning, I took a particular interest in you. After that result you got in the lab... well, let's say my interest has grown."

"What *did* happen in the lab?" Willow asked. "What's a run?"

"You probably would have learned about that in the very class you're missing now," he said. "But no matter, I'll elucidate it for you. In inscribing, there are several attributes of essence that we are concerned with. One is the measure of resistance in the inscription itself. The more complicated the inscription, the higher the resistance. That resistance is measured in a unit called wam.

"The storage capacity of an inscription is also directly affected by how many storage containers are added to it. Those lights in the metrology department will run for a day before they need to be recharged. That capacity is measured in ems.

"And finally, the force with which essence is pushed through a system is measured in runs. All of these units were originally calibrated to a researcher's natural essential attributes. One em is the general amount of essence a person can store in their bodies. One wam is the typical resistance between a user's heart and their hand. And one run is the maximal force with which one can generally push their essence from their body."

"So that device," Willow wondered. "It was pushing essence into my body with the force of 150 mages?"

"Mages generally have a higher run rating than researchers, but not much higher. Two, I think, is the highest I've ever heard measured. And yes, that is what it means. It might go a long way towards explaining why you're reacting that way to the injected essence."

Willow's arm had mostly calmed down, but her fingers still twitched every few seconds. She closed her fist to try and force the muscles to quiet.

"I assume that's not common?" she asked grimly.

"Correct. Humans have a pretty low resistance to essence, which is what allows us to move it around in our bodies so freely. Magical creatures have much higher resistances as their magical effects are constantly engaged, disrupting the flow of essence like islands in a stream. There are some metals that can disrupt essence, but you didn't happen to apply a silver balm to your hands this morning, did you?"

Willow shook her head. "What does it mean, then?"

"Well, it explains why you had such a difficult time producing the magelight in class. You've never conjured the second layer?"

Willow looked down at her knees, then shook her head. There was no use lying. He'd already seen her test results.

"That you're able to do even as much as you have is a testament to your will. If I'm not mistaken, the terms of your probation require you to produce a magelight or similar introductory spell by the end of two weeks, correct?"

"Yes," Willow whispered.

That task seemed all but impossible now. She'd thought before that she wasn't practicing enough, even though she'd practiced hours every day back in Bridgewater. Or that her mental acuity wasn't where it needed to be. Or that her essence control was weak. To learn there was something wrong with her—something *else* wrong with her—seemed to sap all of her drive. For all she knew, it could be related to her wasted condition. How could she possibly work through that?

The professor nodded. "I will assist you in completing this task."

"Oh, no. No, I couldn't possibly—I've got a friend who's going to help me. We'll be practicing every—"

Brandeweiss held up a hand. "Do not reject my offer lightly. I'm talking about one-on-one tutoring from someone who's helped many other students in similar straits as yours. I only require one thing in return."

"And that is?" Willow asked.

Brandeweiss scratched his graying beard. "It would be most unusual for me to continue to intrude on your metrology readings. I'm sure those metrology students will overlook it this once, but if I'm to act as your tutor, I would like your permission to sit in on your measurements. They'll give me a better idea of what we're working with."

"Can't you just read the reports after?" Willow asked. She didn't particularly enjoy the idea of even more people learning just how much of a freak she was.

"I would rather see the tests as they're performed," he said.

Willow sighed. "I suppose that's fine. Thank you, Professor."

"Please," he repeated. "Call me Carl."

CHAPTER 10

Her room was so far away, near the city wall and gate. Too far. With so little time between the end of her half-tardy inscription class and her first tutoring session, Willow opted to stay near the Arcanum and scrounge up something to eat. As it turned out, there were plenty of establishments on the street outside the campus proper which catered to the student rush between classes.

That was where she ran into Leopold.

"How did your first classes go?" Leopold asked with an expectant smile.

Willow groaned and proceeded to tell him about the strange events of the morning after their class together. Complete with the deadly evil eye she'd received from the inscription professor.

"Well, that isn't really your fault, is it?" Leopold grumped as he sat munching on his meat pie. Willow was on her second of three. "Has anyone ever told you that you eat like a horse?"

"No, not like a horse," Willow said. "Like a cow once before. I think I hit him with my cane."

"Ah, well I'm glad you haven't got one of those yet."

"I'm not. My back is killing me."

Leopold glanced around at the alleys radiating off the Arcanum's border street. "I'll see what I can get after lunch."

"What? No, you don't have to do that. I'll go out and get one—"

"You're tutoring with Brandeweiss after, and it'll be too late by the time you finish. It's the least I can do."

"Oh. Okay," Willow said, and she couldn't help but smile. When had he gotten so helpful?

"And besides, it'll give me a chance to choose your weapon," he said. "I'd rather have a nice light caning than a fatal beating with that metal rod you had before."

"Gods, how I miss my old cane. My father got that for me. It must've cost a fortune, but he wouldn't tell me how much he paid for it. I cost them a lot over the years with my disease. They hired a traveling healer, a mage, to fix me once. She couldn't do anything and said there wasn't anything wrong with me. Still charged them though. Bullshit! Of course there's something wrong with me."

"Hey," Leopold said, and Willow looked at him. He looked down, almost abashed. "There's nothing wrong with you," he whispered.

Willow couldn't stop herself from laughing in his face. "Are you joking? What do you see, when you see me? A waif, someone on the edge of death. What do you think when you see this?" She pushed up her sleeve, exposing a forearm so shrunken that the skin fell into the gap between her ulna and radius.

He winced.

"That's what I thought," Willow said and lowered her sleeve. "I always thought... They told me I got the Wasting, that I survived. I guess I thought I was special, that it could've been worse. It turns out I didn't even get the Wasting. I'm just sick."

Leopold scooted closer to her. All at once she realized how ridiculous she was being.

"Gods, listen to me," she said, her cheeks flushing. "I sound like a child."

"You're shook up is all," he said. "The demonstration, the tests. You'll be back to being pissed off at me soon enough."

Willow chuckled. "Yeah, I guess," she said, but she wasn't sure. She hadn't felt so low in years.

It was with a fuller stomach but lower spirits that she made her way back to Professor Brandeweiss' office. She knocked on the wooden door and heard his muffled voice from the other side.

"Come in! I'm sort of trapped back here."

Willow opened the door to see the office completely rearranged from the last time she'd been there just a few hours before. Gone were the stacks of folios and thickets of yellowed pages that had formerly crammed every inch of the room. It would have looked almost clean if it hadn't been for the several small tables Professor Brandeweiss had crammed into the office. They separated his own desk from the door, and each sported a dark crystalline device. A lone chair stood on her side of the barricade.

"Professor?"

"Carl, please," he said, and motioned as best he could to the chair beside her. She gently shut the door and took her seat.

"It doesn't feel right to call you Carl."

"Well, I'm not your professor right now. I'm your tutor. And hopefully I've constructed something that will help your essence flow."

Constructed? Willow looked at the tables again and, sure enough, thin strips of copper connected each of the obsidian halfspheres. The strips were crammed with inscriptions and the whole room felt like it was buzzing.

"What is all this?"

"This is how I plan to get your essence flow high enough to finish a magelight spell," Carl said, gesturing to the domes. "Each of these is an essence capacitor, and they've all been maxed out. Would you mind guessing why I've arrayed these five capacitors before you and unfortunately blocked off any means of escape should this office burst into flame?"

"Um," Willow said. And sure enough, she realized he was right. He would definitely be trapped back there if one of those should explode or something were to catch on fire. The thought made her slightly queasy.

"I really don't know. If they're charged up... are you planning to inject me with them?"

"Oh no, no," he said, then frowned. "I suppose I did make you miss the first half of your inscriptions class. A full essence capacitor has an extremely high resistance to being overloaded. Overloads can occur and are dangerous, but the steep rise in resistance makes them virtually unheard of in inscripted constructs. However, that's exactly what we're going to do here, but on a minor level."

"But... they're dangerous, right? You just said that."

He waved her complaint away. "Dangerous for high essence flows. But from your test results earlier today, it appears that's a problem we won't have to worry about."

Willow felt a moment's pang of shame but gritted her teeth together. If she was going to stay in the school, she'd need all the help she could get. And Professor Brandeweiss—no, Carl—was freely offering it.

"So it's a good thing," she stated.

"For now," he said, directing her attention to the capacitor at the far left. "This is where we'll start. I've wired all these together to absorb any extra essence that might spill out, just in case you push too hard. What you're going to do is put your hand here and try to push as much essence as you can into the capacitor. I'll be monitoring the numbers."

"Okay," Willow said, still unsure about how this was supposed to help.

She put her hand on the farthest left capacitor dome and visualized the essence in her body. It whirled and swirled like disturbed water, and overall, it felt like there was a lot less than during the tests earlier that day—but she visualized anyway. She forced the essence to flow from her heart, down her arm, and sluggishly exit her hand into the capacitor.

It felt like she was pushing essence into a rock. The device was completely unaccepting of more essence, but she put her back into it. Choosing to believe Carl, she trusted that the dome would eventually yield and accept a small trickle.

It took several sweat-drenched minutes before she felt the first wisp of essence flow into the dome. Carl sighed in relief.

"Got it. The first dome is registering an overcharge. Now you're going to slowly lessen your push and accept that overcharge back in."

"I've... never pushed with anything less than my full force before."

"There was never a reason to, but now there is. If you would..." He gestured to the dome again.

Even though she was damp and sticky with sweat under her overcoat, Willow focused on her essence and attempted to attenuate the push she'd been sustaining. It was difficult at first, but she eventually got the essence to flow backwards in fits and starts.

When the capacitor finally stopped pushing against her, Willow let out a gasp and dropped her hand from the dome. She was drenched from crown to foot with sweat, and a headache was setting up behind her eyes. When she looked at Carl, he was beaming.

"I'm seeing we're back to 100 percent capacity," he said, pointing down to the crystal plate she hadn't noticed before. "You pushed into an overcharged capacitor and accepted the pushback. I'm extremely happy about this result."

"Why... so?" Willow panted, rubbing her left hand with her right. Strangely, she still didn't feel any of that buzzing quality that she'd gotten from being injected earlier.

"Because it means that this training method will probably work," Carl said. He began disconnecting the metal strips connecting the capacitor to the rest of the chain. "Take this home, don't use its capacity on anything other than training. And I want you to train like this every morning and night as many times as you can manage."

"How am I supposed to cast anything in class with a schedule like that?" Willow panted.

"Willow." Carl became deadly serious. "If you can't do this, you won't have class two weeks from now. Schoolwork can be made up. Expulsion… not so much."

Willow swallowed, then nodded.

* * *

When she got back to Grave Street, Leopold was already there waiting for her. Dinner had long ago been set out and taken up, but Margaret had saved her portion and the leftovers in the inscripted icebox. Willow wondered if Leopold had said anything about the way she ravenously devoured lunch.

Well, she wasn't going to complain. Leopold peppered her with questions about Carl's training as she ate her second helping of shepherd's pie. Then he examined the capacitor dome she retrieved from her sack.

"Do you know its capacity?" he asked as she was finally beginning to feel stuffed.

"No, just that it's full."

Leopold shook his head.

"What?"

"Just… I have no idea what it actually means unless we get a read on its capacity. Its overcharge resistance could be anything."

Willow shrugged her shoulders.

"You're not even a little bit curious about what you're pushing? A hundred and fifty runs isn't… well, it isn't normal. To say the least."

"It isn't helping me, is it?" Willow sighed. "If anything, it seems like it's partially to blame for my problems."

"I don't think so," Leopold said. "Or Professor Brandeweiss wouldn't be training you to increase your pressure, would he?"

"I suppose not," Willow said.

Leopold set the capacitor down and crossed the room to the corner, where he retrieved a wooden cane.

"Oh, Leopold," she gasped when he handed it over. After her torturous day, the gesture was almost too much and she had to blink back tears. The cane was light, its wood hollow and segmented on the inside.

"It's made of something called bamboo," he said, shrugging. "I thought you might like it after... well, how heavy your other one was. I'm sure Bryan can cut it to size."

"Bryan's not the only one handy with a saw," Margaret chided from where she was washing up at the basin.

"I won't make that mistake again," Leopold apologized as Willow got up from the bench and put her weight on the cane.

It barely bent at all, even with its lightness. And it was only a little too long. It felt... good. To have a cane in her hand again—to take the load off her feet for even a half-step.

"Thank you," she said, and Leopold smiled.

"No problem," he said, adjusting his glasses and turning away. His neck had grown dangerously red. "What are friends for?"

Chapter 11

He'd wanted to practice spells after dinner, but Willow waved it off. With a headache growing behind her temples, she went to bed early. In her dreams she swam through water as thick as tar, flailing uselessly as she sank deeper and deeper into the viscous substance. Something was poised above the surface of the water, reared up in a vicious curve. Something that sucked more than air into its gaping maw.

Willow woke sweating to Margaret's gentle knock at her door.

As much as she didn't want to, Willow laid her hand on the capacitor at her bedside table, as Carl had instructed, and focused on her essence. Her hold on the substance was a little shaky with the dregs of sleep, but she channeled it as hard as she could towards the device.

By the time she was utterly exhausted, she'd managed to push her utmost into the capacitor and slowly accept it back five times.

When she got out of bed, she immediately felt weaker than normal, almost as if half the day was already gone. She hadn't expected her exercise to tire her so—according to her textbook, manipulating your essence was a purely mental exercise, not related to physical exertion at all. Despite her weakness, she forced herself through her morning routine anyway, if only to clean herself of the sweat she'd worked up from her training. It was strange to be sweating and not aching at the same time from some physical exertion, but she supposed that was how things would be now that she was practicing magic.

In the kitchen Willow found that Margaret had cooked her a double breakfast, and she thanked the woman profusely. In return, Margaret gave her a hug that ached all across her back and arms, but Willow didn't complain. When it was time to head out, Willow picked up her newly-shortened cane from beside the door and pushed through to the cold mist of morning.

The first class of the day was an introduction to the history of magic, where she learned about the Arcana and the cities that grew up around them. Magic had been discovered there, and as a result, the city-states that emerged flourished with increased crop growth and healing. Those Arcana and the cities that surrounded them eventually grew large enough and greedy enough to war with one another, which produced the first warbeasts.

"The warbeasts were incubated in potent essence wombs, starting off as magical creatures that were quickly mutated by their essence-laden environments. This gave them strange powers and a propensity to grow to enormous sizes. A warbeast hasn't been grown in centuries, though, and those that remain are the more docile of the final waves."

The portly professor stopped as a student in the back raised their hand.

"Yes, you in the back."

"How old is Durum's warbeast?"

"Well, records indicate it first arrived about 120 years ago. As to how long it incubated before that arrival, we can safely guess decades. So probably 150-ish, give or take a few years. And I wouldn't quite call it Durum's warbeast. It was sent by Raly, so it's really their warbeast, isn't it? But regardless, it's been around for so long that its danger has mostly been neutralized, as long as we use proper precautions when entering and exiting the city. Now, onto the Bloodless Pact, and the prohibition against warbeasts..."

Luckily Willow didn't have any spell-crafting classes that day, because she wasn't sure if she'd have the mental fortitude to manipulate her essence after the morning exercises. Unfortunately, she did have another appointment with metrology. That meant entering the small building with the constellation of inscripted lights and making her way to the back room once again.

Carl was already there waiting with the other students. They had an array of metallic strips and trays of black, crystalline devices laid out on the back table and a seat for Willow beside them. In the corner were a couple of long staves wrapped in strips of shiny copper.

"Alright, Willow, today we're going to try to track your resistance in wams," Daniel said and gestured to the seat beside the long table. There was a device closest to the seat connected to a couple of pads with scripted copper tape. Towards the back of the room, Burket already looked upset.

She hadn't even done anything yet.

"This is our standard wammeter," Steph said and picked up the pads. "This one goes on your wrist and the other goes on your chest above your heart. I'll let you apply that one yourself."

The pad was covered on one side with some kind of golden sap—Willow assumed it had been imbued with copper powder for essential conductivity. It was a pain to work the pad in between the buttons of her overcoat and through her blouse without getting the sap on her clothes, but she eventually got it adhered to her chest. Steph had long ago gotten the other pad on her wrist.

"So this device is going to send a small—very small—current of essence through your body, and the run of the current it outputs compared to the run it receives will give us your resistance. It'll be a pretty good gauge of your resistance when casting," Daniel said. "Are you ready?"

Willow nodded, and Burket tapped on his crystal plate. Carl took up vigil behind Burket's shoulder and watched the display.

Nothing happened for a long time. The room was silent. Steph eventually walked over and took a quick look at the plate before coming back with her mouth pressed in a tight line. Willow assumed that couldn't mean anything good.

"Alright, we're almost at capacity," Daniel said to Burket, a vague hint of warning in his voice. Willow could feel a slight tingling from the pad on her wrist, almost like a light breeze had brushed the skin there.

"Fine," Burket said and tapped the plate. All at once the tickle vanished and Burket huffed in frustration.

"What? What happened?"

"You—" Burket began, but Daniel interrupted him.

"The wammeter isn't as powerful as the emmeter, and even the emmeter barely got any kind of reading. If we push the wammeter that hard, it'll definitely burn out. We got reamed out by the head of the department yesterday for breaking so many."

"Oh, I'm sorry," Willow said, the familiar feeling of shame and confusion settling over her chest.

"No, it's not your fault," Daniel said. Something in his voice made her look up as he swiveled his eyes towards Burket.

Ah, message received loud and clear.

"But we prepared for this eventuality." Daniel headed for the corner and retrieved the two wooden staves wrapped in inscribed copper.

"Rather, Professor Brandeweiss prepared for it," Steph corrected. "He acquired these from the geology department via unknown means."

"A colleague of mine owes me a favor," Carl said with a smile. "Just don't break them."

"That shouldn't be—" Daniel said, then stopped himself, considering. "We won't."

Carl nodded and Steph helped Daniel replace the black crystal wammeter on the table with the pair of spikes, both pointy ends facing Willow. They didn't make her feel particularly safe.

"Um, so what are these?" Willow asked.

Close up, they appeared to be wooden all along the shafts, leading down to what was either copper-plated or solid copper spikes inscribed with spirals of symbols. Thin copper tape twisted up the wooden shafts, which Steph and Daniel were delicately unwinding. They hooked the tape into Burket's crystal plate and a half-dome that Willow recognized as an essence capacitor.

"These are used to survey the ground for copper and silver deposits," Carl said, walking over and touching the copper tip of one of the staves. "At a set distance, solid rock should have a certain resistance. But if that's greater or less than usual, it means there's a deposit in there somewhere messing with the essential flow. Surveyors use them to identify deposits before the miners go to work on the rock."

"You're saying that you have to measure my resistance on the same scale as solid rock?"

"It's worse than even that," Burket said from behind his plate. He tapped frenetically on the surface now that the tape was inserted into the side. "These spikes are supposed to be placed a hundred feet apart. The distance between your heart and your arm is barely, what... three feet? A dead body has less resistance than you. A magical creature has less resistance than you."

"Burket," Carl warned, and Burket clamped his lips together.

He clearly wanted to go on about how fucked she was and about how much work she was making them all go through. Gods knew she wished it was just over on exam day.

"This time it might be a little uncomfortable," Daniel said. "We'll be pushing a fairly high level of runs into your body, so if you start to feel any pain—"

"I'll say something," Willow lied.

Daniel finished hooking the tapes leading from her body to the copper ends of the spikes. He looked at Burket and nodded. Burket didn't nod back and instead began tapping on the plate again.

"Okay, we're starting now. Just remember... be safe."

"Right," Willow said, and immediately she felt the tickle on her wrist.

It quickly progressed from a tickle to a breeze, then to a pushing weight. She felt movement in her arm, her fingers started to twitch, and it felt as though something was pricking her hand at random. Willow clenched her teeth against the phantom sensations.

Steph and Carl both stood behind Burket and the plate. She didn't need to look into Steph's eyes to see that the results were unexpected. Daniel hadn't joined the others though. He was standing by her side, next to the tapes of copper foil, tensed as if ready to pull them at a moment's notice. For all she knew, he would. *If* she said anything. She clenched her teeth harder against the mounting pain.

"Willow, are you alright?" Daniel asked.

The pressure had become excruciating on her wrist, and it felt like molten iron was forcing itself up her arm to her shoulder. Her arm was shaking, but she couldn't help that. Her fingers lost control and began twitching like crazy. She grasped them with her other hand to hide the effect, which only caused both hands to convulse in the phantom pain.

"Okay," Willow managed to hiss through her teeth.

"Burket," Steph whispered, and Willow heard fear in her voice.

Burket's frenzied eyes bored into the dark crystal plate as he tapped on the surface. Steph whispered his name again, trying to snap him out of it. Carl laid a hand on her shoulder and shook his head, never once taking his eyes off the display plate.

Willow gasped as the molten shaft passed her shoulder and spread into her chest. She felt her heart race, skip a beat, and the world became blurry around the edges. Her eyelids fluttered.

"Shut it off!" Daniel yelled, then moved to snatch the leads.

"No!" Willow screamed louder than she'd meant to, but it stopped Daniel in his tracks. "I need this!"

"Got it!" Burket yelled, and all at once the infinite pressure lifted.

The spreading fire in her chest dissipated, but her arm felt worse than ever. Her fingers were still twitching.

Carl grabbed another capacitor off the table and set it down at her side. "Push the extra essence out into this," he said, taking her hand and placing it on the domed top, covering it with his own. "It should help."

If he was surprised at the feel of her squirming fingers, he didn't show it.

Strangely enough, it was easier than normal to push out the injected essence. As it left her arm, she felt strangely better than even after her first test with the emmeter.

"Gods, we finally have it. Finally, her first measurement," Burket said.

"Wait, what about the one with the emmeter? The runs?"

"That was only a measurement of how hard the emmeter had to push to inject essence into your body," Steph said. "It wasn't actually your measurement. Although it should correlate."

"Well?" Willow asked, looking at Burket.

Burket smiled at her over the display plate. "Twelve hundred wam. Good going, silver girl."

* * *

Willow and Carl were back in his office and she had her hand on another capacitor, pushing her essence into it and then letting it flow slowly back.

"Am I really as resistive as pure silver?" she asked tiredly, nearing the end of the relaxation cycle.

"No." Carl sighed. "Almost. Three feet of silver bar at the width of your arm... maybe 1,500 wam."

"I guess that explains why I'm so shit at magic," Willow said.

She felt strangely calm. For her probation, she was happy they'd finally gotten a reading, but the number itself didn't actually change anything. Things were just as hard for her as they had always been. Nothing was worse. Nothing had changed.

"Have you ever heard of anything like that before?" Willow asked, peeling her hand off the capacitor.

Carl had been watching a small plate hooked up to the capacitor the whole time while she pushed and pulled her essence from it.

"Some injuries have been known to increase the body's essential resistance," Carl said. But Willow could tell from the sound of his voice that those increases weren't even on the same level as hers.

"Silver girl," Willow said, then chuckled to herself.

"I do wonder if you might have silver compounds in your blood, but I haven't heard of anything like that before. And you said other people in Bridgewater could cast spells just fine?"

Willow nodded, and Carl set the plate down.

"Well?" Willow asked. Carl sighed.

"In just the past day, you've increased your push force. Even after what you went through in the lab. I'm measuring an increase of five milli-ems in the capacitor at its peak from yesterday, which would normally be great news. It shows you have fantastic potential for growth. Unfortunately, it'll be too slow by far to get you where you need to be to produce a magelight by the end of next week. So we're going to try a different tack."

"Something different? Do I have to keep practicing with the capacitor at home?"

Willow was surprised at how easily the word had slipped from her mouth. Home. She supposed it felt like it now.

"By all means, keep practicing with the capacitor. It'll only help you to increase your runs. I've got a different idea though. You said you've been practicing the magelight spell for five years now, but how long have you been practicing the second layer? The steadfast one?"

"I've... never cast it," Willow said. "The book never said to practice it alone. It said I should just be able to cast it on top of the layer of blazing light. I've been trying to do that."

Carl actually smiled. "Yes, most people should be able to layer pretty effortlessly. But as we saw in the lab, you've got such a high essential resistance that it's taking most of your effort just to get the blazing light layer out. What I would like to try is practicing the steadfast layer. Hopefully you become familiar enough with it that it will be easier to cast on top of the blazing light."

"How do we do that? I mean, I can't keep two layers going at the same time, so what is it going to keep steadfast?"

"My own blazing light core," Carl said.

"Different people's essences can be layered together?"

"They can. It's an advanced technique but entirely dependent on the previous layer in the spell to get it working, so I've got you covered there. It's called a group cast, and you wouldn't normally learn about it until next year. But, well, here we are."

"Here we are," Willow agreed.

Carl positioned his hands in that oh-so-familiar spell-form. As he recited the concept mantra, she noticed each of his fingers begin a little twirling motion, as if he were setting up eddies in the flow of essence. Soon the blazing light core brightened the room, casting their shadows back against the walls.

"Alright, I'll hold it here and you cast the steadfast layer."

Willow nodded and moved her hands into position, the tips of her fingers tingling from the nearby essence core. She pointed her fingertips in a form meant to turn the escaping essence back in on itself. As her fingertips approached the blazing sphere, it wobbled slightly. Carl winced.

"Can you cast from that far away?"

"I can try," Willow said, although her hands were a good three inches away from the core and she'd never tried building up essence from that distance. She concentrated on the essence in her arms and chest, forcing it to move towards her hands. As she did so, she muttered the concept.

"Steadfast." She wove her fingers back and forth like the book described.

She'd dreamed of this moment for years—the moment when her blazing light core would be strong enough that she could attempt the second layer.

"Steadfast," she repeated and felt a thin trickle of essence leave her hands to encircle the core.

She didn't need to watch, so she kept her eyes closed. Her essential perception kept her in tune with her essence's behavior, and the layer she'd just put down encircled the core nicely. It linked up on the far side like stitching pulled tight.

"Steadfast," she whispered. With a final burst of effort, she pushed with the last of her mental fortitude.

A small surge of essence washed out and joined the stitching she'd laid down before, encompassing the core completely in a layer as thick as two or three sheets of paper.

Willow opened her eyes slowly, unable to really believe that she'd done it, but there it was. The core. Encircled by *her* steadfast layer. Self-sustaining! The light from this core would last for an hour, maybe two, and *she'd* provided the logic required to keep it self-sustaining. She felt at that moment like anything was possible. Like she might actually have a chance of getting through this probation after all.

One look at Carl's face was all it took to banish the flooding warmth. His jowls were shaking, wet with sweat and effort, and she noticed that he'd replaced his hands around the blazing core. He was trying to keep it from dissolving, and it was taking all of his considerable strength to do it.

"Carl?" Willow asked.

At the smallest twitch of her fingers, the magelight bowed inwards at the side like an injured beast, and the blazing core itself dispersed within the steadfast shell. The shell folded in on itself and reduced to shreds a second later.

Carl panted with effort. He wiped his brow with a handkerchief from his vest and stared hard at the space where the magelight had been, deep in thought.

"What happened?" Willow asked. "Did the group cast not work?"

"It almost worked."

"Then what happened?"

"Whatever's wrong... whatever the effect is in your body that makes your resistance so high, affects any essence you come into proximity with. Group casts work on fine adjustments between the various mages to ensure their essence doesn't interfere with each other. But your very presence in the room would affect all but the simplest of group casts, I'm afraid."

"Is that what happened that day in class?"

Carl nodded.

"I'm certain I can correct for it. If I overbalance my essence towards stability... yes, yes, I think that should work. Come on, let's try again."

"Again?" Willow asked. She'd barely recovered from the first attempt. "You mean right now?"

Carl looked at her solemnly. "The clock's ticking."

* * *

They cast five times before she was too exhausted to continue. Carl looked as though he was on his last leg, but he didn't have to walk all the way home to the city wall afterwards. Luckily when Willow hobbled out through the door to his office, Leopold was already waiting for her, leaning against the wall. He started at her appearance.

"Gods you look wrung out. What have you been doing?"

"Casting magelight," Willow said, and she found that saying the words lifted her spirits.

The last three attempts had successfully resulted in a magelight, which remained even after Willow carefully extricated her hands from around the web of steadfast essence. Carl grasped each with his glove-spell and gently tossed them into the ceiling.

"You can do it then? Probation's over?"

"Not quite yet. I'll tell you the whole story on the way back, but I might need a hand."

"Yeah."

Leopold stepped in beside her. Willow cast off her inhibitions and wrapped her arm around his shoulders. He was warm in the chill autumn air, and her tender muscles didn't protest as she pressed against his padded overcoat.

They walked together down the twilit road as she recounted her day of testing and training.

CHAPTER 12

The next morning after she awoke and practiced with the capacitor, Willow set off for class early. That wasn't to say that she didn't pack away a double breakfast before leaving the table, but that she scarfed both down as quickly as she could. She didn't want to rush to class and be even more fatigued by the time she reached the Arcanum, especially with training later in the day. Bryan and Margaret waved her goodbye with confusion evident on their faces, while Benny bid her farewell with a ditty, which somehow rhymed her name with the word *ham*.

Willow ran into Leopold as she turned a corner halfway to the Arcanum. He stumbled and looked a little embarrassed, as if he'd been caught doing something he shouldn't have.

"What are you doing this far away from campus?" Willow asked, looking around at the darkened shopfronts surrounding them. There was nothing that he could possibly be doing in this part of the city this early in the day.

"Well." He looked at those same shopfronts and then set his jaw. "I wanted to walk with you to class."

"Walk?" Willow asked, confused. "But your room is right beside the Arcanum. Why would you...?"

And just like that, it hit her. Was it the dawn sunrise—just peeking over the border wall—that highlighted the blush on his cheeks in the morning chill? Or was it the way he'd let her lean on him all the way to Bryan's house last night? Then there was the cane he'd gotten for her, which she was holding at that very moment.

He felt something for her. It wasn't anything she'd had experience with before. Everyone else in Bridgewater had known her since she was a little kid, watching her grow up frailer and thinner than they could have ever imagined. They'd always known that she was sick, that she probably didn't have long to live. The doctor's kid, who even the doctor couldn't fix. She was pitiable. Someone to be helped but never looked upon with anything other than charity.

And maybe it was all those childhood crushes that had gone unrequited, and the way those she dreamed of looked at her—like a freak, like a corpse—that had buried her feelings of desire. But she felt them stir again for him.

"Okay," Willow said, feeling a blush rise to her cheeks. "Yeah. Thank you. That would be nice."

And when he offered his arm for support on that long trek up the hill, she still batted it away with a smirk. She wasn't helpless, after all.

But it was a long walk to the Arcanum, and that gave her plenty of time to think. Inevitably, her thoughts turned to the boys she'd crushed on back in Bridgewater who'd never reciprocated. They didn't want to be tied down taking care of an invalid for the rest of her life. And she didn't blame them, not really. What was Leopold thinking? Or was he thinking at all? Was *she* thinking too much?

* * *

It was weird to see Carl—no, Professor Brandeweiss—in a teaching role again after seeing him for so many hours over the last two days out of class. But, to her relief, when she sat in the front row, the professor didn't even give her a nod. She had enough on her mind without his special attention in class.

She sat beside Leopold as Professor Brandeweiss instructed them in the eight basic spell-forms. And then the sixty-four intermediate forms. They were usually a combination of two of the eight but sometimes seemed to be completely unrelated to the forms they were charted under. She watched Leopold labor to memorize them under his breath.

Each had its own name, and they were expected to have the whole table memorized by Friday for their first exam. This announcement elicited a chorus of groans from the class, but not from Leopold.

Not from Willow either—studying and focusing was something she could do, silver girl or not. Her eyes followed Leopold's note-taking.

Okay, she might have been a little distracted.

When it was time for a demonstration, Professor Brandeweiss picked someone else from the class without his eyes ever meeting hers. She tried not to let herself redden with the resurging embarrassment of the last debacle. She wondered what Leopold had thought—

This was insane! What was she doing? She couldn't let herself get distracted like this. And it wasn't even like he'd confessed. He hadn't really said anything at all. It was just a look and a feeling. Was she reading too much into it? No, she thought she wasn't, but even so, she had to focus. Once the extinction-level threats were dealt with and she secured admission to the Arcanum, she could worry about... whatever this was. Maybe.

Gods.

When class was dismissed and she was packing up her things to leave, the professor very obviously caught her eye and nodded to his desk. She'd been about to rush out to the metrology lab, but she veered off course to meet him across the wooden surface. At the door, Leopold waved before leaving and she hesitated before nodding back.

"Metrology needs a day to set up their next test," Carl said. "So you get a break today from getting injected with high-pressure essence or whatever the hell they're going to do."

"Oh, goody," Willow deadpanned.

"We'll be using the time to practice magelight," he continued, which made her heart sink. If five casts had absolutely stripped her yesterday, what would he expect of her with double the amount of time?

"Right," she said weakly.

He nodded, gathered his things, and she followed him out the door and towards his office.

* * *

Another five milli-ems gained with the capacitor, and Carl actually used his strip of copper tape to get an official reading of her push force for the record. It came out to a tenth of a run, which, according to some quick calculations, tracked pretty closely to the corollary reading from the emmeter of 150 runs to push essence into her resistive body. It was weird seeing two numbers on her official record—only one left to go—but she wasn't allowed to dwell on it for too long before they started casting magelight.

Seven casts is what they managed to do, with a break between the fourth and fifth for lunch. Carl treated her, then bought her seconds after seeing how fast she scarfed down the meat pie. Then it was back to the office, where they cast another three before the hourglass indicated that outside the Arcanum walls twilight would be coming on.

When Willow left Carl's cramped and humid office, she found Leopold sitting on the ground across the hall, nose-deep in a book. How ridiculous that her heart leaped at the sight of him, and she forced composure on herself before she approached. She managed to walk all the way up to him and tap him with the foot of her cane before he realized she was there.

"Oh, hey. How was tutoring?"

"Strenuous, difficult. Impossible. So pretty much like yesterday and the day before. Why? How was class?"

"Oh you know... sort of boring. More boring than I thought it would be. You think all of these things about inscribing magic into copper, but when it comes down to it, there are a lot of calculations and math to make. And that's just so you don't give someone a nasty injection or melt the copper strip."

"Tedious in another way, then," Willow said, and Leopold got to his feet.

Sitting down, getting up—it was all so easy for him. He was at school, in the Arcanum, the way she'd always wanted to be. And she was playing catch-up. If she could just keep up with him, things might be different.

Things might be nice.

"What is it?" Leopold asked. He was looking hard at her eyes, and Willow shook her head.

"Nothing. Let's get home or I'm going to pass right out."

The hot-iron sky faded to violet while they walked the close-fitted stone streets down the hill from the Arcanum. Willow didn't talk much, and Leopold took up the silence beside her. It wasn't until the door to Bryan's house that he finally spoke up.

"Are you too tired to practice more tonight?" he asked. "I know I said... but I didn't know you'd be working on it all day."

"No, I just need to get some food in me," Willow said and walked inside.

Bryan was already home, and he seemed overjoyed to lay eyes on Leopold again. With the house suffused with the smell of roasting meat, they ate elbow to elbow at the small table. And before Willow could object, Margaret gathered up the leftovers and made a second plate for her.

It was strange how quickly a place and people became like a second home. There hadn't been much time for her to stop and think, but she found that touching the memories of Bridgewater didn't produce the acute sting of homesickness she was expecting.

After dinner, Leopold and Willow retired to her room to practice. Margaret gently nudged the door shut behind them.

"And this is how you're supposed to group cast?" Leopold asked.

Willow had molded his hands into the shape she remembered Carl making, showing him the way each individual finger swirled to produce eddies and whorls in the essence sphere.

"That's what it looked like at least."

"This is way beyond the classes we're in," Leopold said. "This is at least second year, maybe even graduate-level stuff. You only hear about mages group casting in stories. And I suppose they had to group cast to raise the walls around the city, but you never see it anymore."

"Well, it's what he has me doing," Willow said. "He said it would help me cast the steadfast layer more intuitively."

"That may do so, but you won't get to a point where you'll be able to cast it without making a spell-form or intoning the concept. Which it seems like you can barely handle now, not even adding another spell on top—"

"I know," Willow snapped.

Leopold lowered his hands from the spell-form and squeezed his lips shut. Willow took a deep breath and tried to get a handle on her emotions.

"I'm sorry," he said. "I just... it's that resistance reading. I can't fathom how you're producing half a magelight. You'd need twice as many runs to layer on top of it. Maybe even more than twice as many. It just seems cruel to expect you to be able to do it."

"I can't give up," Willow whispered. "Not now that I'm finally here. After everything I've been through."

Leopold looked at her for a long time. She wouldn't meet his eyes.

"What do I know?" he said. "Obviously Professor Brandeweiss has tons more experience with this, he said so himself. I'm nobody. I'm just a student. It's just... I don't like seeing you run yourself ragged."

Willow let out a bark of laughter. "I'm always running myself ragged," she said. "I'm always pushing myself to walk faster, to last longer, to stay awake, stay strong, just like everyone else! If I didn't, I'd just be a little invalid back in Bridgewater. I've gotten here *by* running myself ragged."

Leopold almost reached out to her—she saw his hand move to the elbow of her coat, then drop back down. He looked away.

Life as an invalid was full of dreams deferred. Of things you wanted but could *never* have. Of things you desired that would pass you by.

And an invalid couldn't do this.

"Oh, come on," she said, grabbing him by his thin blouse and pulling him into a kiss.

He froze for a moment, mouth hard against hers, before his lips softened and his tongue probed hers. She responded in kind, breathing hard and smelling the sweet scent of his face.

She never wanted to forget it.

CHAPTER 13

Thursday morning. Willow lay in bed a long time after she woke, remembering their kiss the previous night. It was everything she hoped it would be. And more. They eventually practiced casting, although he was unable to cast the first layer so that it would accept her essence. Even approaching the sphere he held between his own hands caused it to warp and fold in on itself.

Eventually she could barely keep her eyes open, and she walked him to the door. The rest of the house was asleep and only the dull coal of the fireplace provided any light. They didn't kiss when they parted—it felt too frivolous to repeat in the doorway open to the night air. As if what they shared was a sacred thing.

Willow hardly believed that it had happened, that she'd taken him and pulled him towards her. She squirmed in bed with equal parts embarrassment and elation. What did it mean? *Something wonderful,* she thought.

By the time Margaret knocked on her door, she was all ready to go. She had to wait at the table for Margaret to finish cooking her eggs, but the double portion filled the gnawing hunger in her gut. Right on cue, as the first wisps of twilight touched the sky, there was a small knock at the door.

"I think that'll be Leopold," Margaret said.

Though he sat at the table with Willow, he refused a breakfast of his own. Margaret forced a biscuit on him anyway. Willow didn't much like the knowing smile Margaret gave them as they headed out the door.

The world was silent as they walked in the dawn hush. Things felt awkward now between them. She hated it, so she reached out and took Leopold's cold hand from his jacket pocket. He held her fingers gently, like you would hold a bird. And she appreciated him for it. She appreciated feeling normal.

Her hands were already tender and noticeably thinner, the knuckles standing out like knots in rope.

By the time they arrived at the large main doors to the Arcanum, the city had woken up around them, and sleepy trolleymen were ushering their horses down the stone streets. Leopold left her at the main hall for his own class but gave her hand a gentle squeeze before they parted. She smiled and watched as he walked away, then set out for her class in the history of magic.

"After the Third Blasted War between Asche and Durum, Raly joined in to propose a ban on warbeast development. Records tell us that Durum and Raly were eager to sign the ban. They wanted to shoehorn Asche into it as well, as Asche's warbeasts were of a different caliber entirely compared to what the other two could produce. But before Durum and Raly could sign the tripartite agreement, Asche fell silent. Not a single emissary has been seen from that land in the last 150 years, and scouts report the mountains have become warped and violent to life from essence oversaturation. It appears as if, in the end, Asche's prodigious skill with warbeasts was their doom."

* * *

When Willow entered the metrology building, she immediately sensed something different in the air. The place had the feel of a conversation suddenly hushed, and when she looked around, all of the metrology graduate students were pointedly looking away. She supposed she should have expected this sooner or later with the readings she'd been getting. She just didn't expect it to feel so alienating.

Things didn't seem any better when she entered the small room at the back of the main building. Carl was there, as were the three metrology students, but the apparatus before them was entirely different than what had come before. There was a chair turned towards a table, and on the table were two low, crystalline devices with twin pairs of metal rods sticking out of their tops. They were wired up with copper tape to Burket's plate.

There was also what looked to be a disembodied arm lying on the table. No blood.

"Well, this looks... interesting," Willow said.

Carl, who was fussing with one of the connections to the devices, turned quickly at her voice.

"Ah, well, yes. Yes, it is. We're going to be doing something... a little out of the ordinary today. I got this setup from the psychology department—"

"Hardly metrological," Burket interrupted. "I have no idea what use this little experiment will have. It's not set up to measure her essential attributes."

"We'll get to those later." Carl waved him away. "Now, I may have to explain some things to you, as the test isn't as obvious as you might think. You'll sit here, and we're going to have to strap this big arm onto your chest."

"Why are you strapping this big arm onto my chest?" Willow tried to ask sans sarcasm as she took the seat.

Carl went to work, gently threading a makeshift harness around her neck. He tightened it until the extra arm sat snug and heavy from beside her left shoulder. Its elbow rested on the table for support, but from the weight of it against her chest, she imagined it would probably pull her over if she stood up.

"And what is this arm?"

"Ah, it's from the medical school. A pretty lifelike simulacrum, complete with veins, arteries, bones, tendons, you name it. They use it to practice using their essence to see within another's body."

"I thought that you couldn't control your essence once it passed very far from your body."

"That's true," Carl agreed. "But this is a very advanced technique where they essentially create a stable vortex of essence, like a funnel, which allows them to probe deep to search for damage."

"Huh," Willow said. The world kept getting bigger and more interesting.

"Now, as to why we're strapping this arm on you, it'll make sense in a moment."

"I doubt it," she said, and Steph stifled a laugh from the side of the room.

Daniel was helping Carl manhandle the arm into place, bending its stiff fingers around the two metal rods sticking up from the black crystalline base.

"Alright, that looks good. If you will, Willow, make your arm mirror the false arm as closely as possible as you reach forwards and grab the device. Same spot on the table for your elbow, same angle, et cetera."

She had no idea what she was doing or why, but she tried to follow his ridiculous instructions anyway. She laid her left arm beside the false arm an inch or two away, then mirrored its pose as she wrapped her own fingers around the twin rods of her own device.

Carl bent down, bobbed around like an anxious parent, and touched her arm a couple of times to push her into alignment. Finally, he smiled and nodded.

"Alright, bring over the box."

"The box?" Willow asked.

At that moment, Steph approached with a deep black box about the size of a small chest. It seemed too big for Steph to carry. But as Steph moved, its cloth sides billowed in. That gave Willow a clue. The whole thing was hollow—just a frame for the sackcloth.

"And… right there. Perfect," Carl said as Steph lowered the box around Willow's real arm. This made the fake one look disjointedly realistic for a moment. It was even wrapped in a sleeve of cloth down to the wrist, which was covered by a glove. Just like her.

Carl moved to the other side of the desk and sat down. He brought with him two objects: a pencil and a thin band of copper packed with inscriptions.

"Are we ready?" he asked.

Burket rolled his eyes behind Carl's back. "Sure."

"Now, Willow, this is going to be a sort of strange test, as I'm sure you can already appreciate. In the psychology department, they do this little demonstration to show how easily you can accidentally associate a fake limb with one of your own. They take a feather," he raised the pencil, "and stroke both your hand and the fake hand at the same time. Eventually, you start to really blur the lines about which one is your hand. This is when they bring out a hammer and smash the fake one."

"Yeesh," Willow said.

"Yes, I don't understand why they do it either, but it gave me an idea. Steph here will be helping me with her own pencil. We're both going to be stroking your real hand and the fake hand. After some amount of time, I'm going to ask you to squeeze these two metal rods together as hard as you can. Go ahead and test that out now."

"You mean… squeeze the rods?"

Carl nodded, and the corner of Willow's mouth quirked down. Whatever the hell they were playing at, it was above her understanding. She squeezed the rods as hard as she could before the pain from her already wasting fingers overwhelmed her ability to continue.

"Alright, I'm finished," Willow said.

"Burket?" Carl asked.

"Eleven pounds even," Burket droned back, as if he thought this was the drollest and most useless exercise in the world. His attitude was infecting Willow, too, but she worked hard to have faith in Carl.

"And what's that?" Willow asked, motioning to the thin band of inscribed metal with her eyes.

"That? Well, you'll find out in a few moments."

"Of course," Willow muttered.

"Follow my lead," Carl said to Steph, and he stroked the false hand with the tip of the pencil.

Strangely enough, or not strangely at all because she should have been expecting it, Willow felt the sensation of the pencil stroke on the back of her hand as well. Steph's eyes were locked on Carl's pencil, and Daniel was hovering behind the two of them, seemingly as interested in the process as Burket was dismissive.

Carl stroked the false hand five more times. Willow could have sworn that by the fifth time she had difficulty remembering that it wasn't her own hand under the glove and sleeve. Then he got up, taking the band of metal as he did so.

"This is where we diverge from the official psychology playbook," Carl said, and she felt him wrap the band loosely around her upper arm. "This band is going to make your arm go numb. It shouldn't cause you any pain, just a complete lack of feeling. After that happens, I want you to start squeezing on the device. Start low and increase your pressure slowly."

"But how will I know when to stop? My muscles—"

"I'll stop you when the reading from your hand gets back up to eleven," Carl said. "Don't worry, I won't let you get hurt."

Willow met his eyes and found nothing she couldn't trust there. She slowly nodded, and he cinched the band down tight around her arm, just at the seam of her overcoat.

Immediately it was like someone had lopped off her arm, but without the pain. Just... nothing. Just a moment ago, she'd had an arm, and now she didn't.

Then something in her mind shifted, and it was like she had an arm again. That vague sense of where your own limb is located without having to see it. But she was still missing any sense of touch or texture. Just a feeling that her arm was still there in front of her, hand wrapped around the measuring device.

"Alright, Willow, now squeeze."

She started low, just as he'd told her. What she imagined was the faintest feathering of her fingers against the device, then finally squeezing in earnest. Steph and Daniel looked at each other as if they weren't sure anything was supposed to be happening. But Burket, with the plate behind them, had gone pale watching whatever it showed.

That felt good. Whatever was wrong with her, however hard it made her life, she enjoyed in a petty sort of way that it also made that asshole's life harder as well. If he was going to be such a dick to her, then he could suffer too.

She kept squeezing. Without any sensation of pain, she was starting to get worried about how close she was to her limit. She caught Carl's eye behind the plate with Burket, and he nodded.

Keep going.

She squeezed harder. There was almost no sensation of effort at all, and she supposed there wouldn't be, not if she couldn't feel anything. Then when would it stop? Would she just top out at a certain reading? Would she reach eleven again? She had no idea—

The device held by the false hand exploded in a burst of white glass dust and sparking metal. Steph and Daniel shielded themselves. Willow felt shrapnel sting her cheek, and she closed her eyes on reflex, raising her right hand to block her face.

In an instant, Carl was at her side and disengaging the metal strap, which had caused her arm to go numb. Her mind shifted again, like the ice on a pond cracking, and she could feel her arm and hand just as they had been. She unwrapped her fingers from the remaining measuring device.

"What—" Willow could barely hear her own voice.

Carl was at her side and dabbing her cheek with a handkerchief, which came away bloody. Steph and Daniel were checking each other for shrapnel, and Burket was still at the back of the room with the plate in his hands. He looked furious.

"I don't know what the hell you think you're trying to pull," he roared. "But this is the last straw. No more tests, no more evaluations. She's broken enough equipment as it is, and if you expect me to believe for even an instant—"

Carl pulled Willow up from her chair. She heard him make conciliatory sounds, something about the infirmary, and then they were out through the door into the larger metrology building. The rest of the department was crowded around the entrance to their little testing room, and they scattered when Carl and Willow appeared.

"My... my cane." Willow tried to look back at the room where something she didn't quite understand had happened. Everything was blurred and stuttering. The lights in the ceiling left fuzzy streaks across her eyes.

"I've got it," Carl said beside her.

When she looked at him, he was grinning like a maniac.

"I've got it."

CHAPTER 14

Willow thought she'd received a head injury because it felt a lot like Carl was taking her back to his office instead of the infirmary. In fact, it wasn't until he barged through the door that she was certain she hadn't hallucinated the winding journey. A woman in a white nurse's outfit stood up abruptly, then sized up Carl and Willow in an instant.

"Over here," the woman said.

She hinged open a complicated-looking contraption that became a table, as if it had hidden inside itself for just such a moment. With Carl under one arm and the woman under the other, they laid Willow face-up on the strange accordion table.

"What happened?"

"A device exploded in her hand," Carl said. The nurse scanned down Willow's arms. "No, not her hand, another hand. Sorry, I think she might've gotten clipped by debris."

"Well that's obvious," the woman said and gently probed Willow's cheek. The flesh there was tender and swollen, like she'd run into a door.

"And I think she's concussed."

"Also obvious," the woman said, then shooed Carl away. Surprisingly, he backed off into the corner. "Willow, can you hear me?"

Willow said yes but then realized she hadn't actually breathed a word.

"Yes," she croaked.

"You've got a concussion and a minor laceration. I'm a nurse with the hospital, and I'm going to treat you here in Professor Brandeweiss' office. Say *yes* if you understand."

There was so much she didn't understand, but Willow said yes anyway.

"This may feel a little strange. Have you ever been magically healed before?"

"When... kid..." Willow sighed.

It was hard to hold onto her train of thought. She wanted to explain about the mage who'd come to her town of Bridgewater, of the royal ransom her parents had paid the woman to heal their daughter, and the disappointment in their faces when she said there was nothing to be done.

Like that time before, the nurse began muttering concepts under her breath while sketching complicated spell-forms in the air with her fingers. After what Carl said yesterday, Willow noticed the spell-form was based on a funnel shape. The better to pierce her body and heal something deep inside.

The nurse lowered the funnel into Willow's forehead, and Willow slept.

* * *

"How long is she supposed to stay out?"

"I would say ten or fifteen minutes more, but her body's unlike anything I've ever seen. You didn't properly prepare me for what I was coming into—"

"Shh, she's awake. Willow?"

Carl's voice sounded close. Willow opened her eyes to find him crouching beside her. At some point someone had flipped her over, so now she lay on her stomach. The nurse sat in a chair further away, watching the both of them.

"Professor," Willow said.

"Carl," he corrected and smiled. "Welcome back. You've been through a hell of a thing today."

Willow groaned and tried to sit up, but when she shifted her right arm, the movement set off a cascade of tingling, burning pain in her hand.

She hissed and drew her hand in towards her body, which only made the pain worse.

"Something... my hand."

She didn't dare look, but at the same time, she couldn't help herself. She glanced down and saw, rather than a heavily bandaged extremity, her normal hand—fingers and all. Just above the wrist was the same strip of metal that Carl had wrapped around her arm at the start of the test.

"How does it feel?" Carl asked.

"How does your *head* feel?" the nurse butted in, finally getting up and striding over to Willow's bedside.

Willow managed to get into a sitting position, cradling her hand near her stomach. "My head feels fine, but something's wrong with my hand. It burns like it's being stung by a thousand bees."

"You've never felt anything like this before?" the nurse asked, and Willow shook her head. The nurse looked back at Carl. "She's all yours then."

"What's going on?"

Willow watched as Carl took the second chair in the room and placed it beside the fold-out bed. He sat down and sighed like someone who needs to say something but is unsure of how to say it.

"I suppose when in doubt, it's best to start at the beginning. On your intake papers, it says you claim you survived the Wasting in Bridgewater, right?"

"Well obviously I didn't," Willow said. "As my examiner informed me, no one survives the Wasting."

"That's right. No one survives the Wasting. Until you."

"What?"

Carl looked down at his fingers, which he was rubbing together nervously. "How much do you know about the Wasting?"

"Just that it kills babies. And now, apparently, I'm the only person who's survived it?"

Carl nodded. "It's a disease, not of the humors, but something that comes from outside the body. It attacks the nerves at the base of the skull, severing them from the rest of the body. Very quickly the afflicted lose all control over their muscles and are rendered unable to breathe. They invariably die of suffocation."

"So... this didn't happen to me? I fought it off?"

Carl shook his head. "No, the disease appears to have progressed as usual in your case as well. But your reaction to it is something we've never seen before."

"But you said the nerves—"

"You've been paralyzed your whole life," the nurse interrupted. "Complete nervous disconnect between the brain and body. Your spinal cord has been severely degraded."

"Well, obviously that's not true," Willow huffed. She rolled her shoulders, then opened and closed her hands. Well, one hand. The other didn't want to cooperate and only stirred weakly, followed by an overwhelming feeling of fatigue.

Willow winced at the sensation, and Carl leaned in.

"While you were out, I had Annabelle reconnect a tiny bundle of nerves back to your brain. Just the nerves she identified as targeting your right hand. Everything else is as it was before."

"What are you saying?"

Willow grimaced and tried to move her hand again. The pins and needles sensation wasn't abating with time, and it felt like her hand was sapping her of energy.

"I can move. I've been able to my entire life. I'm not paralyzed."

"But you are," Carl said. "And you always have been. Have you done any research into the spell *psychokinesis*?"

"No, I haven't. Pretty much just been focusing on magelight."

Carl nodded. "Well, it's an intermediate spell, so it wouldn't be in the introductory text you would've used to prepare for the exam. But its effect is that it allows you to physically manipulate another object at a distance for a short period of time."

"Okay... and?"

Willow was in pain and running out of patience. What she wanted more than anything was just to be back in familiar surroundings. Back in her room on Grave Street, back with Leopold and Bryan and Margaret and even little Benny. Back at home... back in Bridgewater.

Carl gestured to her hand in such a way that she felt as though she should understand what he was implying, but she didn't. She shook her head.

"That's how you've been able to survive. That's how you're able to move. You've been controlling your body with psychokinesis your entire life."

The room was dead silent, and she could feel both Annabelle's and Carl's eyes on her. She tried to flex her right hand again, but it felt like it took nearly all her strength to do it. And then it twitched only the smallest amount.

Suddenly, she began to chuckle. The chuckle grew into a laugh, and the laugh grew nearly into a cackle before she began to choke with the spasms of it. She had to double over, painfully pinching her hand in her stomach, but she couldn't help herself. What the hell were they saying?

"Willow, are you okay?" Carl asked.

"What is this? What are you on about? Why are you trying to get me to believe this ridiculous story? Is it a test of some kind? If so, I pass. No dice."

"No, Willow. This isn't a story. This is the truth. We don't need you to believe it for it to be true, but it would be easier if you'd believe us. There are some demonstrations I can do—"

"Like I'd trust anything you put me through now! What was that back in metrology? Did you put a bomb in one of those things? Is that why it blew up?"

"No, Willow. It blew up because you squeezed the meter so hard that it shattered the crystal base. By the end, we were reading over 2,000 pounds—"

"Enough," Willow said and swung her legs over the side of the fold-out bed.

She glanced around the room and saw her cane propped next to the door. Gingerly, she hopped down from the table, shuffled over to her cane, and leaned on it in her off-hand while cradling her right hand at her abdomen.

"I don't know what you're trying to feed me, but I've had enough. It's been a terribly long day already, too long by far—"

"I told you she wouldn't believe—" Annabelle said.

"Shut up," Carl spat at the nurse, who didn't react in the slightest.

"—but I've got to go home now. I've got to get something to eat, or I'm going to pass out. Thank you very much for rescuing me from your own invented little catastrophe back in the lab, but if you don't mind, I think I'll be doing my own tutoring from here on out. Thanks for all the help, Professor."

"Oh, Willow," Carl sighed as she swung the door open and stepped through. "You don't even need my help anymore."

She slammed it before she let herself be pulled back in by the mystery of whatever *that* meant.

*　*　*

Leopold was nowhere to be found, but she had to get out of there. She stumbled through the main building of the Arcanum, to the courtyard between it and its low outer defensive wall. All of the buildings in the city looked to be made of the same kind of pale stone, but this wall was seamless in such a way that suggested it had been built by magic instead of by hand. Willow leaned her forehead against the cool wall and tried to gather her thoughts.

What the hell had happened back there? That nurse had obviously healed her since her cheek no longer smarted from the shrapnel of the failed metrology device. But she'd also done something to her hand to make it itch and pinch terribly. Once she stopped moving, the discomfort came back to assail her full force, and she rolled her head back and forth against the wall to try to distract herself.

Healed her spine? Unless she was terribly misinformed, a nurse didn't have the training to do that sort of thing. Only advanced magical surgeons could perform treatments on internal organs through spellwork alone. Somewhere along the line, Annabelle was lying—but to whom Willow had no idea.

And Carl! Why would he spring all this on her? This obviously concocted two-bit story? What he was saying was impossible. You had to focus to cast a spell, to shape the spell-form, and conceptualize the essence. Only magical creatures could use essence without those, and they couldn't actually cast spells.

She thought of the salamander with its flame-licked skin and giggled crazily to imagine it human-sized and wearing her clothes.

Ridiculous. Absolutely ridiculous. Willow moaned in agony. Why wasn't the pain going away?

"Willow?"

Willow turned to see Leopold standing a step away, his hand out to touch her shoulder. The sight of him was like home, and she staggered forwards on her wobbling cane.

"What's wrong? Did something happen with the professor?"

"Let's get out of here. I'll fill you in on the way back."

Chapter 15

Margaret gave Willow a handkerchief filled with shards from the icebox to rest on her hand during dinner, but Willow wasn't sure it did much. Sure, the shooting pain lessened, but the feeling of intense cold was almost worse. As was the way it kept flickering to intense heat, as if her skin wasn't sure what to make of the ice. But she kept the ice pack on anyway because it was such a kind gesture. And she didn't know what to do instead.

"You should go to the hospital tomorrow," Bryan told her between mouthfuls of sweet cornbread and chipped ham. "They'll be able to set you right."

"Yeah, of course," Willow said and glanced at Leopold.

He was giving her a meaningful look. After what she'd told him about that nurse, he clearly wasn't enthused about the prospect of leaving her in the care of the medical establishment a second time. She wasn't sure she was either.

After eating even more than usual, Willow thanked Bryan and Margaret profusely and retreated to her cramped room with Leopold, where she shut the door quickly behind them. Leopold began pacing immediately.

"We could take it to the dean. I'm sure this isn't above board."

"No shit it's not above board," Willow said. "Both of them are lying here. But does it stop at them, or does it go higher up? And why me?"

"Yeah, that's a good question." He paused. "I mean, you do have those really strange readings—"

"Thanks for that," Willow said flatly, as if she needed him to bring it up.

"—maybe that made you a target. Or it could be because you're from a smaller town?"

"Plenty of other students from small towns," she said, scratching her arm where the burning, prickling sensation ended. "I just wish this would—"

Wait. There was something there under her shirt sleeve. She raised the fabric and found a band of heavily inscripted copper wrapped around her forearm right above the wrist. She'd seen it before when she awoke, but the pain made it hard to concentrate on anything else. Already she was getting used to the sensation. Or it was going away. She wasn't sure which.

"What's that?" Leopold leaned in.

The small oil lamp on her side table wasn't bright enough to make out the symbols. Leopold cast magelight quickly, and the bright yellow light bobbed above their heads.

"It's the same band from the experiment earlier today. It made my arm go numb, but that was on my left arm. Why's it here?"

"Are you sure it's the same one?" Leopold asked.

Willow shook her head. "No. I don't know. I can't read any of these inscriptions. It could be something completely different."

"It could be why your hand is so weak, why you're in pain," Leopold said. He swallowed hard.

"Should I take it off?" Willow asked.

He stared at the band for a long while, trying to read the inscriptions and obviously failing. "Yes."

There was an obvious seam in the band, and it wasn't difficult to bend the metal back. It wrapped around onto itself, and it took her a moment to unravel it with the tips of her fingers, but it finally snapped off and landed on the bed.

Sensation rushed back into her hand, which was strange because she could already *feel* her hand. She felt her fingers where they should be, but the sensation overlayed the much stronger burning and tingling. The phantom feeling seemed to make the burning even more intense somehow, as if reminding her of the level of sensation she was used to.

Willow grunted and clenched her right hand into a fist. Moving her fingers set off a cascade of pain, which shot up her hand to where the band had been. She screamed as her fingers spasmed, the sensation like her muscles being fed through a meat grinder.

"Gods!" Leopold said and fumbled with the band.

He hurriedly fit it around her wrist again. When the metal made smooth contact all the way around, the secondary sensation disappeared completely. The relief was almost euphoric when only the tingling burning was present again. Whatever had happened to her muscles began to subside.

Willow leaned back onto the headboard of her bed and sighed at the disappearance of the grating pain. There were tears in her eyes, which she awkwardly wiped away with her left palm. What was happening to her? What had Carl and the nurse done? What was wrong with her? And, gods, why was Leopold still standing by her bed instead of running out the door?

"There's something weird going on here," Leopold said. "They did something to you, something that the band's keeping back. What was it they said?"

"Something about my spine. Healing the nerves." Willow laughed. "Ridiculous."

Leopold was looking hard at her, at her neck. For a moment, she had the uncomfortable desire to pull up her cowl, but she resisted.

"It is ridiculous, right?"

"I mean… I haven't heard of such a thing. But that doesn't mean it can't be. That doesn't even mean it's unheard of, just that I'm an ignorant first-year student. Maybe it's all more normal than we thought—"

Willow cut him off with a shake of her head. "No, it's not normal. At all. He said I was the only one, *the only one,* who survived the Wasting. That's not normal. And if it's not a lie, then I don't know what it means. Who else can we ask? Who else do you trust?"

Leopold drew inwards in thought for a moment before fixing her with his gaze. "I know you don't want to hear this, but I can really only think of one person who would know. Or, well, two people."

"Oh, come on!"

* * *

She couldn't face Professor Brandeweiss at the front of the classroom, not after storming out of his office the previous day. So she camped out in front of his office door while he was out teaching the class she was supposed to be attending.

After an hour crawled by, a bell in the towers above rang, and students filled the main lobby at the end of the hall of offices. Professors began filtering in, closing doors as they disappeared back into their crannies to prepare for their next classes. Professor Brandeweiss was one of the last to come down the hall.

"Miss Willow," he said, stopping between her and the door. "I have to say I'm surprised to see you back here. I half-thought that you'd be back home on a caravan by now with how you left yesterday."

"I can't say I haven't considered it," said Willow stiffly. "You have something to tell me?"

Carl nodded and waved her in. The fold-out table was gone, and the office was set up almost in the same way she'd seen it the first time they'd met after class. He motioned to a chair and closed the door.

"Professor—"

He cut her off with a shush and incanted a spell under his breath. The spell-form was tortuously complex, but when he finished, its essence flowed into the door and along the walls in a rushing blue wave.

"There, now we won't be disturbed."

"What was that?"

"A little privacy conjuration. Nobody will be able to hear what is said in this office as long as that door remains shut. I had one on yesterday, which faltered when you rushed out. I have to say, I was prepared to explain a great deal more when you woke, but perhaps I approached the subject matter too obliquely."

A privacy conjuration. Right. Keeping secrets from your colleagues and students was completely normal.

"I... perhaps." Willow sat tensely, keeping a clear line between her and the door. "I was overwhelmed. The things you insinuated..."

Carl nodded. "Before we get into it, how is your hand doing?"

Willow looked at her right hand and turned it weakly over in her lap. Then she clenched the fingers into a fist with little more strength than a newborn.

"Better. Last night it was burning, and ice didn't help. I took the band off—"

Carl sucked in a breath, but his eyes were riveted on her. "What happened?"

"It was excruciating," she said, teeth clenched. "It felt like my hand was being torn apart."

"I thought it might. If you gain nothing else from our meeting today, I implore you not to remove the band again until I instruct you to do so. The results of which may be... catastrophic."

Ominous. It was difficult to decide how much to take Carl at his word. Was this all a ruse? Or had he really done something to her spine? Or... was it the nurse? Who definitely wasn't a surgeon and definitely not qualified to practice neurological surgery. So add *illegal experimentation* to the list of strange things going on here.

"And now?"

"Now, I can barely feel the burn," she said. "It's sensitive, like my skin is raw, but it doesn't hurt all the time anymore."

"Good," Carl said. "Your brain's adjusting to the sensations coming from your body. I had hoped it would over time, but I was prepared to give you a hefty dose of analgesic upon your departure yesterday in case the pain was too much."

"That would have helped," Willow ground out, but Carl waved the comment away. If he'd been so prepared for her to be in excruciating pain, did that make him more trustworthy? Or less?

"No matter. You are incorporating the neurological input faster than I had hoped. I see you've learned how to move it?"

"I just move it like normal."

Was there any other way to move a hand? How much *should* she be trusting him right now? He didn't seem to know a lot about what he was talking about, at least when it came to the side effects of what they'd done. Was he... guessing?

"Hmm, interesting," he said. "The psychokinesis must have taken root in the same portion of your brain which controls motor function. This is most fortunate."

"Psychokinesis," she said, pointing at him. "You mentioned it yesterday. What do you mean?"

"Well before we go into that, I'd like to do a little test with you. If that's alright."

She eyed the door, judging the distance short enough that she could yank it open in a single bound. "I've about had it up to here with tests."

Carl smiled. "You've done this one before. I'd like you to push into a capacitor. Have you been keeping up with your exercises?"

"Um, I didn't do them last night," Willow said, relaxing slightly. Even with everything that had happened between them, he wasn't the metrology department, which gave her a feeling of relief. "But I did yesterday morning."

"Perfect, perfect. If you'll just place your right hand on top of this capacitor."

The crystal dome he pulled out from under his desk looked different than any other she'd seen before. There were thin copper lines circling around at different levels, coming together in concentric circles. It also looked heavier than the one she had at home.

Willow hesitantly put her right hand atop the dome, and the cold crystal prickled her sensitive palm. Carl brought out a rolled blanket and laid it under her elbow.

"I want you to relax. Just try your best to completely loosen your arm, keeping your palm in contact with the capacitor. When you're ready, try pushing into it."

Willow took a breath, felt her arm go slack, and then visualized the essence in her body. But where she normally held a one-to-one image, now her imagined right hand was completely missing, as if it had been chopped off.

"Um," Willow said.

"You're not seeing your hand in the visualization. Try to push through it anyway."

"Okay," she said and attempted to push essence through her hand.

She was used to her essence moving like molasses, but now it was as if that strange darkness was an impassable wall. There was no way for her to control the essence in her hand, or to move essence from the rest of her body into it.

"I... can't," Willow said and opened her eyes again.

Carl was focused on the display on the other side of the capacitor. He hummed. "The block is working then," he said with a smile.

"Is that what this band is?" Willow asked. "Is it the same one from the test yesterday?"

"Ah, I never got to explain it to you," he said and gently pushed up her sleeve. "This band is a creation of my own design, based on essence insulators in high-density inscriptions. What it does is quite simple. When formed into a circle, no essence can pass through the circum-scribed plane. When I wrapped the band around your arm yesterday and it went numb, that was, in itself, a secondary test I was performing. I was, in effect, seeing if my hypothesis was true, if indeed you con-trolled and received sensation from your body through magic alone."

From what little she knew, it seemed like he was making sense. But he could just be bullshitting. And there was one problem. "But I can feel my hand now," Willow said.

"That is due to the surgery my colleague Annabelle performed while you were unconscious yesterday. She restored the connection between your hand and your brain. Thus, whenever this band is on your wrist, you are controlling your hand through your mundane ner-vous system alone.

"Now," he said, lifting the edge of the band with the tip of his finger. "I want you to close your eyes and visualize again. Be ready to push into the capacitor when you see the essence in your hand, but be warned. Do not, under any circumstances, move your hand. To do so will result in nearly unbearable pain."

"Right," Willow said, remembering the excruciating agony of the previous night. She wasn't in a hurry to experience *that* again.

What Carl was saying sounded so good—too good, maybe. That all of her problems stemmed from an impossible situation where she was actually paralyzed and that he had the cure for said paralysis? She couldn't help but feel like she was receiving a well-designed sales pitch. But she also had to admit that she felt something else as well.

Hope.

"And... now," he said.

The moment she felt the band lift from her wrist, her hand appeared again in her visualization. She pushed as she always had before, as she had a million times in her life, but something new happened this time. The essence in her hand shot out so quickly that the limb almost disappeared from her visualization again. The essence in her arm was still sluggish, but as it crossed the unmarked point in her wrist where she felt things differently, it too flashed out of her body at insane speed.

She felt the band go back around her wrist, and she snapped open her eyes. The capacitor under her hand was glowing a dull red, which looked to be some sort of warning. Willow removed her hand from the warm surface.

"What was that? What happened?"

Clearly something strange had happened. She wanted to remain skeptical, to analyze everything he said with suspicion and doubt, but pushing her essence into that capacitor had felt different from anything she'd ever experienced before. It had felt... good.

Carl was smiling. "Something beyond even my wildest imaginings. This is a twenty-five em capacitor, and you've overcharged it to twenty-seven em."

"I pushed two em in just now? That's... impossible," Willow said.

Carl shook his head. "No, and no. The capacitor was empty when we started. You just flash-charged it to twenty-seven em. I don't think a rummeter in the Arcanum could chart the force with which you ejected your essence. These results are far above my expectations."

He was... wrong? How could he be telling the truth? Any mage could be expected to contain a single em total in their entire body, more or less, and he'd just said that she'd flash-charged the capacitor to twenty-seven em? Just from what was in her hand? It wasn't possible, but she'd felt it happen anyway.

"What... what does it mean?"

"Mean? Well, first off, under no circumstances take that band off, especially when casting spells. You've been training these last five years to push against the natural resistance of having hundreds of psychokinetic spells blocking the flow of your essence. With that resistance removed, you have the potential to cause terrible damage with even the simplest of effects. You have to learn how to do the opposite now. Learn how to shoot low and how to feather your power so you don't blind those around you with magelight. Or set the school on fire with a summoning."

"Is this real?" Willow whispered, suddenly confronted with the opposite of what she'd experienced her entire life. That her disability had somehow given her a gift, instead of bestowing curse after curse. As much as she knew she should distrust him, she wanted more than anything for this to be true. If it were... *everything* would change for her.

"This is real, Willow. This is very real, but I must also entreat you. Do not speak of what you are or what you can do to anyone else. We will work together to hide it, to help you fit in, and to pass your probation, but you must not let anyone else gain knowledge of how different you are. You haven't told anyone in the last day, have you?"

The image of Leopold, Margaret, and Bryan came to her head.

Gambling with her own safety, with her own twisted, cursed life was one thing, but she wouldn't expose them to what she didn't yet understand. What did Carl want with her? And what would he do if he found out she'd told others?

"No," she said. "Not a soul."

After leaving the Arcanum through the main gate, Willow hooked a right and hobbled down the street to the crossing at the corner. The wood of her cane chafed painfully on her sensitive right hand, but the sensation meant everything to her. It meant she might not be a failure. It meant a chance at a real life, a normal life. Gods! It meant possibly more healing in the future, after she could control herself.

Leopold waited in a shadowed doorway at the corner, and, catching sight of her, he started forward. She shook her head and motioned into the alley, where he retreated.

She turned into the alley as well and leaned against the wall to catch her breath. A quick look back showed that Carl hadn't followed her out. Or at least, if he had, she didn't see him.

"Gods, Willow, I've been waiting forever," Leopold said. "You have no idea what it's like not knowing if you're even going to come out or not. I was a bare hour from going to the constable."

"No need, not anymore," Willow said and lifted her sleeve. "He explained it. Well, most of it. It's... almost fantastic. Unreal. I never would've believed him if he hadn't shown me."

"Showed you what?" Leopold asked, but Willow pulled her sleeve down in response, hiding the nullification band.

"Not here. Let's go back to the house, I'll explain everything there. You're not going to believe me, but I'll explain it anyway."

"Try me," Leopold said, and they started off.

At the mouth of the alley, a pebble skidded as if being crushed under an invisible shoe.

CHAPTER 16

"Less. Feather your essence, Willow. I need less."

"I'm trying," Willow said, sweat standing out on her forehead.

Her right hand was covered by a glove woven from silver thread. Even so, the first layer of magelight was able to form on the other side in the palm of her cupped, immobile hand.

Suddenly, shooting pain wracked the muscles in her fingers, and the magelight dispersed in a puff of essence. Willow hissed and fumbled for the band, which she quickly slapped around her wrist again.

The pain, as it had before, disappeared.

She didn't need to ask Carl how she was doing—she knew that well enough. For her magelight to form on the other side of the silver glove, it meant she'd been outputting way too much essence. It should've served as an almost insurmountable resistive barrier, but instead, it barely felt like a flimsy sheet of onionskin compared to what she was used to working with.

"Alright. That was less than ideal. Perhaps we should call it a day."

"No," Willow said, shaking her head.

They were in his office. Even though it was lit by magelight as always, the ache in her body told her it was far past twilight on the street outside. Leopold would be waiting for her somewhere on the road back, but she couldn't leave yet.

"I have barely a week left. Barely. And I can't even produce a mage-light. And I don't have a capacitance reading yet."

"You won't be able to get one of those," Carl said and waved the idea away. "The way we measure it, you'll need to avoid casting any spells the whole morning before the test. But as we're now aware, you can't go a single second without casting a spell."

"What if you wrapped one of those things around my neck? Then I wouldn't be able to cast anything, right?"

"If I wrapped a nullification band around your neck, I'm pretty sure you would suffocate," Carl said. "You haven't had those nerves re-connected yet."

"Ah."

"I'll get Annabelle on it once you're more in control of your hand," he said. "There's no way I can isolate your diaphragm the way I'm doing with your wrist, so it's going to be tricky." He looked at her, seeming to take in the state of her for the first time in hours. "Are you sure you don't want to call it a night? Start fresh tomorrow?"

"I'm already skipping all my classes. There's no reason not to work late too." Willow positioned her hand palm-up in the molded pillow on the desk.

She took a breath and slipped the nullification band off her wrist as Carl stifled a yawn. For a moment at least, that secondary sensation of feeling didn't rush in. She was getting used to freeing her hand of the spells that had controlled it her entire life, although the process was a lot like unlearning how to be potty trained.

"Again," she said and tried to let out the smallest stream of essence possible.

* * *

Leopold met her at the Arcanum gate and provided her his arm as they walked home. She hated being so weak at the end of the training sessions every day. But if she was going to stay in school, she needed to be able to produce a magelight without killing herself and the examiner. Poise came second to that. And, she admitted to herself, it was nice to lean on him. To feel supported. Not as an invalid but as one half of a... relationship? How long that would last—how long he would stick around—she was unsure of. But it was nice at the moment.

Dinner was long finished by the time they got to the house on Grave Street, but Margaret set out their chilled plates before turning in for the night. They ate silently, then retired to Willow's room.

"Here are your notes from history of magic," Leopold said, retrieving a sheaf of papers from his bag. "And you've got an essay due Thursday on the Decade Skirmish."

"And what is the Decade Skirmish?" Willow asked, throwing open her history tome. The book was littered with papers and notes, making it even more unwieldy. That was fine. She did all her work in her room nowadays, so lugging it to school wasn't a problem.

"They went over it in class." Leopold pointed to a section in his notes. "But you'll find more on the listed pages."

Essays, homework—and above all of that, the exam that would determine if she could stay in the Arcanum or not. Sometimes it felt like too much, but it was what she'd signed up for. And now she had it. A shot at a normal life, a productive life. She couldn't help but smile at the barest thought of it.

"Thank you," she said. "For going to all my classes for me. I know it's not easy."

Leopold waved that away. "It's no hassle. I'll have to take these classes next semester, and now I'm ahead."

"Well," she said and touched his hand.

The feeling of his skin through her right hand was almost the same as it was with her left, though more intense. It was as if each hair on his skin stood out in stark contrast, like she was looking at him with a magnifying glass. Sometimes it was too much.

"Leopold," she breathed, leaning in.

He leaned towards her, their breath hot together, but then he gently held her at bay. She opened her eyes, surprised.

"You've got a lot of work to do," he said with a smile. "I don't think we've got time for anything else."

"No. I guess not," Willow sighed. She flipped the pages in her history book restlessly. She had wanted all the time in the world.

* * *

"I've got something new for you," Carl said as she came into his office for their morning training.

She didn't even knock anymore, but just came in and sat down to work. It seemed insane that so recently she'd been suspicious of his motives. To be fair, she'd been operated on without consent, and she still didn't know how she felt about that nurse. But Carl had spent hours and days training her to wrangle her innate power, all to keep her at the Arcanum pursuing her dreams. This went beyond what a professor owed their student—it was almost fatherly.

"Oh?" Willow asked.

Carl pushed a copper band across the table. "Another nullification band, but this one's intentionally faulty. Flickers of spellwork and essence will be able to travel across it. Now that you're going seconds at a time without reactivating your spells, it's time to move up."

"Thanks," Willow said. She intentionally focused on relaxing her hand before slipping the old band off and snapping on the new one.

It felt much like the old one, but when she moved her hand to test the sensation, she felt a twinge of pain in the muscle at the back of her middle finger.

"Damn," she said and rubbed it.

"You'll have to concentrate all the time. Concentrate on not moving your hand the way you've always moved it."

"Yeah," she said, not looking forward to the rest of the day. She reached into her bag and retrieved the thin silver glove, wincing in pain as her thumb seized up.

"You look exhausted," Carl observed as she slipped the glove over her hand and laid her arm on the small pillow.

"Cramming all your schoolwork into nights will do that to you," Willow said.

"I wasn't aware you were continuing to study," Carl said, surprised. "I just assumed you'd drop this semester and re-up next."

"I don't have that kind of money," she said.

* * *

After lunch she had to postpone her training with Carl in order to take a test in inscription, which she hadn't attended since her first class. A few of the students did double takes when they saw her walk in, no doubt at her ghoulish appearance. She sat down at an empty desk anyway and retrieved her inkwell and pen. Even the professor looked startled to see her there.

As it turned out, the half-period lecture she had to sit through before the test began showed her that the professor was much less adept at conveying information than Leopold's notes were. This was further confirmed when she breezed through the test with nearly no difficulty whatsoever.

As she wrote a long-form answer on engraving depth—her right hand twinging painfully every few seconds—she imagined what it would be like to be any of these other students. Going to lectures and living on campus in the dorms. What did they do with all of their free time when the tests were this easy? When they didn't have to worry about being kicked out in two days?

She couldn't imagine it. *Wouldn't* imagine it. Not yet.

When she got back to Carl's office, he was just finishing up lunch at his desk. Willow sat down and began to arrange herself for further training.

"Willow," he said, then coughed on the remains of what appeared to be a roll of meat and cheese. "Wait a moment. I don't know if you know this, but they're not going to let you use any inscribed materials during the test." He motioned to the glove she'd slipped over her hand. "That, or the band," he added, pointing to the band on the table.

"Um, okay," Willow said, not quite getting what he was trying to communicate.

He coughed again to clear his throat, then threw away the remainder of his wrappings.

"What I mean is, we're going to have to get all the way there before Friday morning," he said. "All the way."

"So a day and a half left," Willow said, fear twisting her gut. "That should be plenty of time."

Carl nodded. "Just so you know."

* * *

Leopold sat at the other end of Willow's bed, watching her whisper the concept for blazing light and carefully twitch her fingers. The key was to not move them so much that her reflexes started up her psychokinetic spells.

A faint glowing sphere spun out into the air above her silvered hand, about the same luminosity as her previous magelights before Annabelle had healed her. Willow sighed, and the magelight dispelled.

"The magelight shouldn't even be visible," she said, rubbing her brow in frustration. It was proving almost impossible to keep her new-found power back. And the most infuriating part: trying harder wouldn't solve anything. She had to do less, and that was something she was not used to at all.

"It was... barely visible," Leopold said, but it was clear he was trying to offer her encouragement even as he eyed her with concern.

She plucked at the silver glove. "If this thing wasn't on, we'd probably both be blind."

"Why not use a different concept?" he suggested. "How about *nearly-invisible light*?"

Willow wearily shook her head. "The concept is standardized. I have to use the same one in the text. If I could just change my idea of the concept... but that probably wouldn't work either. That light's going to burn the examiner's eyes right out of their head."

"Well, just make sure you keep your eyes closed," Leopold joked, then sobered. "It's still hard to believe."

"It's harder for me." She sighed, not from physical exhaustion, but from the mental and emotional drain the practice and time crunch were putting on her. She knew she had to stay calm to make any progress in controlling her powers. "I was weak my whole life. Now I've got the opposite problem. How am I supposed to deal with that?"

"The same way you've always done," Leopold said. "Raw grit."

* * *

Raw grit—what a terrible idea. Good to keep her going, but not so good when she's on her last legs. If she'd listened to Leopold and tried to bull her way through, she'd be walking into this exam going on three days with no sleep and destined to fail.

"Willow Tremont." The examiner was a middle-aged woman with short-cut hair, wearing a heavy gown stitched with the Arcanum's symbol: a sphere surrounded by a brick wall.

"That's me," Willow said, bubbly with nervous energy.

She'd just entered the small room—one of the many tiny rooms in the main hall of the Arcanum. It was similar to the one in which she'd had her first disastrous examination two weeks before. Somehow it seemed like a lot longer ago than that.

The woman motioned to the chair across from her. Besides that, the room was entirely empty. It resembled a storage closet more than an auxiliary classroom.

"Please take a seat, and we'll begin the examination."

Willow hooked her cane on the chair back and sat gingerly in the seat across from the examiner. There was hardly three feet separating their knees. The examiner turned a page in the sheaf she was holding.

"We've only got the spell demonstration scheduled. Which spell will you be casting?"

"Magelight," Willow said and shifted in her seat, trying to find a comfortable position. That was proving to be impossible though, so she determined to just settle down and get it over with.

"When you're ready," the examiner said, pen poised over the sheaf.

Willow had the brief thought that being *ready* would require a few more weeks of practice, which she didn't have. But she was as ready as she was going to be. She reached over and slipped the band from her right wrist, the metal straightening out like a ruler as she laid it on the ground beside her. The examiner's eyebrow quirked up, but she didn't make a note.

Willow held her right hand loosely, opposite her left. Both formed matching halves of a sphere-form with her fingers pointed inwards, just as she'd practiced the night before. She closed her eyes, breathed out, and hoped beyond hope that her hand wouldn't seize up on her now.

"Blazing light," Willow said, focusing not on her right hand but on her left.

The essence there moved sluggishly, and she pushed it with all the force she'd trained herself to use over the last five years. Even at full strength, the essence barely leaked out through her palm into the spell-form. Willow angled her fingertips, coaxing it into a rough sphere—not her best work by far.

She could feel it holding together. Barely. It wouldn't hold together with her meager control if she began to push with the same force in her other hand, so she didn't. Focusing on her right hand, she coaxed the essence within.

"Steadfastness," she whispered.

The surge of essence that exploded from her ungloved hand was almost too much to control while keeping the core intact. She bent her entire will towards encapsulating the steadfast layer around the core of blazing light—manipulating the form surrounding the sphere, while still eking out a thin stream of controlled essence from her left hand. She felt, more than sensed, the steadfast layer fully wrap around the core of blazing light. The spell solidified into its final form.

Willow let out the breath she'd been holding and slowly opened her eyes. Sure enough, hovering right between her palms was the palest magelight she'd ever seen. But it was magelight nonetheless.

While the examiner made notes on her sheaf, Willow allowed herself to smile and almost laughed. She'd done it. *She was in.*

CHAPTER 17

Unfortunately for Willow, all the dormitory rooms had already been claimed by students and their overflow admissions. Fortunately, Bryan and Margaret didn't seem put out at all by the prospect of lodging her for the rest of the semester. Willow found it difficult to express the depth of gratitude she felt, but Bryan seemed to think it was all in due course. To hear him tell it, he'd never really be out of her debt for that one strange night in the caravan.

She was so elated at passing her exam that the moment she saw Leopold, she kissed him full on the mouth, right there in public. She could feel the other students' eyes on them, but she didn't care. She was in. Finally, out of probation! Carl had swung it so she didn't need the capacity measure, making her a fully honored student. She hadn't felt such relief in weeks.

Willow stopped by Carl's office before her inscription lecture to let him know. Immediately he noticed the pale sphere she carried in her hand.

"Is that…" He trailed off, as if he couldn't believe what he was seeing.

"Oh, yeah," Willow said, holding up the magelight.

It was as light as air and stayed wherever she put it, but its surface was solid like warm glass. Leopold told her that none of his magelights had ever been corporeal like that. When he tried to touch them, his fingers just slipped through.

"My passing grade," Willow said, grinning.

"May I?"

"Here," Willow said and handed the magelight over.

Carl cautiously grabbed it, and the expression on his face said more than words. It said she'd done something weird again. Something impossible.

"How did you make this?" Carl asked. "It's really magelight?"

"It is," Willow confirmed. "I couldn't get my right hand to cooperate by Thursday night, so I decided to cheat a little."

"Cheat a little?" Carl asked, as if he couldn't believe what he was hearing.

"I laid down the light core with my left hand, then used my right for the layer of steadfastness."

Carl's eyes flicked from the magelight to Willow, then down to her right arm. She wondered if he could sense that she wasn't wearing the band at the moment. She'd decided after the exam that if she was going to really be in the school now, she'd have to step up her training on looking and acting normal. That meant dealing with her hand seizing up. That meant gaining conscious control over her psychokinetic spells.

"You layered both... at the same time?" Carl asked.

Willow nodded. "I figured I couldn't keep the core stable if I finished laying it down before I started on the steadfast layer, so I..." She trailed off. "That's not normal, is it?"

Carl sighed. "You've never done it before, have you?"

"It just seemed like a good idea."

"It would be," Carl said, rubbing his face. "It would be the best idea—if anyone else could do it. Spells could probably have twice as many layers if others could apply two layers at the same time, instead of having to maintain the more and more unstable core layers after they're done depositing. But no. No one else can do this."

Willow looked at the magelight, which had benefited from the extremely active steadfast layer in a way she hadn't expected. She wondered if the only way she'd been able to apply the much stronger layer had been because she was actively putting down the core at the same time. What would normally feel like another way she was different and broken was now starting to feel a lot like a benefit.

"So, how can we take advantage of this?" Willow asked, holding her hands out.

"I'll start thinking," Carl said and handed the magelight back. "Congratulations, scholar Willow."

When they got home, Willow and Leopold discovered that Bryan and Margaret had prepared a celebratory feast. An entire side of boar, potatoes, and some kind of delicious leafy green—all roasted to perfection. Margaret must have been cooking ever since Willow had finished the exam. How they'd found out about her passing grade before she got home, Willow never discovered.

They called for magelights again and again. Willow delighted in producing the little baubles and watching Benny chase them around the dining room, batting them into the ceiling to bounce off the rafters. For dessert, Bryan extracted a tub of whipped, chilled cream from the icebox. It was the first time Willow had eaten the delicacy. He served her up a healthy dollop, and she savored the rich, strawberry-flavored cream bite by bite.

It was, if at all possible, the best night of her life.

They talked late into twilight and then even more after Benny was put to bed. Bryan wanted to hear everything about the tests, about her tutor, and about the exam. Margaret seemed to delight in Willow's animation. And every now and then, Leopold would put his hand on her back. But eventually it was time even for Bryan and Margaret to call it a night. After Leopold and Willow helped them clean up, they found themselves alone in the dining room under the twinkling canopy of magelights.

"Help me shepherd these into my room?" Willow asked.

They spent an enjoyable half hour jumping in silence, trying to snag them from the rafters using any tool they could manage. By the time they were finished, Willow's feet were sore and her back ached something terrible, but she closed the door to the bedroom and pulled Leopold in for a kiss.

"Congratulations," Leopold said when she finally pulled away.

She fingered the ties on his jacket, then pulled one until it came undone. Leopold's eyes went wide.

"I'm not ready for the night to end," she said and pulled another tie undone. "Are you?"

"Gods no," he said and gently slipped the toggles from their loops in her stiff overcoat.

It slipped free of her shoulders, and she shrugged it to the ground. She eased his jacket away, then ran her fingers up his chest as she lifted his shirt over his head and nearly knocked his glasses off. He seemed to hesitate, and for a moment, she became self-conscious.

"I wish I hadn't made so many magelights," she said, suddenly aware of the brightness of the room and how she would look to him. The effect she had on people. What would he think when he saw all of her?

He tugged the hem of her undershirt gently, then raised it over her head. She closed her eyes, suddenly exhausted of initiative, suddenly afraid.

"You're beautiful," he said, hugging her gently to his chest. She rested her cheek on his collarbone.

"Thank you," she whispered.

They moved to the bed.

* * *

If Bryan and Margaret were surprised to see Leopold there in the morning, they didn't make any sign or mention of it. It was the weekend, Willow's first weekend where she didn't have the exam hanging over her head, and Leopold had promised a trip as they cuddled together in bed before falling asleep. Willow had barely heard his words, caught up in post-coital bliss, and had drifted off to sleep even as he spoke.

But he had been serious, because after they ate a hearty breakfast—they needed it—Leopold practically shoved Willow out the door in his excitement. They held hands as he guided her down the street towards the giant wall which encircled the city.

"I found out about this only last week," he said as they got in line.

Ahead of them were a few guards and another couple who looked as though they were also sightseeing. What looked like an iron birdcage large enough to hold eight or so people descended from the tall, dark wall, lit from within by inscribed lights.

When it reached the bottom, a porter inside swung the door out. The guards, the couple, Willow and Leopold all gathered in the cage, where the porter closed the gate and latched it. He slid a little brass lever up on a heavily inscribed plate, and the basket began rising. Willow looked up and couldn't see any rope hauling above them.

"Is this thing floating?" Willow asked in a whisper.

Leopold nodded. "They have larger lifts down the wall for supplies and such. This is just one of the smaller people-movers for the guards and anyone else who wants to reach the top."

The view out of the birdcage was equal parts enthralling and terrifying. The city of Durum spread out beneath them, shadowed by the large protective wall into almost perfect darkness until it began to rise towards the center. The Arcanum, surrounded by a warren of streets and half-hidden by double-story shops, stood at the central crest of the city. The very tops of its spires gleamed with morning light.

As the cage rose higher, the city began to take on the aspect of an anthill. Thousands of tiny tunnels—once her eyes adjusted, she realized the streets of the city were the same way. They twisted and wove with a logic all their own, islands of houses and shops in the scurrying stream of early-morning risers. She saw a cemetery near the wall and knew that Bryan and Margaret's house had to be nearby on one of the connecting streets.

The ascent began to slow, and Willow hoped that they were near the top of the wall. The city had grown so minuscule beneath them that, although she hadn't considered herself a person fearful of heights before, she was beginning to feel a definite queasiness in her stomach from the sight. Looking up, she saw the crest of the wall slide past the top of the cage, then down until it locked level with the floor. The porter moved across the cage along the outside bars and swung an opposing door open onto a paved path.

The guards left first, followed by the sightseeing couple, and then Leopold practically had to pull Willow over the small gap between the cage and the wall. Once on firm ground, she let the size of the city wall impress itself on her for the first time. She'd been unconscious when they made their way from the wilds through the warded tunnel and under the fortification, but she'd heard her whole life of the impressive walled cities in fairy tales. Those stories didn't do justice to the wall she stood on now.

At least forty feet wide, a stone-flagged road, spacious enough for passing carriages, ran down the center. Willow turned slowly on the spot and took in the ancient weapons of war mounted every 200 or so feet along the rim, all pointed down at the outside world. She also studied the broad sweep of the wall's hard line as it encircled the city mile after mile. Truly, something so massive could have only been made by magic, and only by the combined spellwork of hundreds of mages.

"What do you think?" Leopold's voice was a whisper in the morning hush. Further away, guards were changing shifts with a smattering of chatter and the clanking of equipment, but for the moment, they seemed to be in a little bubble of quiet.

"It's incredible," Willow breathed. "Magic built all this?"

"In a single year, so they say," Leopold said and pulled her towards a battlement on the far side of the wall.

The crenelation was waist-high at its lowest, with stone spires rising up to either side. She supposed they might give some kind of protection from attacks launched from below, although she couldn't imagine anything powerful enough to land a blow this many hundreds of feet up.

The sun rising over the landscape was incredible—it was as if the world itself was on fire from the clouds above to the waves of rolling hills below. From this height, Willow could even make out the ancient winding tracks of generations past—an elder civilization whose roads one could still find in quieter parts of the world. Sometimes farmers in her own town would turn up shards of glass when plowing, or stringy wisps of ancient flimsy. These artifacts were all that remained of the world that existed before the discovery of magic.

"It's beautiful," Willow breathed, and she felt Leopold's arm encircle her waist before gently pulling her close.

She leaned her head against his shoulder and looked out on the dangerous wild that had nearly claimed her life before it even started.

"Where's the warded tunnel?" she suddenly asked, barely leaning over the battlement to scan the miniature world at the base of the wall. She had to grit her teeth against the vertigo, but she searched anyway.

Leopold leaned in beside her, scanned the base for a moment, and then pointed.

"There's the gate," he said.

Sure enough, Willow could just make out a disruption in the seamless structure of the wall to her right. To be visible from so far away, she thought it must be over fifty feet wide, or maybe even larger. She couldn't make out much detail, but something bugged her.

"I don't see anyone coming into the city," she said, looking out again.

For several miles outside of the walls, the world was entirely barren of animal life, both magical and mundane. Dark patches of forest clumped together in the distance, where she knew diminutive tree sprites lived. But between the wall and the forest was nothing much besides a few scraggly tracts of grass. Even into the rolling hills, the ground was mostly covered with great gouts of upturned earth.

Warbeast tracks.

"You can't see them once they're in the tunnel," Leopold reminded her. "Traders, woodsmen, they have to cross the warbeast's territory on a daily basis. The invisibility wards are our main defense against it."

Willow scanned the ground again but couldn't see anything moving down there.

"Could you see it from up here?" she asked, suddenly eager to see the enormous magical creature. From this high, behind the battlement, it didn't seem nearly as terrifying as, say, a deathworm up close.

"I think so," Leopold said and looked out again. "Maybe it's on the other side of the city."

"Huh, damn," Willow grumbled. "I don't know why I wanted to see it so much."

"You'll see it someday," Leopold said, smiling. "I'll make sure you do."

"Oooh, a romantic monster encounter," she teased. She could barely remember a half-fever dream of Leopold telling her about the warbeast as they trundled into the city.

Strangely enough, she felt cheated of the experience—especially if she was going to spend so long within Durum's wall. She had no reason to leave, and another caravan ride was going to be expensive. She only planned to return home once her studies were complete in almost two years. Until then, she'd be on her own.

Willow pushed back from the battlement and dragged Leopold towards one of the colossal, ancient weapons that rose above the wall-top road.

Speaking of expensive...

"What do other students do for money?" she asked.

They passed guards newly relieved of duty, sporting sweaty mops of hair from the helmets they'd recently relinquished.

"For money?" Leopold asked.

"I can't be the only one here who's been sent without a full ride," Willow said. "I assumed there would be some way to make up the rest of what I need."

"I suppose you can try to find a job doing whatever you'd like in the city," Leopold said. "As for magework, I haven't heard of anyone doing spellwork outside of class for pay. But... it must happen, right? We're in too high demand for it not to."

"Maybe it's a big secret," Willow mused as they came up to the war machine.

It resembled nothing so much as a giant cannon, of which Willow had only seen illustrations in books. Great iron plates adorned the outside of the device, deeply inscribed with what she recognized now as essential inscriptions.

"They must have fired essence through this," Willow said and touched the cold, black surface gently with her hand. "To battle the warbeasts."

"Can you even imagine?" Leopold came up beside her and searched the surface of the cannon. "I can't find any commemorative plate saying what it did."

"That's because it's still active," a guard said as he came around the other side of the cannon. "Hasn't been fired in centuries, but it could be powered up again in a jiffy. We'd need twenty mages to work it, and a whole team of guards to aim the thing, but it once took out a giant salamander before it reached the city's wall."

"And this is your charge?" Willow asked, trying to imagine what firing such a device would even look like. The guard nodded.

"It has to be manned at all times. Though the bloodless pact is still in effect, better to be prepared than too trusting."

"Of course," Leopold said.

The guard took a step closer and lowered his voice. "As for what you were talking about before, a scholar at the Arcanum can make a mite more than pocket change if you know the right places to go calling."

"Oh," Willow said. She couldn't help a conspiratorial smile creeping across her face. Leopold looked taken aback, but she leaned in closer. "And where might a scholar at the Arcanum peddle their fledgling skills, might I ask?"

"Do you know Geoff's, in the market square?" He leaned in to meet her. "I would speak to him. Tell him you're a student and you're looking to fatten your pocket. If you're not a'feared of doing some abnormal work, there's plenty to do."

"Thank you for your recommendation," Willow said. She went back to Leopold, who had taken an unusually strong interest in the casing of the cannon. "Would you like to take a stroll to the market square?"

CHAPTER 18

"I still don't know if this is such a good idea," Leopold said as they entered the large market square. It was easily several hundred yards to a side and absolutely crammed with covered stalls. Willow doubted that this *Geoff* would be set up in a stall, but she had no idea where else to look.

"We're just going to take a peek," she said. "We're not marrying the guy."

"What if it's against the rules? You know, I never did read through all that scrollwork they threw at me when I signed admissions."

"Well, I did," Willow said. "A student is not to, under any circumstances, misrepresent themselves as a fully licensed mage. Such is an expellable offense and prosecutable by the full weight of the Mages' Guild."

"It says that?" Leopold paled.

Willow laughed and pulled him along. She was getting used to her strong right hand and how she could actually use it without the pain in her muscles flaring. Carl said it was because her muscles had begun to reverse the process of atrophy.

"But I'm not misrepresenting myself, am I?" Willow asked as she pulled him up to a covered stall.

Within sat an elderly lady who was selling all sorts of leather and brass tools. Willow saw several hammers hanging from the awning, a steel awl, and a book of needles. Perhaps this was a leatherworker's stall?

"Hello, dearies, how can I help you?" the old woman croaked.

"Sorry, but I'm looking for someone named Geoff," Willow said. "You wouldn't happen to know where he'd be, would you?"

The old woman leaned forwards and squinted at them, which served to make her already wrinkly face nigh unrecognizable as anything more than a bundle of crepe. She looked down the aisle of stalls, towards a wall of shops.

"You'll find Geoff down that way," she said. "The shop with the anvil shingle."

"Thank you so much," Willow said, preparing to take off down the aisle, but the old woman stopped her with a hand.

"You're students at the Arcanum, aren't you?" she asked.

"What gave it away?" Leopold sighed.

The woman gestured to them as a whole, as if it was obvious. "Don't let him gouge you. He'll haggle. Don't leave unless you're paying half or less of his asking price."

"Wow, thanks," Willow said.

The old woman nodded, then sat back in her chair. Willow yanked Leopold down the colorful aisle of awnings towards the wall of shops. Leopold groaned.

"If he'll haggle down fifty percent, how reputable could he be?" he asked. "Why are we even doing this? You've got enough money without lodgings, right?"

"Enough money for now," Willow said. "But next year things are going to be tight, even without lodgings."

And if she were going to keep staying with Bryan and Margaret, she'd be damned if she didn't find some way to repay their generosity.

Even now, so early into the term, she felt like a moocher taking advantage of their generosity.

"I always planned on getting a job in the city. I just assumed I'd have to work as a seamstress or something equally debilitating. If I can use my magic to make money, that's wear on my body I'd gladly give up."

"R-Right," Leopold said, and she felt his hand flush with sweat under hers.

It was so easy for him, with his perfect body, to forget how hard things were for her. Even with this burst of morning energy, her feet were already aching and her left hand was stinging something terrible from managing the cane. Magic would be the only way she'd be able to make anything of herself in the world, and she was eager to start.

The shop was easy enough to find once they knew what they were looking for. It was a wide-set wooden and white plaster building, like many of the structures in this part of town, with an anvil and sparks displayed on the swaying shingle above the open door. Willow led the way into the dim interior, dragging a reluctant Leopold in behind her.

"I thought you said you wanted to take me shopping," she whispered to him in the dusk.

There were objects of every sort hanging from the ceiling and mounted on the walls in racks. Freestanding tables held an assortment of strange odds and ends. There was a dagger beside them which shone with a brightness not easily attributable to the light coming in from outside.

"Yeah, for trinkets or snacks," he said. "Maybe even some flowers."

"We can buy flowers later, romantic," she said, but his grip on her hand tightened as he froze.

There was a large-set man sitting behind a wooden counter, watching them in the gloom. Willow made her way across the showroom, her arm around Leopold's waist.

The corpulent man smiled at them. His nose was fat and pocked and as red as a tomato, like his veiny cheeks. Willow looked upwards as they approached and saw inscribed lights set into the ceiling.

"Hello there," the man said. "Welcome to Geoff's. If you're in the market for artifacts, there's no better place in Durum, and I've got the best prices. And the best pieces. But you can judge for yourselves. What are you in for?"

Willow tore her gaze away from the inscribed lights and pointed up. "Your inscriptions, who powers them?"

"Ah, you must be scholars," he said, smiling as if he were looking at a particularly naive couple of marks. "I have a contract with one of your fellows to top them off every couple of days. Always work to be found for the enterprising student."

"That's what I'm here for," Willow said. She disengaged from Leopold to hobble to the counter.

Geoff took a quick look down at her cane, then scanned her body with an appraiser's eye. His eyes flicked back to hers, and a small smile touched his lips. "Are you new in the city? Here for the term?"

"Yes, first year," Willow said.

"I don't have much work that a first-year could do," Geoff muttered. "Besides refreshing inscriptions. You must've come in on a caravan."

"I did," Willow said, a bit confused.

"Was it an eventful trip?"

She looked closer and saw his narrowed eyes. He knew something, something about the attack. And then she realized: of course he did. This man had been recommended to her by a guard on the wall. He probably knew all of the caravan guards. He might even know Bryan.

Willow nodded. "Deathworm attack. I almost lost my hands."

He looked down at the hand clutching her cane. "Looks like you got all healed up."

"Lucky for me, my guard had some favors to call in."

"It hasn't affected her spellwork," Leopold interjected. Willow knew he was trying to be helpful, but she felt that something else was going on here. Geoff was angling for something.

"You wouldn't have had anything to do with that worm, would you?" Geoff asked, his face entirely placid. It was only his eyes that told her he was itching for the answer.

"Apparently I killed it," Willow said, gripping the cane so hard in her right hand she felt a twinge of psychokinesis along her wrist. She forced herself to take a breath, and the twinge went away.

Geoff nodded. "I've heard of you. Shut the door, young fella, and run the bolt. I'd like to see you both in back."

With the door shut, the display room was much darker. The inscribed lights in the ceiling were barely enough to see by, but the workroom behind the counter was lit by a much denser constellation of inscriptions, and Willow noticed several oil lamps mounted to the walls too. Apparently, Geoff needed to see clearly in this place, whereas the gloom at the front of the shop probably worked to his benefit while haggling.

Once they were in the brighter workroom, he motioned towards a thick wooden table set into the wall, and they gathered along its edge. He turned to them.

"I haven't properly introduced myself. Geoff," he said and held out his hand.

Willow was surprised when his handshake didn't crush her, although she was using her right hand to squeeze back. Leopold shook too, and then Geoff retrieved a sheaf of papers from a high shelf among racks of tools.

"Apparently you saved the guard on your little caravan," Geoff said. "He was very impressed with you."

"Bryan talked to you about me?" Willow asked, astonished.

Geoff nodded. "It isn't every day that something gets the jump on a caravan guard. It's good money for a reason and Bryan's one of the more careful sort. He's got a kid. He's got to be."

"Benny, I know. I'm staying with them now."

"You are, are you?" Geoff asked, and she saw a smile touch his fat cheeks. There was some kind of relationship between him and Bryan, more than she'd suspected. She supposed it might work in her favor.

He turned to the papers on the desk. "I've got a set of jobs here, pretty standardized. Refilling essence in inscriptions, probing artifacts, they each have a payout associated. It's not much, but it'll be a little pocket money for you in school."

Willow looked at the sheet and was unimpressed. Refilling ten light inscriptions paid only five copper, probing unknown artifacts was two copper a piece. When a meal was easily fifteen copper if she wanted to eat something that Margaret hadn't made, it was even less than pocket change.

"I was told I could make more than this," Willow said.

Geoff laughed. "By who? Aye, if you were a second-year, I've got more on the docket. Inscribing, repairing artifacts, you name it. You can make a lot from that, but you can't do any of it yet, can you?"

Willow hunched her shoulders, feeling slightly offended. "I'm in an inscriptions class now."

"If you're not specializing, there's little use I can get from you in inscribing. I'm not selling trinkets here. The best artifacts in Durum, that's what I offer, and that's what I have. Some I get from the caravans coming into the city, found in the wilds, but most I have made custom. Things nobody else has."

Things nobody else has.

Heat rose in her cheeks at the insinuation, however oblique, that nothing she could do was worth anything. That had once been true, and it was the future she'd worked so hard to change. She wasn't an invalid anymore, and there *were* people counting on her. As much as Bryan and Margaret hid the costs, she knew she ate twice as much as anyone else, and they only had Bryan's income to support the family.

Willow slid the sheet of paper away, leaned her cane against the worktable, and cupped her hands. She barely had to concentrate now to envision the concepts, to affect the flow of essence through her good hand. It was still too strong by far, but not for this.

"And how much for this?" Willow held out the pale, solid magelight. Geoff reached out and, surprised at first, accepted the physical spell. "I guarantee you nobody else has anything like it."

"Willow," Leopold whispered into her ear, but she shook him off. It felt good doing something. Being useful. Being more than a cripple. Being special in a way that meant something.

"What in the seven—" Geoff began, then cut himself off with a cough. He held the magelight up to the inscribed lights above and turned the perfect sphere this way and that.

"It's not very bright," he said, tapping the surface with his fingernail. "How long will it last?"

"I don't know," Willow admitted.

Geoff hummed to himself as if he'd suspected as much. "I'll give you fifty copper for it," he said. "It's really very pale, it probably won't last the day."

"It'll definitely last the day," Willow said, remembering the constellation of magelights that hovered against the ceiling when she and Leopold awoke together that morning. "And you're fleecing me."

Geoff shrugged. "Take it elsewhere then. Nobody else will know what to do with it, I guarantee you that. Fifty is generous. It's barely shining at all."

"I can make brighter ones, brighter by far," Willow said and found that she was seething at his insinuation. She was proud of her mage-light. It had guaranteed her admission into the Arcanum. She felt personally invested in it.

"Well, I'd love to see them," he said, holding out his hand.

"Fine," Willow said and cupped her hands in the spell-form.

"Willow!" Leopold said, louder this time as he shook her shoulder.

It was like a cold splash of water in her face. She remembered the silver glove back in her room and how Carl had warned her not to cast magelight without it. The result, he'd said, could be disfiguring.

Willow forced her hand into a fist, then lowered it to take hold of her cane again.

"Not yet," she admitted and felt Leopold's frenzied clutch on her shoulder slacken.

"Well, fifty's the best I can do."

"Seventy-five," Leopold said from beside her, and she turned to look at him.

Geoff laughed. "You don't have room to bargain, first-year. I doubt I'll be able to sell this as it is."

"Seventy-five, and you get exclusive purchasing rights to the solid magelights. Even the brighter ones," Leopold said. "That is, assuming you'll buy them."

Geoff's face pinched as he calculated in his head. Willow wrapped an arm around Leopold's waist and squeezed him in appreciation. He squeezed back.

"Nobody else gets them," he said. "Nobody."

"So long as you don't say who's making them," Willow amended, thinking of Carl. She'd gone against his instructions, she knew, but she hadn't been able to help herself. At the very least, she could try to keep her name out of it.

"Why would I go and reveal my source," Geoff scoffed, "if I've got an exclusive contract?"

"You'll be the only one," Leopold confirmed. Geoff moved to hold out his hand towards Willow. "And we'll renegotiate for the brighter ones."

Geoff hesitated for a moment, then extended his hand fully. "You've got a deal."

Willow took his hand, and his grip was much stronger this time. She forced herself to squeeze back as hard as she could and met his eyes as they shook.

"Deal," she said.

Chapter 19

Monday came all too soon, and that magical first weekend of freedom vanished like so much mist in the morning sun. Leopold didn't stay with her Sunday night—he had his own business to attend to back at his dormitory room—so Willow slept alone in the house on Grave Street. For the first time it felt as if it were strange.

It was difficult to get to sleep. She couldn't stop thinking about the seventy-five copper stored in her pack. After so long being less than, being pitied, she'd done something valuable. And not only that, but she was the only one who could do it, who could create a solid spell. She found the thought—of not only being normal, but being *better*—intoxicating.

Leopold arrived at the end of breakfast, as he had every day the last week, and they walked together up the long, low hill towards the Arcanum in the wan morning light. The school seemed to shine in a way it hadn't before, like it really was a pinnacle of hope in the walled city. She had everything to look forward to and nothing to be afraid of.

She went to class, her first class as a full student, and sat in the front as Carl demonstrated triple layering on a spell that would produce water from a rock. Then he set the class to the assignment. Willow slipped on her silver glove, hidden under a tight-fitting leather one, and once again practiced modulating the power that coursed through her right hand. By the end of class, the essence she was able to pass through the glove was almost as weak as the essence oozing from her left hand.

Carl left class at the first clanging of the bells, and Willow followed closely behind as he dodged students in the corridors back to his office. She didn't even knock when she reached his door. She just burst right on through. He briefly looked up as he arranged a set of documents on his desk.

"I want Annabelle to heal my left hand, too," Willow said, the door barely closed behind her. The wards against eavesdropping weren't even up, but she assumed this conversation would be so inconsequential that they wouldn't need to worry about anyone overhearing.

"Don't you have a class to be in?"

"Not until after lunch," said Willow impatiently. "Inscription. I used to have to go to metrology now."

"Ah, yes," Carl said, and he smiled. "Poor Burket, I wonder how he's doing. You sent him into a nervous fit, you know."

"That's not my problem," Willow grumbled and thrust out her left hand, holding her cane. "This is. I can barely push any essence out through it. If we could just heal it like my right hand—"

"Out of the question," Carl said with finality.

"What? Why?"

The professor turned. "Cast magelight now with your right hand. Go on."

"Um..." Willow raised her right hand in the spell-form.

"Without the glove," Carl amended, and Willow closed her hand.

"I... I can't do it safely yet," Willow said.

"And that's why."

"But I could just use another glove."

"I only have the one," Carl said. "Do you have any idea how expensive that thing was?"

As a matter of fact, Willow had no idea at all. She supposed it would be worth at least its weight in silver. But then she considered the tooling—drawing the silver into fine wire and weaving it into cloth. It wouldn't be cheap, and who would it even be made for? Battle mages, most likely. They would need armor against enemy spells. How had Carl gotten a hold of such an artifact? And, she couldn't help but wonder, why was he dedicating so much time, energy, and coin to bringing her up to speed?

Willow set her jaw and kept eye contact, nonetheless. She needed to have her hand healed, and she needed to keep moving forwards. If she had access to the essence in both of her hands, she could really start working on down-regulating their pressure. This high-low shit had to stop, and fast, because she felt intuitively that it was holding her back.

"The time will come, Willow," Carl said, his voice softer now. Understanding. "You'll master the essence in your right hand, and we'll move onto your right arm. It'll be a long process, but it will come. You've spent your entire life like this. What's a few more years?"

Willow's mouth dropped. Years? She found her plans, the solution to all her problems, vanishing before her eyes. She shut her jaw quickly, not wanting to clue him into her shock and indignance.

She didn't have years. She wanted to master her own body—this body she'd never known she had before—and she wanted to do it *now*. If she could work her muscles, if she could move her body, she'd have access to her full essence capacity. And she could also begin the long, painful process of building herself up for the first time. No longer would she look like a waif. She would just be normal, like everyone else.

More than normal.

But she could see he'd made up his mind—after all their time working together, she could tell that much at a glance. She knew it had been a good idea to keep secret her deal with Geoff. Undoubtedly Carl would have made her back off and slow down, just as he was doing now.

Willow gave a slight nod, then turned and left the room. She felt Carl's eyes on her back as she exited, but she couldn't turn to face him again. Years? How could he expect her to wait so long when it was all within her grasp now?

There had to be a better way.

"What are you doing?" Leopold asked as they sat together in the high-ceilinged dining hall over lunch.

Without metrology breathing down her neck, she finally had a proper period of time to enjoy some food. And there was just something special about spending the coppers that she'd received from Geoff for the solid magelights. She had helped herself to a double portion of the broiled chicken, and both platefuls had been picked to the bone already.

She was staring at her left hand, lying limp on the tabletop. Leopold was also staring at it.

"Trying to..." She grunted. "Shut it off."

"You're trying to—" He looked around, then leaned forwards and whispered, "restrain your psychokinesis?"

Willow nodded. Her left hand lay on the table, but it was harder to surrender control over than her right hand—probably due to the fact that it hadn't already been reattached to her nervous system. But maybe if she could consciously calm the storm of spells in her hand, she'd be able to push essence through her palm without the impossible resistance she'd lived with her entire life.

The best she could get were flickers—instants where, in her mind's eye, her hand flashed clear, suddenly free of the tortuous turbulence that plagued the rest of her body. Now that she knew what she was looking for, she could see the psychokinetic spell effects in the mangled flow of her essence. The way her flow twisted around them, slowed and redirected, forming eddies and back currents in her stick-thin limbs. It was a miracle she'd been able to cast anything at all!

Her hand flashed clear again, then clouded with turbulence as Willow involuntarily twitched her palm. She let out a sigh of frustration and picked up her fork to push around some of the soggy, oiled vegetables on her plate.

"I take it the talk with Professor Brandeweiss didn't go well," Leopold observed.

"Years, he said. Years! I can't wait years."

"Why not?"

Willow looked over at him, incensed that he could even ask such a question. But then again, he knew nothing of living in a body that held its secrets from you. Of always looking the freak, of being crippled both physically and magically. What was it to him, a game?

"They're reconnecting your spine, Willow," he leaned over and whispered. "It's going to take time. Lots of time."

"I can't stand it," she snapped. "I just can't stand to wait."

"Why?" he asked again.

"I want to..." She paused. How could she even express the desperation that clawed at her innards every moment of every day since that fateful discovery? "I want to be me. Me as I was meant to be. The me that was always under the surface, held back."

"You're already you," Leopold said, placing his hand over hers on the table. "This other stuff, yes, it's another part of you. But you're already Willow. The Willow I love."

That word. How could he use that word when she was… like this? He could have a normal love, a normal lover, and he wouldn't even have to wait. Ardor and self-pity warred briefly before the former won out. *It must be real*, she thought, *if he loves me like this.*

She scooted closer to him, giving up the nearly futile experiments on her hand to press herself into him.

"I love you too, Leopold," she said.

He leaned against her, mouth to her ear. "It's dangerous too," he whispered. "It must be. I don't want anything to happen to you."

"What's the worst that could happen?" Willow asked, gently squeezing his hand. "I can't be even more crippled."

"I don't know," he said. "But sometimes… I'm scared."

"I won't let anything happen," she said seriously. "I promise."

* * *

In inscription class, they were practicing graving copper strips adhered to wooden boards with lacquer. The symbology of the inscriptions was easy enough to understand with Leopold's notes. It was a simple essence-redirection effect. It would shunt essence from one location in an inscription to another, or from one side of the board to another once they were done with the graving.

Unfortunately, all of Willow's studying prepared her little for the realities of handling hammer and engraving chisel. Even though she knew what she wanted to set down, the graving head kept getting away from her, and she had to wrangle it back to the symbol sketched on the thin strip of brass. By the end of class, she had a mangled strip. It weakly shunted essence across its face to the other side of the board —while spilling a great deal more essence off to either side.

Luckily this wasn't a test, because she was pretty sure she would have failed.

It wasn't just her inability with the chisel—her mind kept wandering. With what she'd done with her magelight, the possibilities kept spinning out in her mind. Could this excess power be applied to inscription? What could she do here that no one else was capable of trying? Her thoughts went to the cannon on the city wall. Could she fire it all by herself?

It was strange getting out of class with light still in the sky. For so long, she'd been tutoring with Carl until after twilight. Now he wanted her to work on her own until she mastered holding her essence back through the silver glove, and then moved on to regulating it down to something that wasn't blinding. It meant she had a lot more time to herself to work, and theoretically, she could work on anything she wanted.

There were unused classrooms all over the Arcanum, especially after a class as late as Inscription. Willow found one and boarded herself up inside. The thick stone walls of the college left the sounds of students walking through the halls muted—just what she needed to concentrate.

Willow laid her left hand out on the table, palm up, and concentrated on letting go. It had been days since she'd felt a twinge in her right hand, so she knew she could do it. It was just hard to start again with another limb. But she had to, damn what Carl said. She couldn't let all of this power just lie on the floor unused. Couldn't leave it pent up inside of her, moving limbs that should rightly be moved by her own muscles. It was a gods damned waste.

Her hand flickered, and the clarity lasted for longer than an instant. A half second, a full second, then gone. She began again, periodically forcing herself to release control. Now that she was aware of what saturated her bones, she began to feel the psychokinetic spells soften. Begin to give way.

Another flicker. Was it a second? Or even longer? She settled down in the hard-backed chair and steeled herself for a mental workout.

CHAPTER 20

Willow was free.

She was no longer in danger of being thrown out of the Arcanum—she was, in fact, a full student at the magical college, which was what she'd always dreamed of. She was in a relationship. A *real* relationship. One where someone saw her as an equal, as someone to cherish, and not as someone to care for or pity. And she had income. For as long as she kept producing magelights for Geoff, he kept paying her. And she was well on her way to repay Bryan and Margaret for everything they'd done for her since her disastrous arrival at Durum.

She had everything she'd ever wanted.

So why wasn't she happy? Why was she still pushing herself harder and further than she could take—practicing into the late hours of the night, gaining control over her hand second by precious second?

It was because, as simple and pure as those invalid's dreams were, they weren't her dreams anymore. At least, not all of them. She'd been given a glimpse of a world brimming with possibility and wonder. A world where she wasn't just normal—she was better than normal. A world where she wasn't weak, but strong. Unbelievably, impossibly strong. And after that taste, everything else was bland.

It was in this unsatisfied, worn-out state that she emerged from her bedroom after completing her morning training. Leopold was already there, talking with Bryan at the empty table with the ghost of bacon still on the air. Benny sat on the floor, amusing himself with a pair of carved wooden toys, which he forced to battle again and again. If Willow didn't know any better, she'd think the precocious young boy was simulating warbeast battles. Had Bryan been entertaining his son with stories of the rotting warbeast outside Durum's walls?

"Good morning," Willow muttered as she crossed the room to sit beside Leopold.

He turned, a smile on his face, which immediately transmuted to a frown. He was taking in her general exhausted state, looking at her bloodshot eyes, and it was clear he disapproved. Willow leaned over, and they shared a short kiss. When he came away, the small smile was back, though tempered.

"Willow," Margaret said, retrieving a plate from the chilled larder and sliding its congealed contents onto the frying pan. Even with just the heat from the coals, the smell of bacon suffused the air.

"Mmmmm," Willow hummed, closing her eyes.

When she opened them again, Margaret had crossed the room and was holding out a letter to her. Willow's eyebrows creased in confusion, and she took the letter, but not before she saw the same look of concern on Margaret's face. She glanced at and quickly broke the seal, trying to steer the conversation away from its inevitable destination.

"Who's it from?" Leopold asked beside her.

"Arcanum," Willow guessed, though she wasn't entirely sure. The seal had shown a sphere surrounded by a circular wall, though above the sphere had been a pair of calipers. It was a small letter, only a single sheet, whereas the ones she'd gotten before from the Arcanum had all been packets. She unfolded it to read.

As the bacon sizzled, Willow smiled. Then let out a chuckle. Then a laugh.

"What... What's going on?" Leopold asked.

"It's Daniel. They want me to come in for another test. Must not have gotten the memo that—" Willow stopped cold at the last paragraph.

"More tests?" Margaret asked. "I thought that was all over now. When you were admitted..."

"It should be. It is," Leopold insisted. "They can't make her do anything they couldn't make any other student do."

"If they're trying to pull something—" Bryan added from across the table, his brows low and bulk shifted forwards.

"No," Willow assuaged slowly. "They're not. They're... I'm going to go."

"Why?" Leopold pleaded. "What could they possibly—"

"They know how to get my capacitance."

* * *

The metrology building looked the same as always, but things felt different now. Willow initially thought it must have been herself that had changed as she walked through the large room towards the door at the back. Then she realized nobody had looked up at her entrance, and nobody's eyes followed her on her way back. That made the real change all the more conspicuous.

They were ignoring her on purpose.

Willow knocked softly on the door to the small room, but nobody answered. She raised her fist to knock again when Daniel spoke up from behind her.

"Willow," he said, sticking his head out from another door along the back wall. He motioned her over and she left the first door with not a little confusion. Were they in a different room now?

Daniel retreated into the room, and when Willow entered, she found that it was much larger than the previous one. Along the back wall were four large tanks banded in silver and copper, capped with hemispheres of dark crystal. She had a feeling she knew what they were.

Steph was there, and she smiled when Willow walked in.

"It's good to see you again," Steph said and gently shook Willow's hand. Daniel shook next, with a wide smile on his face. Willow looked around for the third metrologist.

"Where's Burket?" she asked.

"Ah, well. He's not coming. We're sort of spearheading this on our own," Daniel said, his smile slipping nervously.

"On your own?"

"Well, nobody's ever done a capacitance reading like this before," Steph said excitedly.

"Why?" Willow asked. Not that she was complaining, of course. Capacitance was her last essential attribute they'd yet to measure. After what they'd found with the other two, Willow was excited as to what *this* test might reveal.

Not only would she know more about herself, about this strange power contained in her broken body, but she hoped the reading would prove to be valuable ammunition in her quest to convince Carl to step up her body's reintegration. Maybe she could tempt him with the reading, the way she was tempted now thinking of that cannon atop the wall. The possibility that she alone might be able to fire it.

Willow stepped over to the large capacitors against the wall. Sure enough, the bands running horizontally across their surfaces were so heavily inscribed it was almost impossible to pick out individual functions. Even this far away, she could feel a strange pressure in the air— thick like jelly.

"Ah, please don't get too close!" Daniel blurted. "They're not— I'm not sure how they'll react to your..."

"To my what?" Willow turned.

Daniel had gone red, and he looked at Steph. She had her gaze locked on Willow, eye to eye.

"We figured it out, eventually," Steph said. "Professor Brandeweiss didn't tell us anything, wouldn't tell us anything, but we figured it out. How we could never get a capacitance reading from you before. Your ridiculously high resistance. Monstrous push force."

"It should have been obvious," Daniel said, and Willow sensed embarrassment in his voice. "We should have seen it right from the start. We just weren't... prepared."

"Prepared for what?" Willow asked, puzzled, unsure what they were trying to get at.

"You're some kind of magical creature, aren't you?" Steph asked, excitement raising her voice to a near-squeak. "Something that looks human. Half-human?"

"It's the only explanation," Daniel said. "The only thing that makes sense. Only magical creatures do the things you do."

Willow felt her eyebrows narrow into a scowl, but caught hold of herself before she began yelling at them. They thought she was some kind of... animal? *Offended* couldn't begin to describe how she felt about the insinuation that she wasn't a real person, but only some creature pretending to be human. Or half-human, whatever that was. But the temptation of that reading, of knowing herself, of maybe convincing Carl to stop wasting her potential and just finish up her damn reintegration already, was too much.

She twisted the scowl into a grimace—the best she could do given the circumstances—and tried to look cagey. "I can't say much."

"Of course." Steph patted the air placatingly, then moved over to the capacitors. "We got the equipment by fibbing we were going to test it on a salamander," she explained.

"Well, we fibbed that for the first tank," Daniel said. "A manticore for the second."

"Griffon for the third," Steph smiled.

"And what for the fourth?" Willow asked.

"An essence shadow," Daniel said. "We thought that was the closest we could come to describing you. We wanted to make sure our professors thought the idea was sound."

"Essence shadow? You mean ghosts?"

Steph shook her head. "They're not ghosts, not really. When a powerful enough mage dies, especially in active combat, their spellforms can become self-sustaining. It's not really the spirit of the person. It's just an echo of their power. Like a shadow."

Daniel cleared his throat. "Now that we've got you here, are you ready to start?"

"Yes," Willow said, which elicited grins from both Steph and Daniel.

"Then go ahead and sit down in that chair right there," Daniel said, motioning to a chair beside the four essence tanks.

It was banded with copper strips, and there were thick plates where her hands and feet would go. A chunky rubber cap was on the floor as well, connected by a thick copper strip to the rest of the chair.

"After our last evaluations, we thought maximizing surface area would allow us to inject more essence at a lower pressure. Kind of like water going through a thick pipe versus a thin pipe. And it should be more comfortable for you as well."

"We think," Steph added.

Willow blinked, looking at the frankly frightening assemblage of timber and metal that constituted the chair, but she firmed her resolve. They were just going to inject essence into her like the other capacitance test. She would be fine. She leaned her cane against the wall and gingerly sat in the chair. The inch-thick copper plates felt warm against her hands and, when she removed her shoes, her feet as well. Daniel busied himself at her arms with a set of leather straps, which he snugged down.

"This is just to ensure you maintain contact with the plates," he said, though the tightening straps did elicit a spike of claustrophobia. She shifted uncomfortably as he tightened straps at her legs too. Then he picked up the rubber dome from the floor.

"And this goes on your head, like so," he said. Willow saw radial strips of copper on the inside of the cap as he brought it over, then snugged it down over her hair.

Steph had picked up Willow's cane from against the wall and was weighing it in her hands.

"We got a hold of the report from the caravan you came in with," she said. "The deathworm attack."

"Moment of glory," Willow said sardonically.

"It makes sense," Steph said. "Deathworms only ever attack other magical creatures. It was probably lured to attack the caravan by you."

Willow opened her mouth, then shut it with a click of her teeth. Let them think what they would. She'd get this number and then be out of here. They couldn't offer her anything else, so she needn't ever see them again. Steph and Daniel moved to sit side-by-side behind a small desk that hosted crystal displays wired to the contraption with copper lines.

"We're ready to start," Steph said. "This may feel... a bit uncomfortable. I think it would kill a normal human."

"What?" Willow blurted, then it was as if a horse had kicked her back into the chair.

The essence barreled into her hands, feet, and head like a raging river, stopping her breathing and causing her to throw her head back and clench her teeth together. Her body convulsed, and her limbs writhed against the straps completely out of her control. Willow grunted, hissing through her teeth at the full force of the essence pouring in. The pure pressure forced itself in through her limbs against her sluggish psychokinetic spells, disrupting them and causing her body to go haywire. Every time her psychokinetic spells were disrupted, another spurt of high-pressure essence would surge through, filling her up. It was as if she were being exhausted and replenished at the very same time.

"Less resistance than we thought," Daniel muttered to Steph.

"The curve is rising," Steph said back. "We're almost topped out."

"Looks like it," Daniel said. "Let's start the extraction."

The extraction?

Willow wanted to shout at them to stop, but her jaw wouldn't unclench and her lungs were fluttering. She couldn't catch her breath. Daniel touched something on his display plate and the sensation from the chair and cap changed instantly.

Where before it had been like a torrent crashing into her, as if she were embedded at the bottom of a waterfall, now it was as if she were at the center of a terrible whirlwind. The sensation of sucking, of vacuum—she'd only ever felt it in her life once before.

The deathworm.

"Holy shit," Daniel said, shaking his head. "Look at these numbers."

Willow's lungs came under control, just for an instant, and she let out a short scream before they collapsed again. Neither Steph nor Daniel looked up. She tried to breathe, but it was as if she had no control of her body at all. She tried to squirm against the restraints, but the only thing that moved was her neck and right hand.

If she was drained of essence, she realized, she wouldn't be able to control her body anymore. She'd suffocate, just like she should have as an infant.

Willow tried to move, tried to call out, but nothing happened. The chair was still taking from her, sucking her dry, and she couldn't get a grip on any of the coursing essence. Her body was completely clear in her mind's eye, absolutely devoid of psychokinetic spells. Absolutely devoid of resistance.

"Gods, can you believe it?" Daniel said, his eyes wide.

"Keep going, she's still got more!" Steph said.

Willow had to stop this, somehow. She had to stop this, or she was going to die. She focused on her hands, on her feet, and put all her effort into moving them. Psychokinetic spells flickered to life for an instant in each, but the force of the rushing essence destabilized them instantly.

She couldn't resist the torrent; she couldn't resist the terrible sucking vacuum. There had to be another way. She had to find something! Or they were going to kill her. And then what? Would Leopold find out? Did anyone besides Bryan and Margaret even know they were together? Who would tell her parents? What was the protocol for disposing of a dead magical creature?

And that's when she realized—that's all she was to the metrologists. Just another dead salamander. They'd never intended her to leave this room.

Her body went clear again, but her awareness expanded at the same moment. Not of her body, but of the chair she sat on, of the tanks against the wall beside her. Of the wall itself. It was as if she had become that chair, those tanks, that wall. The snaking copper cords that drained her of every last ounce of power. She could feel her own essence in them, as if from outside her body.

She'd never felt anything like this before.

Willow needed to stop the process before it killed her. And now she *was* the process. Or at least some of its equipment. She moved her cord—not *the* cord, but *her* cord. It was inextricably a part of her now—and it slithered along the floor, coming tight against the chair she was strapped to.

"What was that?" Steph asked.

"Eddy current," Daniel murmured. "None of these cables are rated for this essence throughput."

Willow snaked the cord again, and it strained against the copper plate at her right hand. She felt the weld, was the weld, and peeled the metal apart like it was her own hands stuck fast with sap. The cord snapped and fell to the ground.

"We just lost contact with point two," Steph shouted, looking up from her display plate towards Willow. Her eyes went to the cord on the ground, hissing with high-pressure essence. "Shit!" she said.

Willow peeled the second cord off the copper plate to her left, and it dropped similarly to the ground.

"Point three gone," Steph shouted.

"We're almost done," Daniel said. "Almost finished. The curve is flattening."

Willow could feel it too—she was almost dry. There was barely enough energy left in her body to take a single hitching breath, but she tried, nonetheless. That part of her body, the part made of meat, was so much smaller than her now. She was more than she'd ever been.

"We're approaching zero," Daniel called out, just as Willow's chair exploded. She'd disassembled it all at once, the joints and fastenings working out of contact instantly. Her body rose into the air, trailing brass plates from her hands and feet, and hovered over to the wall.

Towards the tanks of essence.

"Gods, be merciful," Steph whispered.

In some far-off place, Willow heard her say it. She was vaguely aware that Steph and Daniel were cowering behind their desk, clutching each other as if afraid for their lives. Willow moved the flesh part of her body over towards her first tank and laid her copper-plated palms on the contact bundles at the top.

"No!" Steph screamed.

Essence flooded back into Willow's flesh like a raging river. She lost control over the part of herself that was the chair, and the wood began twisting and splintering against the floor behind her. She was vaguely aware of a high-pitched keening from somewhere in the room.

Dry. She needed more. Her second tank had more for her flesh body, and she slid the body from the top of one tank to the top of another. There was the smell of roasting meat.

A door opened, and then she was alone in the room. She sucked greedily from the tank, filling her flesh up with the essence. Her body was clear, thrown over the contacts, and the essence flowed freely into her blood.

The third tank.

She was beginning to feel full again, but she needed more. The world around her was swimming, coming in and out of focus as she probed it with the fringes of her awareness. She became walls and floor for an instant, combing their substance with her perception and then retreating back into herself.

The essence was all that mattered.

She threw her flesh body across the contact points atop the third tank and rejoiced in the feeling of filling up. She was almost full again, but the last tank still held a portion of herself within. She needed it back, though she couldn't remember why.

An older, fat man ran into the room and began shouting, but it was hard to concentrate on him. He seemed familiar, in that vague way that flesh bodies could sometimes be. Not familiar in the way the wall was and the splinters of chairs were. Not familiar like she knew the tanks to be. They were her body. They were her soul. Everything else... that was nothing.

She opened her flesh body's mouth and slid it over a contact point on the final tank, pushing the body's hand against the other. The final burst of essence slid through her body, filling it up the rest of the way.

Now she was full again. Now she was complete.

But the world was turning blurry. There was the smell of roasting meat again, and that man was trying to pull her flesh body off the tank. She let him, releasing control of the charred thing. He could have it if he wanted to. She was so much more than that now.

But her world pulled in again. Her sphere of body inched inwards, and she lost control over the splinters of chair. They clattered to the ground, but she couldn't hear the sound. Everything was silent and senseless. The man was bending over her flesh body, pushing down onto her chest, breathing into her smoking mouth.

Why did he bother? The flesh body was already dead.

Her awareness reduced to a small sphere, centered over the man's body as he pushed mercilessly against the flesh body's chest. She probed his body, sliding the fringes of her consciousness along the fibers of his muscles. He stopped his compressions, shivered, and raised his hands quickly in a spell-form. What was he trying to do?

He said something she couldn't hear, and her feelers were immediately rejected from his skin as if pushed away by a mighty wind. She felt offended, attacked, and bent herself towards coming into contact with him again.

This time, she would take his body by force.

But the sphere of her awareness shrank even further until she was barely the size of an apple. The man yelled at the flesh body. She saw tears on his face. The flesh body stared up at the ceiling, senseless.

And then, her awareness snuffed out like a candle.

CHAPTER 21

The flesh body awoke.

Willow came back to herself and opened her eyes. She was in a small room lit by a dim inscription set high in the ceiling. The walls were pale stone, and at the edge of her vision, she saw the top shelf of a bookcase.

Willow turned her head and suddenly there was pain. Oh, the pain! It swept from her neck to her feet like an avalanche, then back up again until it filled her with nausea. She'd felt pain before, terrible pain, but not like this.

She moaned and moved her arms weakly at her sides. She was on some kind of padded surface, something that accordioned out of a large case.

The portable bed. Someone moved in the room, and she saw Professor Brandeweiss come into view.

Carl.

"Willow," he whispered, laying a hand on her forehead as if checking her temperature. Strangely, she did feel like she'd come down with a fever. She tried turning further but he stopped her. "Don't move. Not yet. You're still healing."

"Healing?" Willow croaked, and Carl looked across her body.

Willow turned her head—suffering another wave of nausea—and saw Annabelle sitting at her other side. She was directing a glowing green sphere of light that hovered over Willow's abdomen. Annabelle didn't acknowledge that Willow had awoken at all.

"What happened?" Willow whispered, turning back to Carl. She clenched her teeth to keep from vomiting and vowed to herself not to turn her head again.

"What do you remember?" Carl asked.

"I was with… Steph and Daniel," she said. "Metrology wanted me to come in for another test. Capacitance."

"They were nosing around," Carl said. "Tried asking me all sorts of things. They came to the wrong conclusion."

"They thought I was a magical creature. An animal."

"And they treated you like one," Carl growled. Willow saw his face change color, his forehead ripple, and realized he was furious. Furious for her.

"There was a chair. And a terrible force."

"They extracted nearly all of your essence. At least, that's what they told me. They nearly killed you."

"There was…" Willow said, but she had difficulty finding the words for the memory. Something about a sphere. "I wasn't myself," she continued. "I was… everything."

Carl was silent, eyes boring into her. But nothing else would come.

"How did you know?" she asked.

Carl shook his head, raised his hand to his brow, and let out a chuckle that sounded a lot like a sob. He wiped his eyes and looked away from her.

"There were spells. Leftover scryers from before we met. This was my fault. I should not have held you back. If I'd just given you your other hand, maybe this wouldn't have happened."

"What?"

He shook his head. "Nothing. I'm just tired I suppose."

"How... bad was it?" Willow asked. "*Was* it bad?"

"As bad as it could get," Carl said. "Rest, and let Annabelle finish her work. Afterwards, we'll have a discussion about your future."

Willow swallowed the lump in her throat and nodded slightly, then closed her eyes. She was out before she had the chance to consider his words.

* * *

It was everything.

Earth and stone and metal and flesh. It reached and touched and became. A body all-encompassing and ever-shifting. Moving at the speed of thought, adopting whatever form it wished. It sprang up through the walls of stone, passed through mortar and door. Spread through the teeming river of flesh in the hall outside and touched a hundred at a time.

They shivered, but knew not what it was. It was them, if it wanted to be. It was everything.

The flesh body awoke.

Willow awoke.

She was in a high-ceiling room made of pale stone, lying on a padded mat beside a desk and a chair. Carl was standing over her, a pulsating ball of pale blue energy between his hands. He let out a sigh and canceled the spell, which boiled off into the air.

"What were you doing?" Willow asked, gingerly getting up onto her elbows. Her stomach felt tender, and so did her chest, but the pain she remembered from before was mostly gone. Just her normal gamut of aches.

Carl shook his head in exasperation and walked around to sit behind his desk. Willow presently heard the rapid tap of engraving hammer on chisel and the high squeak of cutting metal.

She worked herself up into a sitting position and found that her clothes had been refastened strangely. She supposed it made sense that Annabelle would have had to undress her, but she still felt a pang of embarrassment.

There was a charred hole in her overcoat, right over her stomach.

Willow squeezed the edge of the cloth between her fingers, and it crumbled into charcoal. Her underclothes were blackened but were at least still present under the hole.

What happened to her?

"Steph and Daniel?" Willow asked.

Carl tapped for a few more seconds before he flicked away a curl of metal and let out a held breath. He considered whatever he was working on under a stand-mounted magelight, and then he peeled the metal off the lacquer backing.

"Steph and Daniel are alive, unfortunately," he said. "They were sitting far enough away from you when... Well, they're fine. Expelled, but alive."

"Expelled?" Willow asked. She would have expected them to be arrested for attempted murder. Carl's face didn't change at her reaction. He was inspecting what looked to be a small silver medallion.

"They destroyed three 200 em tanks. That's not an expense the Arcanum can overlook."

"I think I destroyed them," Willow remembered, and she saw a smirk touch Carl's face.

"I know, but they shut up long enough to take the fall. I suppose I should give them a little credit."

"But they're getting expelled, why would they—"

"They're missing. Apparently their experiment caught someone's attention, and they were made another offer. Disgraceful, but at least I could mitigate the damage to you."

Willow considered his words. "Does everyone know now? About me?"

Carl shook his head. "Nobody does, not even those two idiots. They were planning to publish on you. Postmortem," he sighed. "The dean knows you were grievously injured, but besides that, nobody knows about your condition."

He looked towards the door, as if expecting something on the other side.

"There's a young man who's been threatening me for the last few hours," he said and smirked again. "He seems quite taken with you."

"Leopold," Willow sighed. "He won't have known what happened to me."

"I filled him in with most of the details," he said. "As for the rest, you'll have to figure out how to lie well, and fast."

Carl slid the small amulet onto a thin chain and walked around his desk to Willow's side. He motioned with the two clasps of the chain, and Willow raised her hair.

"What's this?" she asked.

Carl fastened the chain around her neck and laid the inscribed silver disc just under her throat. She didn't feel any effect.

"Something happened in that metrology lab," Carl said. "Something I can't explain. This acts as a planar nullification field. It'll keep you from... well, I don't know."

"What don't you know?" Willow asked. "What really happened in there?"

He shook his head. "Something I didn't expect, as usual. Just don't take it off, whatever you do. Especially when you sleep."

* * *

Willow found Leopold hunched over, sitting against the wall in the hall outside Carl's door. He held her for a long time, painfully tight, but she didn't tell him it hurt—she welcomed the pain. It seemed to anchor her. They made their way back to the house on Grave Street, mostly in silence. He tried asking her what happened, but she found it difficult to talk about. Difficult to remember.

Margaret took one look at her and began fussing immediately. Bryan wasn't much better when he came home. Mention was made several times to her bruised eyes. She shrugged them off after stuffing her face with potato stew. She and Leopold retreated to her room soon after, where she gently shut the door and lay down on the bed, fully clothed.

Leopold lay down beside her.

"Willow," he whispered. She turned her head towards him and felt the familiar creak of her spine. Was it her spells that turned her head? Or her muscles? Where did the paralysis start? How much of her was a real working human body?

Willow closed her eyes and tried to banish the thought. Of course she had a human body. Why would she think otherwise? Was it what Steph and Daniel had thought—that she was a magical creature or some kind of half-breed? No, it wasn't that. The idea seemed even more ridiculous to her now that she was out of the metrology lab.

It was something about a chair. And a wall. The tanks against the wall. She felt, strangely, like they were a part of her too. That she was, somehow, more than just her body.

Her thoughts weren't going anywhere, and she turned to look at Leopold. He was here—he was still here after everything that had happened. She couldn't tell what had occurred in that metrology lab, but she knew he was here with her, and that was something real.

Leopold watched her carefully, and then his eyes slipped down to the small pendant at her throat. He reached over and stroked the metal.

"Inscriptions," he said. "In silver. Did Professor Brandeweiss give you this?"

"He made it for me," Willow said, touching the pendant too. The graving was rough, and the metal raised enough to bite into her thumb. She still couldn't feel any effect from it.

"What does it do?" Leopold asked.

"I have no idea," Willow said and turned over.

CHAPTER 22

Life returned to semi-normality after what happened in the metrology lab. If any of the metrology students thought anything strange about her, she didn't have a clue. She'd never go back to the metrology lab again. Classes continued, with their scattering of homework and essays, and life at Grave Street became comfortably regular. Leopold was patient—more patient than she had any right to expect—and he waited as she slowly emerged from the stupor of what happened in the lab.

Carl had wanted to see her the next day in his office. She arrived there to find Annabelle waiting with the accordioned table as well. He told her that he thought it was time to grant her access to her left hand, and she didn't complain as Annabelle guided her face-down onto the fold-out bed. She slept through the operation. When she awoke, her left hand was twitching and seizing just like her right hand had weeks ago.

It was easier this time bringing her psychokinetic spells under control. Was it because she'd been practicing with her hand already? Or was something different about her? It was almost as if she had more control over her psychokinesis. She found it nearly trivial to remove its influence from her arms above the wrists—unfortunately resulting in her arms flopping about uselessly.

Leopold took her out into the city again and again. They went to a glass-enclosed garden where plants from all over the world thrived. She'd never seen so many colors or smelled so many strange smells. Slowly she came back to herself and felt the cotton padding between her and the rest of reality fall away. Sensations became sharper, feelings stronger. Her feelings for Leopold were strongest of all.

They went to Geoff's shop with a small wooden box tucked under her arm. He closed up and took them into the back room—but not before Willow spied one of her wan magelights on a shelf in the display room. In the back Willow opened the box and revealed five brilliant solid magelights, which Geoff took out to inspect one by one. Leopold bartered with the shopkeeper—never Willow's strong suit despite her father's attempted instruction—and managed to procure a silver apiece. They ate out that night to celebrate, and Willow took him into her bed again for the first time since that day in metrology.

Things were going well—better than well—when Willow arrived at Carl's office for their scheduled training to show him the single magelight she'd saved from Geoff. To show him how much better she'd gotten at throttling her essential power without the glove.

She knew something was wrong the moment she opened the door. Carl was hunched over his desk, head in his hands, staring blankly at a stack of papers. He was muttering to himself, and his eyes looked sunken and dark.

"Professor?" Willow asked, and he jumped at her voice.

"Willow! Oh, Willow." He sighed in relief and attempted a smile that resembled more of a grimace. "Please come in."

He took a paper from the top of the stack and slid it into a drawer as she walked in.

"What's wrong?" she asked, beginning to weave the privacy spell. It was technically an advanced form from the end of the second year, but Carl had used it for their simultaneous-layering practice. She finished the triple-layer spell in a single movement, and it spread out across the walls like a ripple of water.

"Ah, nothing. Nothing," he said unconvincingly. He shifted some papers around on his desk, then shuffled them back to where they were before. Willow sat in the uncomfortable wooden chair between his desk and the door.

"Did I ever, ah, tell you what Steph and Daniel found? In their botched experiment with you?"

"No. I just assumed they weren't able to get any results."

"Nothing stable, but they got a range. Or an estimate. Some inkling anyway, before things went wrong."

"How did you find out?" Willow asked. "Where are they now?"

"They're with... a colleague," Carl said nervously.

A colleague? If he knew where they were, shouldn't they be headed for prison? She wanted to ask, but the promise of an answer to the question she'd almost given her life for was too much to turn her nose at.

"And?" Willow prompted. "What did they find?"

"What?" Carl asked, his eyes a million miles away.

"Steph and Daniel. Their experiment?"

"Oh, yes. Well, after filling you up to the brim, they were able to siphon off somewhere around five hundred em. Somewhere in that range."

"Five..." Willow breathed, her mouth lolling open. It wasn't possible, was it?

"Yes, five hundred." He gave a nervous laugh. "Five hundred. What a catch."

"What do you mean?" Willow asked.

"You've got more essence in your body than all the mages in the Arcanum combined," Carl said. "The stakes are so much higher," he muttered to himself.

"What stakes?" Willow asked. "I've learned how to control it. At least mostly. I made this all by myself." She opened the box and handed over the solid magelight. Carl took it but barely seemed to notice. "I didn't use the glove. That's how good I've gotten."

He turned it in his fingers, then handed it back across the desk. The shadows in the room moved strangely as Willow took the small sphere and replaced it in the box. Had she done something wrong? He didn't even react to what had taken her so long and so much effort to accomplish. What was happening here?

"We're going to change tack," Carl decided, resolution in his voice. "You've got to start training to release this power safely. To shove as much essence into a spell as you can without killing yourself and everyone around you. We're already so far behind."

"Wait, I thought the most important thing was to learn how to control my essence. To turn it down to other people's level."

"And you've done so admirably," Carl said and shook his head a little. "That magelight, really exemplary. I wonder how long it'll last—ah, but that's not the point."

Not the point? Willow could've told him they lasted at least three weeks. Her original pale magelights still hovered among the rafters of her bedroom like a luminous cloud.

"The point is, we've got to start channeling this power. Learn how to release it in a savage attack."

"Attack? I... But I don't want to become a battle mage," Willow protested. She'd been considering going into construction magic—raising walls and supplies to assist in superior fortifications. If it took a dozen mages to fire that essence cannon on the wall, and she could power it herself, what could she create with her power alone?

"We don't always have the luxury of choosing if or when we're forced to protect the ones we love."

* * *

From that day on, her training regimen resembled what it had during those first two weeks at school. It wasn't the direction she wanted, but Carl made a persuasive argument. Her suppressed powers had already caused one attack—if she didn't consider what Steph and Daniel had done to her an attack. She could very well find herself in a similar situation in the future, and he suggested that any magical creatures drawn by her newly integrated body parts would be worlds above what she'd seen before. And, in the end, he'd saved her in that metrology room. Everything he'd ever done for her had been in her best interest, and she couldn't bring herself to go against him again.

For training, Carl somehow procured a device that resembled a tunnel of inscribed rings welded to each other. Each one contained a powerful nullification field, and all together, the effect was slightly disorienting to be close to. He set it up in an abandoned workshop at the edge of the Arcanum, and Willow made the mistake of asking him why they were practicing there instead of in his office.

"Because," he'd said as she got her breath back after casting a gust of directed wind into the device. "If this thing fails, or you overwhelm it, you'll take out half the school if we're in my office. Here, you'll only blow the building down and kill us. It's just the responsible thing to do."

He had her practice with wind, with water, and with fire. She shot beams of light into the dark tunnel of rings. The luminous lance that was impossible to look at directly as it erupted from her fingertips diminished to nothingness just past the second ring.

For Carl, it wasn't good enough.

"You're not pumping the spells. Not enough essence is getting through."

"Then heal my arms," Willow snapped, covered in sweat. She was overcharging the spells as much as she could, but so much essence was still locked within her body behind those resistive psychokinetic spells. If only she could access that power.

"You're not ready for it yet."

"Ready how?" Willow spun on him in a fury. "I've been busting my ass in here with you."

"You can't take it," Carl said, grabbing her arm.

She winced.

"Look, look at this." He shook her limb. "There's almost nothing here. Nothing! Do you know how much pain you'll be in when we reconnect these nerves? It'll be excruciating."

"You have to do it sometime!" Willow screamed at him. Something in her voice made him back away. "I'm nothing. Nothing! I need this power, or I'm useless. I'm just a cripple."

Carl's mouth opened in shock, and he gaped for words. Willow turned away in mortification, hugging her frail arms tight. Did she really mean that? She knew she should be happy. She had a family that loved her, Leopold, and a plan to integrate her body. Why couldn't she be satisfied? Was it not enough?

"Willow, you're not nothing," Carl said and gently touched her shoulder. "I misspoke. You're doing fine. Great even. Better than I could've hoped."

"But not good enough," Willow accused, shrugging away. "Not for you, and not for me. But... you know something, don't you? What's going to happen? What are you so afraid of?"

Carl was silent, and when she looked back, he was shaking his head slightly.

"I don't know," Carl whispered.

He reached out and touched the ring device, his thoughts obviously far away on some unknown and indeterminate eventuality. Then he looked back at her, grim determination hardening his face.

"Let's get back to work."

* * *

It wasn't hard to find Annabelle at the Sisters of Mercy. She had to be a surgeon there. Or a nurse. And there were only so many of the white-robed figures fretting about from bed to bed, changing bandages and delivering food. Willow stalked into the hospital, fueled mostly by anger and impatience, and found her in a sub-wing dedicated to burn victims.

The smell was almost overwhelming.

"Annabelle," Willow said softly, and the white-robed woman turned around in surprise.

"Willow, was it?" she said, then continued on with a tray of food in her hands. Willow hobbled behind her, the clacking from her cane echoing off the stone walls.

"Yes," Willow said, not for a moment buying that Annabelle didn't remember her name. Not after what she'd done. "I need you to fix my arms."

Annabelle let out a bark of laughter, but never once broke stride as she pulled up beside the bed of a man covered nearly head to foot in white bandages. There was a smell, and in some places the bandages had been stained with leaking yellow fluid. The man's eyes were unwrapped, but he appeared to be asleep.

"This is Patrick," Annabelle said as she sat in the chair beside his bed. There was no second chair, so Willow remained standing.

"Okay," Willow said. "Did you hear what I—"

"Patrick here won't last the week," Annabelle said and slightly adjusted the bowl on the tray. The matter-of-factness of the statement caught Willow off guard.

"But why?" Willow asked. "Couldn't you heal him?"

"Yes, I could," Annabelle said. "In an hour, I could have most of his skin regrown. He'd be going home to his wife in two days. He has a daughter, you know."

"Then why don't you?" Willow asked.

Annabelle plucked at her robe. "Do you know what this means?" she asked. Willow shook her head. "It means I'm a glorified servant. I change bandages. I make notes for the doctors and surgeons. I take things here, and I move them there. And I give comfort to the dying."

"But you healed *me*," Willow said. Annabelle sighed.

"Carl's one of the few who knows of my... education," she said. "You were lucky you knew Bryan when he brought you to the Arcanum. Even if you could've paid for it, you'd have been laid up for at least a month waiting for your operation if he hadn't pulled about every string he could. Would your hands have even made it? Or would the bone have rotted away?"

"You can't heal him because they won't let you," Willow said, realization slowly trickling in. "Because they won't let you be a surgeon."

"You're not the only one who's held back, Willow, by the way things are," she said. "There are customs here. Norms in the cities. Things that can't be bent, that can't be broken. Only by working outside those systems, outside the law, can we begin to see who we truly are. What we could become, if not for all this."

Annabelle gestured Willow closer, then grabbed her hand and pushed her sleeve up. Willow winced at the sudden exposure, but Annabelle's fingers were gentle even as they played upon the stripes of bruise that Carl's grip had left earlier that day.

"You'll not know pain like this," Annabelle whispered. "You think you've felt pain? You'll be using muscles that have never moved unassisted. I can't even imagine how it'll feel. Laudanum won't help if you want to work through it."

"I can handle it," Willow insisted. Annabelle dropped the sleeve and picked up the spoon beside the bowl.

"Meet me in your little practice arena after sunset," she said, gently pressing a spoonful of broth to the bandaged man's lips. Surprisingly, he responded and drank the thin liquid.

"I'll be there," Willow said. Annabelle cast her a doubtful look like she didn't think Willow would, and then turned back to her patient.

* * *

The pain hit like slamming into a wall before Willow came completely awake. Her eyes flung open and she took a shuddering breath to scream, but Annabelle shoved a rag in her mouth. Still, the piercing scream filled up her whole world, temporarily blotting out the cascade of torment.

Her arms writhed with seizures. They burned and twisted like someone was wrenching them out of their sockets. Or like someone was breaking them in a vice. Muscles she'd never used before tensed at the conflicting signals from her psychokinesis and her newly connected brain. The excruciating pain was almost so much that she forgot where she was and why she was suffering.

Almost.

"Shh," Annabelle hushed, laying her hand on Willow's forehead.

Willow moaned in response, lost in a tempest of torture and suffering. A pain she'd never imagined coursed up and down her arms between her wrists and shoulders. Slicing, like she was being flayed. Burning, like she was in a bonfire. Freezing, as if she were encased in ice.

A wave of nausea rose up, and Willow spit out the cloth. She gritted her teeth and willed herself not to vomit. She wanted to be strong, especially in front of Annabelle.

Willow moaned again, but Annabelle seemed to catch her intended question.

"The operation was a success," Annabelle said. "Connection restored up to your shoulders on both arms. However, your muscles are jumping, and I'm not sure why."

"Carl said... it would happen," Willow said, catching her breath. She focused on calming her muscles and on releasing the bones from her psychokinesis. Slowly, in her mind's eye, her arms flickered between clear and opaque.

It was going to take a lot of work.

"Can you make it home?" Annabelle asked.

She took Willow by the shoulders and gently tilted her up until she was sitting on the accordioned table. It was hard for Willow to catch her breath, and her mouth kept filling with saliva, but she answered.

"I have someone... waiting for me," she said and spit on the ground. The nausea was only increasing, and she wanted to be out of there before she vomited.

"That boy," Annabelle said, snapping Willow out of her pain for a moment as she jerked around to look at her. Annabelle stared into her eyes. "You must keep him a secret from Carl. You've already told him too much. If Carl finds out..."

"What?" Willow asked.

She knew she wasn't supposed to tell anyone about what was happening to her, and for a long time she hadn't wanted to. Every procedure, every training, had been evidence of her deficiencies. But after what she'd discovered about herself, she didn't feel that way anymore. What kept her tongue still now was a vague dread hidden behind every warning Carl issued, and every comment he'd made about preparations or her progress.

"There are powerful interests that want to ensure word about you doesn't get out until the proper time," Annabelle said. "This boy is a hitch in that."

Powerful interests? What was she talking about? Did more than just she and Carl know about her? And why would they care when she graduated from the Arcanum?

"Who, Annabelle? Who else knows about me? About… this?"

Annabelle pressed her lips together and ground her teeth for a moment. Then she leaned forward until they were almost touching. "He used to be a professor here," she whispered. "A long time ago. He was pushed out. They thought his ideas were too… extreme. Too subversive."

A professor? Was he here at the same time Carl was? Were they… colleagues? Wait, was this the same person who'd spirited Steph and Daniel away?

"What were they? The ideas?" Willow asked.

Annabelle sighed. "There are things in this world no one should meddle with, things best left alone. He was digging deep in the archives and mistook danger for opportunity. When they found out how far he'd taken it, even his initial results… *poof.* They were afraid he'd restart the city wars."

"All by himself?" Willow grunted, trying to keep her mind off the pain. Her arms were writhing less now, as long as she kept them completely still. It was hard to concentrate on doing nothing at all.

"He could," Annabelle said. "If anyone could, it would be him."

"You've met him?" Willow asked. Annabelle nodded.

"A long time ago. Carl introduced us. He was Carl's mentor, years ago. I doubt you could even find mention of him in the records anymore. It was like they scrubbed him from reality when he was told to leave."

"But he's out there. In another city?"

"Yeah, something like that," Annabelle said. She leaned closer to Willow. "He's a dangerous man if you get in his way. If you're some kind of obstacle to him, he won't think for a second before blasting you apart. That goes for anything else that muddies his plans. Carl is a little like him, but not nearly as ruthless. If the order came down... I don't know what Carl would do."

"Order came down? To do what?"

"To get rid of any witnesses," Annabelle said solemnly.

"Oh, come on!" Willow said, and only just barely stopped herself from laughing. "Carl wouldn't... wouldn't..."

"Don't be so sure about Carl," Annabelle said. "I've known him a lot longer than you, and even I'm not sure where his allegiances truly lie. He's been forced to walk a tightrope for years. There's no telling what the pressure might make him do. It's a long way down for people like us, and the end is almost in sight."

"What end? Is something going to happen?"

Annabelle sighed. "Maybe. Someday. But not yet. Not unless I'm further out of the loop than I thought."

Willow remembered Carl's ashen face, his sunken eyes, and the way he couldn't keep track of their conversation, like something else was on his mind. Then of their changed training regimen. More than anything, she felt confused.

"Are you safe to leave now?" Annabelle asked. "It's late."

"Yeah. Yes, I am," Willow said and gingerly scooted off the table. Her arms spasmed as she tried to push off the bench and Annabelle had to catch her.

"Thanks," Willow said. "For this. For everything."

Annabelle pressed her lips into a tight line and said nothing, but steered Willow towards the door to the large building. It opened out on near pitch-darkness, and Willow fumbled weakly in her overcoat for the wooden box she'd brought Carl. With limp fingers, she extracted and then held the magelight as she let her arm drop to her side, lighting up the street.

"You *have* been improving," Annabelle said when she saw the light.

"That's the goal," Willow quipped, taking her first shaky steps out into the dark.

"Maybe," Annabelle said to herself as Willow stumbled towards the edge of the Arcanum grounds. "Maybe it will work after all."

Chapter 23

Things got harder after Willow's arms were reconnected to her brain. What progress she'd gained in controlling her hands was lost as the much larger muscle groups of her arms writhed out of her control. What use was it to have dexterity when she mostly flopped around like a fish? Sometimes, when she was having trouble even getting the straps of her bag around her shoulders, she harbored the thought that perhaps going off on her own and getting Annabelle to heal her hadn't been the best idea in the world.

Carl knew immediately, of course. She didn't know if Annabelle had told him or if he could just tell from the way her arms jerked and she winced in response. Either way, he sighed heavily when she arrived for her first practice session after the procedure. They didn't get much done that day. Willow couldn't hold her arms up for more than a couple of seconds at a time to finish a casting, and Carl refused to let her sit and do the castings in her lap. They were—as he explained—much too dangerous to weave that close to her body.

But Leopold understood. He understood why she needed this, even if he didn't agree. He spent long hours massaging her never-used muscles, working blood around the tissues even as she winced and gasped in pain. They were so stiff, so weak, and so useless. In most ways, she was more disabled than she'd been before the procedure.

Shame threatened to overwhelm her, but this was Leopold, with whom she'd shared so much already. It was hard for her to understand his dedication to her, especially in this state, but she did her best to accept it.

He suffered with her in silence, and slowly her strength grew from nothing to slightly more than nothing. She picked up a fork again for the first time two days after the procedure. Bryan and Margaret both noticed, but they didn't say anything as she brought the small bite of meat to her mouth and just managed to get it in. Leopold rubbed her back as she caught her breath, satisfied.

Even Benny was better at using silverware than she was, and he decided to mimic her regression on the fifth day. He stopped after a sharp word from Margaret.

A week after the operation, Willow could write in her notes for class again. She'd feigned an injury for inscription class, but half a week after that she attempted work with the hammer and engraving chisel again. It was somehow even worse than the first time she'd picked them up. Still, she doggedly persisted in the project even when everyone else in class had left after the bell. In the end, a small vortex of her essence flitted above the graven surface of the copper plate in much the same effect that had been described in their assignment. Willow sighed in relief.

Two weeks after the operation, she was finally able to hold her arms up for long enough to weave a three-layer spell in the practice room. This one was a gust of wind shaped by a supplementary layer into the shape of a vortex, to keep it from losing power as it spread out from the casting point. The layers locked into place at the same time as Willow's arms shook from holding up their own weight.

She let go of the spell in her mind's eye, letting it finally execute its intended purpose. The spinning sphere exploded away from her into the tunnel of nullification rings. The room rumbled with the passage of so much wind, even for just the few inches it was exposed.

Carl walked around to the other side of the nullification setup and probed the rings with his fingers.

"You're getting to the third ring," he said. She'd started off only activating the first, with his assurances that as each ring was overloaded the next would take any spillover. There were five rings in the device.

"Pretty good then," Willow wheezed as she let her arms fall to her sides. She was exhausted from holding up their weight, and it felt more like she'd been hauling a bale of hay than just standing there with arms outstretched for a few seconds.

"Not good enough," Carl responded, and came around the device.

"What?! Not good enough my ass! I'm pumping as much essence into these spells as I can."

"And they're still not strong enough," Carl said. Willow looked at the nullification setup and saw a heat haze in the air above it. They had to wait for it to cool down between casts now, limited more by the device's recovery time than Willow's.

"So what if I can't win on the first cast. I can try again."

Carl shook his head. "Some enemies you only get one cast at. Some enemies have enough resistance to block all but the most concentrated of essence attacks. What if you were to come up against Durum's warbeast? It once withstood a blast from a wall cannon. That's thirty em right there, concepted as pure force, right into its side. And it shrugged it off. What then? Do you think it's going to let you get in a second shot?"

"Um, have you seen that thing?" Willow asked, even though she hadn't seen it herself. She'd seen a drawing of it once though, in the market. It was a truly detestable creature. "I don't think it shrugged that attack off as well as you think."

"If you're talking about the rot, that happened to it in the decades following. They're not meant to live forever. They're not even really meant to live for more than a few months. It's a miracle it lasted so long."

"When do you imagine I'll be facing down a warbeast all by myself?" Willow asked, exasperated. "They can just use the cannons. That's what they were made for."

"Its natural resistance was too high," Carl continued, as if she hadn't said anything. "The essence from the cannon couldn't get through, couldn't penetrate to scramble its organs. The cannon blasted it back, but that did almost nothing to it. If you want to overwhelm resistance like that, you have to overload your spells even more."

"I'm not—" Willow stopped herself.

What did she really want to say? What did she really feel?

"I'm not interested in killing warbeasts," Willow continued. "I don't want to fight. Once this... process... is over, I want to live a normal life. Once I have my body the way it should have been, I want to be a normal mage. Work in something boring."

"Willow."

Carl walked over to her. She took a step back reflexively but bumped against the chair and just barely managed to keep from sitting down hard. He reached towards her neck and touched the amulet he'd carved for her after the disastrous metrology experiment.

"You will never be normal. I can only protect you for so long, but once people find out what you are, they will never stop trying to get at you. I'm just trying to keep you alive until you can fend for yourself. Like a little chick who can't yet fly from the nest."

"Do you mean the Arcanum?" Willow asked, and Carl's lips went tight. "Would they do something to me?"

Carl sighed. "Let's put it this way. If you were to find an inconceivably powerful inscripted device just stuck in the ground, would you leave it alone? Or would you take it, damn what anyone else said? Damn the law, because it wouldn't matter. Not once you had the weapon."

Willow opened her mouth to answer, but she realized that it didn't matter what she'd do. It mattered what Durum would do. What Carl would do. And what his unnamed master would do.

That evening, when Willow got home, she received a letter with the wax seal of the Arcanum on the back. She broke the seal in her room with Leopold and unfolded a letter from the dean of the school.

"The *dean*, dean?" Leopold asked as she was reading the letter. "Corinth Weatherby?"

"Dr. Corinth Weatherby," Willow said, reading the signature again to assure herself that this wasn't some unfortuitous prank.

"Well, what does he want?"

"He wants to meet with me. Tomorrow," Willow said and handed the letter over to Leopold.

"To discuss the events in the metrology lab," Leopold read aloud from the letter and returned it to Willow. She smoothed the paper, folded it, and then smoothed it again, unsure what to do with her hands. They were shaking and sweaty.

"What do you think he wants?"

"I don't know," Willow said, hating the hitch in her voice. Carl had scared her, and now this letter from the dean? What if it was more apparent to him what had happened in the lab than Carl imagined? What if he figured things out? What would happen to her? Was it really as bad as Carl made it seem?

"I guess you have to go," Leopold said as Willow finally made a decision and folded the letter up for good, setting it on her bedside table. "I mean, he *is* the dean."

"I'm going to make you something," Willow said, turning on her bed until she faced the wall towards the street. If anything went wrong, she didn't want to destroy the part of the house that had Margaret, Bryan, and Benny in it.

"Make me what?" Leopold asked, and Willow looked up at the ceiling. The pale magelights were still floating up there, swaying softly on the invisible currents of natural essence.

"Something for emergencies. Just in case," she said and started in on the spell.

It was the same spell Leopold had tried to cast on the deathworm a lifetime ago, but she shoved an unnatural amount of power into it. The spell-core shone brighter than any of the magelights along the ceiling. Finally, above the layer giving direction, she laid down an encompassing layer of steadfastness, just like the hovering lights.

It had been easy, but Leopold's eyes were wide with fright at what she'd done. He could sense the essence she'd poured into that destructive concept, and at some point had scooted away from the bed to stand against the wall. When the spell was safely encapsulated, Willow patted the bed beside her. Leopold sat back down.

"Here," she said and handed the closed spell to him. He took it gingerly and examined it. Within the misty glass of the final layer was a small, whirling firestorm. It moved of its own accord, like a raging tempest responding to a hurricane they couldn't feel.

"You've preserved a spell," Leopold said, fascinated.

"Temporarily," Willow said and touched the glassy surface of the sphere. "It's a spell capsule. I've left a crack in the protective coating. Do you feel it?"

"That's dangerous." Leopold stared down at the sphere, his face lit yellow from the whirling fire.

"It's for you," Willow said. "If you need to use it, just force your essence into the crack. It should open up then... let loose what I've stored inside."

"What could possibly need this much essence to destroy it?" Leopold marveled and looked at Willow. His eyes asked another question. What do you know that I don't?

"I don't know," she said, putting her hand on his leg. "Just keep it with you, okay? I can't let anything happen to you."

"It's you I'm more worried about," he said, but she saw him pocket the spell capsule anyway.

* * *

The meeting with Dean Weatherby wasn't until after Willow's introduction to essence manipulation class, and she found it difficult to pay attention to Professor Brandeweiss and his instructions as worries flitted through her head. They were working in groups to attempt their first multi-mage spells, and Willow nearly blasted her partner across the room when their combined gust of air got away from her. Carl gave her a warning look as she helped her stunned classmate back to his seat.

"Willow," he said to her as the class was emptying out. "Can I see you in my office?"

"Sorry, Professor Brandeweiss," she said. "I have a meeting with the dean."

That caught his attention, and he jerked up so fast he spilled a sheaf of notes onto the floor. Willow smiled and nodded against the rolling nausea in her stomach. She tried to affect nonchalance as she left the class, but the way he was staring at her only made her more frightened of what might be coming.

The dean's office wasn't with the other professors, which Willow supposed made sense considering she wasn't sure if he actually taught any classes. She went back to the main hall and continued down the opposing wing, which seemed to house a lot of rooms with administrative names. She'd never been down this way before, but she found the dean's office easily enough at the end of the wing.

Willow knocked on the arched door, but when she couldn't hear a reply over the general commotion of the changing classes down the hall, she tripped the latch uneasily and pushed inside. The interior was much brighter than Carl's office, and the room she stepped into was larger as well. A little further in, a woman sat behind a desk beside another door.

"Hello?" Willow asked. "I thought this was Dean Weatherby's office."

"This is," the woman said. "Do you have an appointment?"

Willow nodded her head. "Willow Tremont?" she asked, as if she were unsure of her own name. The woman looked down at the blotter on her desk, made a note, then gestured to the door.

"He's available now," she said. Willow crossed the anteroom to the indicated door. She grabbed the latch and looked back at the woman to make sure she was doing the right thing, but the woman had already dismissed her and was busy writing something down.

Oh well. Willow tripped the latch and opened the second door. On the other side was a richly furnished office, probably the nicest room she'd seen in the whole place. And sitting behind a large wooden desk was a portly man with a bushy mustache.

"Miss Tremont," the man said.

Willow nodded from halfway behind the door.

"I'm Dean Weatherby. Please, take a seat." He gestured to several plush chairs set out in front of the desk.

Willow softly closed the door behind her and took in the room as she lowered herself into one of the smaller chairs. There was a window that featured a small stained-glass portrait of someone raising their hands up to the sky below a ball of blue fire. Heavy curtains draped to either side of the window, and around the edges of the room were bookcases and trunks that surely stored innumerable knickknacks and folios. She imagined Carl's office would look neater if he had this much storage space.

"Well, how has your week been, Miss Tremont?" Dean Weatherby asked. He leaned forwards, as if he hung on her every word, which did a great deal to quiet her jangling nerves.

"It's going fine," she said. "Homework, classwork, all that."

"Your professors keep you busy?"

"Yeah," Willow lied. The fact was that she'd never felt particularly busy with her coursework. Even now with her increased training with Carl, it felt like she was breezing through school.

"The reason I called you here today is due to the incident in the metrology lab," Dean Weatherby said, steepling his fingers under his chin. The effect in part made him look serious and contemplative, but Willow couldn't help but notice that the posture also hid his mouth. He could begin concepting at any time, and she wouldn't know.

"*Incident* is an interesting word for it," Willow said, dodging his open-ended statement. She wasn't sure what he was getting at or what he wanted from her, and until she was sure, she didn't want to give anything away. He looked at her steadily, never taking his eyes from her face to glance at her neck or rake down her arms.

Dean Weatherby sighed. "You're right. *Incident* is much too trivial a word to describe it. Disaster, more like. Near-lethal cock-up. Academic negligence. Criminal negligence."

"Attempted murder," Willow added.

"Premeditated," the dean nodded. "You may not be aware of what those former students had set up in that lab, but they'd primed the tanks with enough essence to fry you to a crisp. They were under the insane impression that they could extract some ungodly amount of essence out of your body. And from Professor Brandeweiss' report on the incident, they nearly injured you in the process."

So, Carl had done some creative accounting in his incident report. *Nearly injured* wasn't at all what had happened. In fact, she'd been injured by her own stored essence, not the top-up amount they'd procured initially for the tanks. If Steph and Daniel ever returned to correct the dean, what might he do to her? And if what Annabelle said about Carl's mentor—however much Willow disbelieved her—was true, was the dean in danger? Was that why the metrologists disappeared so suddenly from the city? Did Carl have something to do with it?

Whatever Carl's involvement may or may not be, she needed to play this close to the vest.

"I didn't know I was in any danger."

The dean shook his head. "Nobody knew what they were planning to do. Believe me, if we had, it would've never gotten so far. They fabricated research projects to several different professors in order to obtain materials. Professors, I might add, who had no idea of each other's involvement. All of which have been disciplined, I'll have you know."

"Oh, I don't think that's—" Willow began, but the dean cut her off with a wave of his hand.

"As for Steph and Daniel, they've disappeared without a trace, but we're working with the city guard. We'll find them soon enough, and they'll be tried for their crimes."

If the city guard had been called in, how long could she hope that they'd remain lost? Willow became instantly paranoid. Did the dean suspect that she knew more than she was letting on about their disappearance? She willed her face to become expressionless.

"They're gone now, though," Willow pushed back. "Do you really need to try so hard to find them?" Was there any way she could get him to lighten the search?

"Laws, and more importantly, Arcanum rules were broken, Miss Tremont," the dean said. "We have panels, especially regarding new processes involving humans. Panels to ensure safety and to maintain ethics. They bypassed all of these, and if things had gotten out of hand, someone might have been terribly injured. It's not just your life that was in danger, Miss Tremont. They could have been killed too."

A fragment of memory came back. A chair with leather straps holding a body. But the body wasn't hers. The chair was, and she shattered the chair with her will alone. The body tumbled to the floor.

The flesh body.

Willow jerked in the chair and blinked the memory away.

"Miss Tremont?" Dean Weatherby prodded, and Willow shook her head. The reverie dispelled like cobwebs brushed from their corners, and she was back in the dean's office again.

"Sorry, I just..." she said, but she wasn't sure how to finish the sentence. She just what? Was that a memory? It didn't seem real.

"You've been through a lot regarding this matter," Dean Weatherby said. "If it wasn't for Professor Brandeweiss, well, I'd hate to think what might've happened. I wanted to invite you here to clear the air and to explain what steps the Arcanum will be taking to ensure nothing of this sort ever happens again. And to assure you of your place here, and your continued safety."

Willow nodded slowly, but there was still something bugging her.

"They... Steph and Daniel... got those tanks from different professors, right?" she asked, vaguely remembering that they'd also said this. "If there are panels and such, how did they get access to that kind of equipment?"

"That's where the fraud came in," Dean Weatherby said patiently. "They told the professors that they were extracting essence from a captured magical creature."

She braced herself and asked the question that was really troubling her. "And that would've been okay?" Her right arm twitched painfully, causing her to grimace. "To just... drain something like that?"

Dean Weatherby nodded. "They're not human, Miss Tremont. You are."

CHAPTER 24

Willow was off during her next training session with Carl. Dean Weatherby's words ricocheted around her head, but it wasn't until her second less-than-satisfactory cast that Carl stopped her.

"Something's on your mind," he said and sat on the bench to her right. She was covered in sweat, as usual, and breathing hard. He was still holding the pitcher he'd used to douse the nullification rings.

Willow nodded.

"What did the dean want?" he asked. From the way he fingered the pitcher handle, she could tell he was nervous.

"To assure me that the Arcanum wouldn't let what happened in metrology ever happen again. I learned some interesting things, too. Like Steph and Daniel aren't just missing; they're fugitives on the run."

Carl sighed. "I suppose I should've realized you'd find out sooner or later."

"You told me they'd been expelled!"

"They would've been," he said. "And then imprisoned. I got them out of the city as fast as I could."

"So you secret away criminals now?" Willow said, unsure if she was upset about it or just bewildered at the situation in general.

"I've done it before," Carl said. "There have always been students who... cross the line. Is it wrong to offer them another avenue? A new start at life somewhere else far away?"

"If it lets them keep doing the things they got in trouble for? Yes?"

"They will never endanger you again, Willow," Carl said. "I don't know what they're even working on now, but it has nothing to do with you. Nor could it. You're here, and they're..."

"Yeah?" Willow asked. "And where is it exactly?"

"To the west. There's a city in the mountains."

"Asche," Willow said. "There used to be a city there. Now it's... what?"

"Asche is still there," Carl said.

"I thought we'd lost contact with it a long time ago," Willow said, probing. "How do you know so much about it?"

"There are things about myself that are best left unsaid," he said. "For now, anyway. I suppose since we're just sitting here, I can try to teach you cycling."

"Cycling," Willow said. She was a little annoyed that his topic change had worked, but she was interested in learning even more about magic.

Carl nodded.

"It's an advanced technique used by mages to squeeze out a little more power into their spells. Up until now, you've been directing your essence through your core, down your arms, and out of your hands. This technique would have you keep your essence on the move, cycling around in your body. Each pass through your organs picks up a little more essence, as your regeneration doesn't go to storage but to building up the mass you're manipulating. When you finally concept and cast the spell, you can expect a modest increase in power."

"It's all about power with you," Willow grumbled. "Where are the days when you wanted me to throttle my essence? To cast like everyone else?"

"From what I've seen in class, you already mastered that ability," Carl said, motioning to her arms. "Even with your little unauthorized session with Annabelle."

Willow tried not to feel chastened, like a child caught with her hand in the cookie jar. "It's my body. I have a right to have it fixed."

Carl nodded. "You do."

The agreement shocked Willow more than she was expecting.

"But you need to stay safe," Carl continued. "If you heal yourself too quickly, you risk brain damage from the cascade of sensation. Believe it or not, I do actually care what happens to you, Willow Tremont. Now, breathe in through your nose. Visualize your essence flowing. Up your arm, through your chest, and down the other arm."

Willow breathed, pushing the essence up her arm, but as it crossed her chest, it took up a strange vibration, and there was suddenly so much more of it.

"Carl—"

* * *

Leopold started running the moment he heard the detonation. He was in the west wing of the Arcanum, close enough that he was one of the first on the scene. And it was he who found Willow wandering in the street, covered with a dusting of crushed stone. He rushed to her side and carried her to a wall in an alley, coughing with the dust that clogged the air. When he'd gotten her propped up, he tried to speak to her, but Willow couldn't understand what he said—the world was muffled and ringing.

"What?" she yelled.

"Are you okay?" he screamed into her face. She barely heard it. She looked past him to the end of the alley and the cloud of pulverized stone rising into the sky. He took her face between his hands and gently swiveled her head down again.

"Willow," he shouted.

"I'm okay," she said, but she wasn't sure if that was the truth. She looked down at her hands; there wasn't a scratch on them. She'd managed to find her cane sometime between the cast and when Leopold had found her in the street, because it was still gripped in her right hand.

"Where's Carl?" Willow whispered. The words didn't feel like they had any specific meaning to her, but she said them anyway. There was someone named Carl, wasn't there? Where was he?

"We're going to the Sisters," Leopold said. He leaned over, and before she knew it, Willow was thrown over his back, her cane dangling ineffectually from her fingers.

She didn't mind the ride.

* * *

Leopold, bless him, wouldn't stop pestering the Sisters until Annabelle came by name. When he saw her nod, he finally let the Sisters take Willow. He followed close behind as Annabelle led them to a bed at the far side of the main hall.

Willow heard Annabelle make hurried explanations, but she couldn't understand any of the words the other woman was saying. There was something wet on the sides of her face, and when she absently wiped her ear, her hand came away smeared with blood.

That probably wasn't good.

Annabelle pulled a man in a white coat over and said some things close to his ear, but Willow couldn't hear any of it. Leopold wouldn't leave her side; he'd grabbed her cane and still had it hung over his arm. He was holding her hand. He was crying.

The man—a doctor, probably—leaned over Willow and produced a device that shone with magelight at the twist of his fingers. He flashed it over her eyes, and the world whited out for a moment before it came back into focus. He turned her head gently to the side, then to the other side.

Annabelle got him a chair, and the doctor sat behind Willow's head. The vaulted stone ceiling swam with colors and patterns that Willow was sure hadn't been there the last time she was in the hospital. She should really stop making it a habit to come here.

A green glow rose to the left and right, almost like a second sunrise, and Willow closed her eyes at the knowledge that someone was working on her. Whatever was wrong, it would soon be fixed.

* * *

"I've never seen anything like it," a man was saying.

Willow hadn't been asleep, had she? She'd closed her eyes to the green glow, and then opened them a moment later, but the doctor wasn't at her head anymore. He was at the foot of her bed, and she could hear him. He was talking to Annabelle. Leopold was still beside her, holding her hand and looking into her eyes. The bed was curtained off from the rest of the hall.

"It would be in your best interest to forget what you saw," Annabelle whispered harshly. Willow heard the sound of coins being exchanged out of sight. The doctor looked down, shook his head, and pocketed the fistful of gold.

"What in the seven hells?" he muttered, then swept out of the curtained alcove. The white curtains rippled with blue energy as he passed through.

The privacy spell.

Annabelle stood at the foot of Willow's bed for a moment, huffed in exasperation, then swept her hair back again and secured the loose strands with the rest of her bun. She turned to fix Willow with a stare, then moved to the side of the bed and took the doctor's chair.

"Willow, what happened?" she whispered. Apparently she didn't trust the privacy barrier as much as Carl did.

"Carl and I, we were training," Willow said. The memories were fuzzy, like they were dampened with a layer of cotton. It was hard for her to pick up a chain of events.

"You were in the building collapse?" Annabelle asked, and Willow nodded to her great regret.

"Don't move your head. You're still healing, although you'll be fine in a couple of hours. Concussion, your eardrums were ruptured. It wasn't just a building collapse, was it?"

"No," Willow whispered.

Leopold was leaning close to hear too. She swallowed and licked her lips. Her mouth was terribly dry.

"He was showing me a new technique. We were all set up to cast again, into the nullification rings."

Annabelle's face was as still as stone, and Leopold only gripped Willow's hand harder. Weeks ago it would have been excruciating, but she'd had time to build up her muscles again.

"I cycled, just like he told me." She felt tears sheet her eyes and run down the sides of her face. She didn't know why she was crying. "I told him it was too strong, that there was too much essence. He told me— Oh gods," Willow gasped.

She saw herself, shaking, afraid of what was happening inside her. Carl, pointing to the nullification rings. She shouted the concept and pointed into the rings, but the essence was still cycling up her arm. She hadn't imbued it with a shape when she released it.

"I did it," Willow sobbed, which brought on a wave of nausea. Willow turned to the side and retched. Annabelle didn't even need to dodge as Willow's lunch of cornbread and beef stew came up and splashed on the floor beside her.

"You blew the building up," Annabelle said in realization. "It must've been overpressure."

"Carl, where is he?" Willow asked after spitting the last of the bile from her mouth. "Is he okay?"

Annabelle took a breath, preparing herself. Willow knew the answer even before Annabelle said it, just from the look in her eyes.

"Carl's dead."

CHAPTER 25

Willow was physically better by the end of the day. Her eardrums had been regrown, her concussion healed, and the doctor who'd been called in to do the procedure paid off to overlook her... stranger attributes. When Leopold took her home, she should've been fine. She should've been alright.

She wasn't. Willow couldn't stop crying. Leopold held her close as he slowly directed her towards the house on Grave Street. When they entered, the energy in the place immediately changed. Benny started crying—he was obviously scared because Willow was such a wreck—and Margaret took him into another room to calm him down. Bryan sat with Leopold and Willow at the table as Leopold told him what happened.

"Dead," Bryan repeated, and looked Willow over. His eyes stopped at her pendant, and he pointed. "Any chance that's the reason we still have our Willow with us?"

"No," Willow managed to choke out. "It's not... it doesn't work like that. I never really understood... Now I'll never know."

Leopold held her closer as a fresh wave of sobs wracked her body. Bryan smoothed his fingers over his forehead.

"I saw the plume from the wall. I never thought... I didn't even think Willow would've been there. It was right on the edge of campus, by the inner wall."

"That's where he took her to train," Leopold said. "I think he always knew something like this might happen."

Carl stared, fear making his eyes wide, as he pointed into the nullification rings. He shouted at her to release the essence, to cast the spell. She pointed into the rings...

Willow couldn't breathe. She clawed at her overcoat, still gritty with stone dust, and tore at the fastenings. Her tongue was too big for her mouth, and her eyes were bugging out. She had to get air.

"Get her coat." Bryan moved around the table until he was eye-to-eye with her.

Leopold worked the fastenings, sometimes pushing Willow's hands aside as he unclipped each. Bryan took her face and stared into her eyes.

"You're not there anymore," Bryan said, leaning his forehead against hers. "You're here. You're right here."

"Can't..." Willow gasped, and Leopold finally got her overcoat off. Willow began tearing at her blouse. "Air..."

"You can breathe," Bryan said, holding her face steady in front of his own. "Breathe now, Willow. Breathe with me. In... Out..."

"*Move your essence with your breath,*" Carl said. "*In... Out...*"

Willow shrieked and tried to push Bryan away. Her arms and hands spasmed as, for the first time in weeks, her psychokinetic spells tried to reassert control over her limbs. She cried out in pain and Leopold grabbed her arms.

"Her muscles are like snakes," Leopold grunted as she struggled against him.

"Lay her out on the table," Bryan said. "She's going to hurt herself."

Willow screamed as they picked her effortlessly from the bench and stretched her across the cluttered tabletop. Plates clattered and mugs overturned, but Leopold held her arms and Bryan leaned on her legs. She tried kicking and turning, but the pain in her limbs kept her from putting her all into it. The wooden-beamed ceiling waved back and forth in her vision, and as the seconds passed something about the dark wood soothed her.

It wasn't the light stone of the Arcanum. It wasn't the vaulted ceiling of the training room.

Willow's breathing grew shallower, and she stopped struggling. She whimpered now, her legs severely bruised and her arms twitching with her momentary loss of control. The ceiling blurred and her eyes filled with tears again.

Gods, would she ever stop crying?

And that's when she really let it out. The shock, the pain, not just physical but emotional. Reacting to the knowledge that she'd been the one to kill Carl, that it was all her fault. She sobbed on her back on the tabletop. Leopold moved over and cradled the top of her head with his hand. Bryan let go of her legs and just sat at the far end of the table.

She cried for what felt like hours, too exhausted to move.

At some point she must've fallen asleep because she woke up in her room to the view of a loose constellation of magelights against the ceiling. She didn't want to look at them—she turned over, gingerly moving her wracked limbs, and tried to sleep.

If only Carl would stop haunting her dreams.

The next morning, she slowly got up, feeling like she'd been hit by an oxcart. There was a wrapped plate on the table for her—she'd slept through breakfast—but she didn't touch it. Instead, she used a broom from the kitchen to knock the magelights down from the ceiling. She swept the lights out through the front door and cast them into the sky where they slowly floated away on invisible currents.

Using her cane, she hobbled alone through the twisting streets of Durum towards the shining top of the hill. She didn't know where Leopold was and she couldn't think about him. Not right now. What did he think of her?

It only took a few minutes at the admissions office to take care of business. And she was surprised that when she left, she didn't feel any better. Still the lump of rock in her stomach wouldn't lighten. She felt queasy with hunger and made her way back down to the house by the wall.

She was eating cold leftovers in the empty house when Leopold walked in. He sat beside her and they didn't say a word as she finished her plate.

"I looked everywhere for you," he whispered, and she could sense a quivering rage beneath his voice. Worry for her, wasted.

"I was at the Arcanum," she said.

"I thought you'd found out about... the funeral."

Willow's breath hitched. "He was buried? Already?"

"He didn't have any family in the city," Leopold said. "There was nobody to hold vigil over him."

"I would've done it," Willow said, but she knew that it was a lie. She was in no state to hold vigil over the body of her professor.

"What were you doing at the Arcanum?" he asked.

Willow smiled mirthlessly and felt the swell of despair rise up to her throat. Saying it would make it true. "I withdrew," she said, ignoring Leopold's open-mouthed look of shock.

"You..." He wavered, uncomprehending. "You withdrew? From his class?"

He knew what she meant. He just didn't want to believe it.

"From the Arcanum," Willow said.

"But... but why? Why would you do that? You fought so hard to get in, to stay in! You almost died on the caravan—"

"I wish I had," Willow whispered to her empty clay plate. "If I had, then Carl would still be alive."

"And you'd be dead," Leopold said. "Maybe I'm prejudiced, but I'd take you over him any day."

"You must be," Willow said. "Look at me. I'm worthless. I was never anything more than a sick girl who wanted to run away from home."

Leopold grabbed her arm and shook it. It didn't hurt like it would have weeks ago.

"What about this," he said. "What about everything you've learned. About yourself? About what you can do?"

"What I can do?" Willow spat.

"You're incredible. You've done things—"

"I killed Carl!" Willow screamed. Her plate broke, and Leopold's eyes went to it. Her hands hadn't been anywhere near it. Willow looked too.

"Look at this," she said, holding up the two pieces, fitting them together. "Look at me. I can only destroy."

"That's not true," Leopold pleaded. "Carl forced you into it. You don't want to be a battle mage; you want to build. Remember? You told me you could build a house all by yourself with your power. By the gods, you could even raise a city wall!"

"No," Willow said and separated the halves of the plate. "I'm too dangerous. I brought this on myself."

"No you didn't. Carl—"

"I was the reason for the deathworm attack," Willow interrupted. "The worm probably thought I was a magical creature. That's why it attacked the caravan that night. Because of me."

"Because of you, we were all saved," Leopold said. Willow felt sick.

"I want you to leave," she said, tears blurring her vision. "Please just leave."

Leopold spent a long time watching her, then got up quietly and walked to the door. A stray thought caused Willow to cry out.

"Wait! That spell I gave you, give it back! It's dangerous."

Leopold opened the door and looked out. "They're still floating up there, you know," he said. "Geoff's going to be pissed."

"You're not carrying it on you, are you?" Willow asked. She felt so stupid. Why did she ever give him something like that?

"You gave it to me," he said. "It's mine." He shut the door, and then she was truly alone.

* * *

Willow went to the forestry guild located two streets over from the gate into the city later that day. She asked for a job, then begged for one. The man directing the hauling of stripped logs onto carts sighed heavily, looking her over. She knew what he saw: her wasted body. Even her arms were much thinner than they should be.

"Why?" he sighed in exasperation. "Why not the sewing houses? They're always looking for more women."

"I want to get out of the city."

"You runnin' from something?" he asked, eyebrow rising high.

"No," Willow lied. She wasn't, at least not in the way he probably thought. She could never tell him, but she didn't imagine he would ever believe her if she said that *she* was the danger that needed removing.

"The traders then. You sound like you've got an education."

"I don't... want to go that far." Willow barely kept herself from flinching at the memory of the last time she'd been out in a caravan.

He shook his bald head and walked away, back into the guild hall. Willow was sure she'd been blown off, until he emerged with an ax slung over his shoulder and pointed at a three-foot section of log. He told her that if she could split the log in ten strikes, she could have a job. It felt like an impossible task, especially for her.

Willow hefted the ax in her hands. It was heavy. The iron head weighed almost as much as the wooden handle. Her hands could grip it, but her arms could barely support its weight. What was she doing?

Willow closed her eyes and breathed.

"*In...*" Carl said.

Her eyes snapped open. No, she wouldn't let him come back. Not here.

The large man watched her, waiting patiently. He seemed to sense that she was running, and whatever kindness was in his heart made him stay for the inevitable result of the task.

She couldn't go back home, not now. Her parents would take her—of course they would—but they shouldn't. She was a murderer. And she was dangerous. If she'd attracted a deathworm before, what else might come after her now? Would her village be in danger?

The haft of the ax was smooth from years of use, polished by hands rougher and stronger than hers. She ran her thumb along the wood and felt it through her skin, but in another way as well. Slightly familiar, it was the way she used to feel the world through her hands.

Essence induction.

She let the feeling spread... and she knew the ax. Inch by inch she became it, spreading down to the bulbous foot of the handle up to the head where the wood was split. She sensed another foreign slice of wood embedded at the tip, and felt the pressure that the split was putting on the ax head. Her awareness spread to the iron, along the edge. She felt gouges from a file running across the face of the blade.

"You need to be strong to do this sort of work," the man said as Willow really felt the ax for the first time. "Maybe the caravans would be a better fit—"

In a single, fluid motion, Willow appeared to raise the ax above her head and bring it crashing down into the segment of log, splitting it through and ringing the ax head against the paving stone of the street. The man stood aghast, staring at what he thought he'd seen.

But that's not what happened. Willow raised the ax itself, her arms going along for the ride. She brought it down as an extension of her body, like an extra joint, and it passed through the log as if it was made of spun candy.

As she retrieved the ax, she made it bend its blade back from where she'd rolled it on the stone, then handed it to the burly man. It was like losing a limb to release the ax, but she did it anyway.

If she couldn't be normal, she could at least act the part.

He drew up a contract and signed her with the guild as an apprentice, a shocked look on his face all the while. He'd be her master, as his own apprentice had recently passed to journeyman. She suspected he just didn't believe what he'd seen and didn't want his mistake to be discovered by another when she couldn't recreate her stunt out in the field.

Her first trip out past the walls was the next morning, and she didn't get any advanced pay to put together an outfit for the trip. But she had a year's tuition of gold still to her name—minus a small sum set aside in a thick leather pouch—and enough time before sunset to find a place to stay.

She retrieved her cane from the drainpipe she'd hidden it behind and began stalking towards the worker housing her new master had mentioned.

* * *

Willow didn't have much to move from the house on Grave Street, but she stayed until Bryan got home that night to tell them both she was leaving. They took it well, better than she expected, and didn't try to talk her out of it. Bryan asked for her master's name, and she gave it while wondering why he wanted to know. He nodded in approval.

"He'll treat you right," Bryan said, but there was a threat in the statement, although not towards her. Margaret came around the table and embraced her.

"We love you, Willow," she said. "Nothing else matters. You'll always be family to us."

Nothing else matters. It was the worst thing Margaret could have said, because it was a lie. She only thought that because she didn't know the woman she was embracing was a murderer. She didn't know what Willow really was, what she'd always been deep down and had allowed herself to be molded into.

But if it was such a lie, then why was she crying?

Benny didn't understand, and he bawled at the silent tension in the room. Margaret took him away and left Bryan and Willow to say their goodbyes.

"You know where we are," Bryan said. "If you need anything—"

"Thanks," Willow smiled. "It feels like I'm going away, but I'll just be five streets over."

He smiled. "I've grown used to you, I guess. Will Leopold be staying with you?"

Willow's mood soured, and she looked at her feet. "No. He shouldn't... I'm a danger to him."

To everyone.

Bryan gripped her upper arm, and she looked into his face.

"That's not true. And the sooner you realize that, the better you'll feel."

She nodded, even though she didn't agree. It seemed like such a waste to argue with him on the night of her departure. He hugged her gently, and she tried to wrap her arms around his broad back but failed.

When she left the house, the leather pouch of gold on her bedside table was the only evidence of her long stay. In the twilight, she saw only a single one of the pale magelights still hovering over the nearby roofs.

CHAPTER 26

The woodworkers were a silent bunch, but Willow liked that. The workers' housing had someone come around an hour before dawn and pound on each door in turn. Willow awoke in the room she shared with another woman—who did something in administration—and stretched after getting out of bed. The muscles in her arms were losing their tenderness and becoming more normal by the day.

It was chilly with fall coming up fast, which would spread into winter soon enough, so Willow donned a set of heavy canvas workwear. The fabric was waterproof and sturdy, as the man who sold it to her had claimed. They were called tin pants for some reason, although she was unclear as to why.

Willow quickly grew hot with her outfit on in the workers' housing, so she went outside after stashing her breakfast and lunch in a crosswise sling around her back. Lights shone from the woodworkers' guild hall and a few other facades down the twisty street, but for all else the world still seemed to be in that twilight state before real wakefulness began.

A time of new beginnings. Of new starts.

She found her master at the small caravan, tightening straps on the equipment. His name was Tyrone, and he stood out from the others not just because of his sheer bulk, but also for his jet-black skin. Since coming to Durum, she'd seen a few others with dark skin, but never that dark.

He looked around, caught sight of Willow, and waved her over. She hobbled across the street with her cane to the empty caravan.

"Are you gonna use that while we're in the forest?" he asked, eyeing the cane.

"If you want me to get anywhere," she said.

Tyrone rubbed his jaw, then shook his head. "You're a mystery, Willow. That's for sure. Help me secure the tools."

He showed her knots—ways to weave rope that cinched in just the right way so the strain of so many long tools wouldn't loosen them. It reminded her of weaving essence into magic, but infinitely more practical. And there was little chance that tying a knot could get you or someone else killed.

She felt something in the bundle as she passed her hand over the tools to pull a rope tight. A familiarity she wasn't expecting, like touching your own hand in the darkness. She shook her head and cinched the knot like Tyrone had shown her, then stowed the loose end of the rope.

It was time to roll out. The guild members took their spots on the three-wagon caravan, of which the back two wagons were uncovered and girded by thick vertical poles along their sides for the felled logs. Tyrone called her name, and she shimmied up into the second wagon to sit beside a bundle of long saws.

The caravan began to move, and it wasn't long before the city's gate reared up above them. The wall was thirty feet thick, and the tunnel under it was sealed by a gate at either end. She recognized in-scripted light bars set into the arched stone ceiling, dispelling what shadows might've gathered in the damp tunnel.

Sooner than she'd thought, the caravan emerged through the second gate, and she was out of the city for the first time in months. With the curved city wall at their backs, the world seemed to open up in a vista from horizon to horizon. The sky was just beginning to lighten, but even in the pale morning she could see the strange refractions of the warded tunnel and how it warped the surrounding hillsides.

The track they followed out of the city was well-worn and utterly invisible from outside the city. She looked around, but the warbeast wasn't in sight. Tyrone didn't seem worried. In fact, he was dozing with his back to one of the vertical wooden pillars of the logging trailer. Willow tried to settle down as well, but the constant jostling and her uneasy heart kept her from nodding off.

They traveled until the sun's disc crested the horizon. On the packed earth of the warded tunnel track, they made great time to the edge of the warbeast's territory. The end of the tunnel was obvious from the way the straight line of the path branched out into a delta of churned earth. The caravan doglegged left towards a forest in the middle distance.

It was another hour until they reached it—a much rougher hour of bumps and rocking over the uneven ground. Willow held tight to the pole of the logging trailer and tried to force herself to relax. She couldn't be this fragile anymore. If she was going to work and earn her way in the world, she had to be strong.

When they reached the edge of the forest and pulled the caravan up alongside the outermost trees, Tyrone automatically stirred from his nap. How he knew they'd stopped for good, Willow had no idea, but he jumped off the trailer and began undoing the knots around the stowed tools. Willow gingerly hopped down and helped.

The familiar feeling came again. She got it when she worked the knot around a brace of axes, and when the bundle finally opened, she saw where it was coming from as plain as day.

The ax she'd used yesterday. She saw where the edge of the head was slightly crumpled from her inexpert fix. The wood of the handle, just as she remembered. It was like seeing a long-lost friend. Poor replacement for Benny playing warbeasts on the kitchen floor or Leopold adjusting his glasses, but it was all she had now.

"Grab an ax," Tyrone said, then nodded towards the tall trees. "We're going to fell until the first few are down, then you'll be chopping them to size."

"Shouldn't we use the saws for that?" Willow asked. She looked over to the other cart where pairs of workmen were taking the flexible metal saws into the forest.

"They're trained for it," Tyrone said. "They'll fell all day. We're just helping until we can do our own work."

Willow picked the ax that felt like home and used it instead of her bamboo cane to hobble into the forest. Tyrone went in ahead of her and kept glancing back to make sure she was keeping up.

She picked up her pace. She didn't want to be a burden here, like she'd been to Leopold.

A few trees in, Tyrone stopped at a trunk seemingly at random. He knocked it with the back of his ax and listened to the sound of the wood. Willow wondered what he was listening for, as it just sounded like wood to her.

"This one will do," Tyrone said, and Willow hefted her ax. "Wait. What do you think you're doing?"

"Um," Willow waffled. "Cutting down the tree?"

Tyrone shook his head. "Which direction will it fall?"

"Which..." Willow said, then looked around. She supposed there were some safe directions for it to fall and some unsafe directions. Was the caravan far enough away that it wouldn't hit the wagons if it fell towards it? Where were the other guild members? How would they drag it out of the forest?

"I don't know," she said, and he nodded.

"The cut of the tree is key in controlling the fall. A tree fifteen feet tall is heavy enough to kill a man if it hits him right. A tree *this* size would demolish a house."

She imagined it, even though she tried not to. The tree falling, landing on a building of light stone. Smashing through the roof, blowing out the door. Pulverized stone, nullification rings spinning in superheated arcs through the air. Carl under the trunk, a trickle of blood coming from his mouth.

"Hey, hey!" Tyrone grabbed her shoulder.

It was above where Annabelle had fixed her arm, and she hissed as the pain brought her back and she instinctively jerked away. She stepped back, almost took a tumble, then steadied herself with the haft of the ax.

Tyrone was staring at her.

"I'm fine," Willow said and walked back to the tree. "Felling direction," she prompted.

Tyrone paused for a moment, and the silence was pregnant with questions. Questions about her past, about her life before. And why she was here taking Tyrone up on an offer that was meant to be an easy let-down. Questions she didn't offer any answer to.

"Right," he said. "Well, the caravan is due south..."

They worked until midday to fell the one tree, both going at the trunk on opposite sides to cut the hinge on which it would pivot. Willow didn't recreate the stunt that had gained her admission into the guild, not with the tree looming above them. She was afraid it would crash down prematurely, crushing them both and maybe even others.

Finally, after a back-breaking morning, the tree began to lean, followed by a cracking sound.

"Timber!" Tyrone bellowed into the forest in three directions. It was not the first time they'd heard the shouted warning. The tree tilted slowly over, so slowly, but when it hit the ground the earth shook under Willow's feet. Tyrone was right. It was much more dangerous than it looked.

They walked out of the forest to the caravan, where two other trees were already lined up, and Tyrone retrieved two sets of wicked-looking iron clamps. He gave one to Willow and latched his at the base of the tree, the metal biting into the wood. Willow finagled hers around the upper branches, and Tyrone started dragging.

She was dead weight. Without the ax, which she'd deposited back at the caravan, she stumbled along after him. The claws were barely in the tree, and Willow wasn't even pulling, but Tyrone didn't look back to see what the problem was. He just hauled the trunk in fits and spurts out of the forest and into the clearing beside the wagons.

By the time they got the tree positioned with all its multitudinous branches sticking hither and thither, Tyrone was drenched in sweat. So was Willow, just from the exertion of walking while attempting to pull up on the top of the tree. Tyrone returned the clamps and brought out their axes.

"Here." He offered her one, but it wasn't right.

She reached past him and grabbed the other in his off hand, which elicited a smirk from Tyrone that was indecipherable to Willow. Did he think she was just weird or quirky? Was he regretting signing her with the guild even after she'd passed his test?

"First, the branches," he said, motioning to the many cracked and broken-off remains of the proud tree. He got straight to work hacking with the ax, lopping off the wood and throwing it into a nearby pile.

Willow hefted the ax, *her* ax, and it felt once again like a part of her body. She could almost sense touch through it. She supposed that was how she'd been getting along her whole life, but it was strange to have it happen to any other object.

She swung again and again, paring branches off the trunk. The morning chill burned away to a cool autumn day as they worked in the relatively bright light of the plain beside the forest. Willow tried to keep pace with Tyrone by holding herself back. In this place, in her new life, she didn't want any strange questions. She wanted to stand out as little as possible from the crowd.

After paring the tree down to the bare trunk, it was time to section it up into logs. They worked together with a smaller saw than the two-man teams in the forest to slice the trunk. With each thrust of the thin metal, Willow began to feel it more and more. Her arms began to rest, her hands taking the strain of holding on. Eventually she realized she wasn't pushing against the blade at all on the forwards thrusts. It was just moving on its own to her will.

Again. She'd done it again and hadn't meant to this time. She felt disappointed and worried as well. How often would this happen if she pushed herself? Why was she latching onto objects like this so easily? Was it because she had unused potential from freeing up her hands and arms? Where would it end?

With a thin metal ring, the sawing was complete, and Tyrone looked back over the log sections. He grabbed a set of metal claws, and Willow likewise grabbed her set from before. They dragged the sections to the cart and loaded them up against the stanchions so they wouldn't roll on the trip back. Tyrone explained all of this as Willow barely felt their dragging weight. Was it the claws this time? Or the logs themselves?

The problem was it was almost impossible to tell. She didn't feel any great affinity for the claws, and each log leaving her to go into the cart didn't provoke the same sensation of loss as the ax had.

Why? Why was this happening? Why couldn't she just be normal? She ground her teeth and wrenched the log so hard onto the cart that it nearly rolled off the other side. Tyrone looked for a moment like he would reprimand her, but apparently thought better of it, and they went back to haul more.

They broke for lunch, all of the woodworkers leaning against the cartwheels or the outer trees of the forest, soaking up the sun and chowing down. Willow unwrapped the field rations she'd purchased from a store near the guild hall and bit into hard bread topped with seasoned meat.

It wasn't nearly as good as Margaret's fare, but she had to forget that. That life in the small room off the kitchen. The room where she first laid with Leopold. That room where she felt love blossom for the first time.

Where she'd finally belonged.

She couldn't go back. She'd kill one or more of them, eventually. Accidentally. It would happen again, just like it had with Carl. There was no way to stop it since she didn't even half-understand what her body was capable of. If she just kept herself here, away from magic, she could live in peace.

She was sure of it.

Lunch was over deceptively early, and then it was back to work. This time they cleared branches from trees the sawing teams brought in, not venturing back into the forest for the rest of the day. Chopping, sawing, hauling. Again and again. The work was repetitive, and Willow's mind went blissfully blank.

She didn't realize the sun was nearing the horizon until the conglomeration of woodsmen around her and Tyrone forced her to acknowledge the fact. The cutting teams were back, hacking at the remaining trunks, and everyone pitched in to segment the logs into manageable lengths.

When everything was done, Tyrone held out his hand and Willow breathlessly handed back the ax. It parted easier from her this time. She didn't care why. She was bone-tired and sweaty. But she'd done it. The woodsmen were tying their harvest down with ropes, and Tyrone was gathering the tools to do the same. Willow hobbled off to find her cane, still propped on the wheel of one of the wagons.

They all rode together in the front wagon while the other two carried their harvest. Willow squeezed in between Tyrone and another burly man, paying little attention to the raucous conversation around her. It was nice to be unnoticed, to be invisible. Someone as small as her among men so large, she could just disappear.

The delta of turned earth marked the entrance to the warded tunnel, and only after they'd lined up with the tunnel could Willow see the rammed-earth road that led to the city gates. The illusion really was quite magnificent—it was no wonder it had kept the warbeast at bay for so long. She looked across the denuded horizon and thought she saw movement near the city's wall to the north, but she couldn't be sure in the failing light.

She'd expected to go straight back to her shared room after disembarking and unloading the logs for processing. But after she'd dragged the last section of wood to the workyard, Tyrone approached her in the falling dusk.

"Good work today, Apprentice Willow."

She smiled but couldn't meet his eyes. She was leaning on the articulated claws—her cane was back leaning against the guildhouse—
and she knew he'd seen things today he couldn't easily explain. Nothing supernatural, nothing impossible, just improbable. Like a wasted
girl keeping up with a band of experienced woodworkers when she
wasn't hobbling from place to place.

"We're going to get a bite. The guys usually do after we finish.
Would you like to join us?"

Willow thought back to the chamber she shared with the woman
in administration, the tiny space with barely enough room between
the beds to shimmy out. And how hard it would be to find somewhere
open to get food at this hour. She nodded.

"That would be nice."

* * *

As it had been described to her, the tavern was almost unnoticeable between the workshops and warehouses on the twisting street.
Everything smelled of sawdust and hot iron—this was the worker's
district, where she now belonged. She supposed she should get used to
these smells and forget as quickly as she could the scents of parchment
and paper, chalk and roast beef.

When Tyrone opened the door for her, absent of any mark or
shingle that might identify it as a tavern from any other workshop, the
roar nearly blasted Willow off her feet. Yellow light spilled out onto
the street, along with the strong funk of sour ale and boiling stew.
Tyrone placed a hand at her back and gave her a little push into the
tavern before shutting them in.

Another cheer went up across the small room. Willow realized
that everyone was looking at her. Cheering for her. She wanted to fold
into herself and hide away, but Tyrone placed his arm around her
shoulders and steered her to the long central table where most of the

men she'd worked with that day were seated. With an incomprehensible shout, Tyrone summoned a barmaid and Willow found a pint of ale sitting before her on the slick wooden tabletop.

"The woman of the hour!" one of the woodsmen shouted, clearly already half-drunk from the slur in his voice. Another cheer went up at the proclamation.

"What's going on?" Willow leaned over and shouted into Tyrone's ear, the only volume that could possibly register in the rowdy space.

"Cutting a new apprentice is always something to be celebrated." Tyrone barely had to raise his deep, gravelly voice over the crowd to be heard. "But with you it's something special."

"What's special about me?" Willow asked, then snapped her lips shut. She shouldn't prod or poke and should just disappear. Willow tried to hide her face behind the large wooden pint as she gulped ale.

"You swing like a man," a hairy fellow beside Tyrone shouted. "I've never seen such a thing from a woman before. You're strong as an ox."

"Keep it up, and Tyrone will have to raise you to journeyman tomorrow," someone cheered, eliciting another clinking of mugs all around. Two clanked into hers, spilling ale all down her work clothes. Surprisingly, the ale just ran off onto the floor as if slipping on a greased skillet.

"It's months before that," Tyrone shot back and elbowed Willow slightly. "But I wouldn't be surprised. Our new apprentice has shown us all up, hasn't she, boys?"

Another cheer drowned out the instinct to fold into herself, and Willow was surrounded by a chorus of "drink, drink, drink!" She drank, sucking back the sour ale until she couldn't hold back anymore and let out a mighty belch. This, too, elicited a cheer.

The night grew hazier as the drinks continued to flow. Her confusing mélange of emotions—fear of standing out, of being a freak, mixed with pride at having been impressively useful—bled away until there was only pride and comradery left. Eventually a stew was served and Willow tucked away four helpings, which again caused such an uproar that new toasts were proposed. Willow the bankbreaker. Willow the logsplitter. Willow the apprentice.

It was better, much better, than being Willow the waif.

A woodsman, who she didn't catch the name of, helped her back to her dormitory. He almost had to carry her with how she was wobbling on her cane. If any of the woodsmen were confused about the juxtaposition between her cane and her performance out beside the forest, they didn't mention it. It was almost like she could just *be* as she was. It was nice.

Willow was still pleasantly buzzed as she opened her door, but that ended quickly when she saw who was sitting on her bed.

Annabelle. Illuminated by a handheld magelight, she rose from the floor bed and slipped silently by Willow's roommate. Did she enter after her roommate had already gone to sleep? Or had she been here for hours? Willow shook her head to try and clear it of ale, but all that did was cause her to nearly topple against the doorframe from dizziness.

"Willow," Annabelle said, looking her up and down.

Willow, too, sized Annabelle up and found that she was carrying a bag over her shoulder. Whatever she was here for, Willow didn't want her roommate to hear it. She didn't want to mix lives.

Willow reached out, grabbed Annabelle's night cloak, and pulled her into the hallway. It was dark save for a slow-burning candle at the far end opposite the door. The other woodsmen had already shut themselves away to sleep off their hangovers until morning, when they'd all start anew. And when Willow would start with them.

"You're drunk," Annabelle said, wrinkling her nose in disgust. "What are you wearing?"

"What does it look like I'm wearing?" Willow thought she had a witty retort loaded, but she was fairly certain that her words had slurred when she spat them.

"You look like a laborer," was the reply.

"Well, good," Willow said, swaying against the wall. "Because I am."

"Stop playing games," Annabelle snapped. "You've dropped out of school. Why?"

"That's none of your business," Willow said. "How did you know?"

"Leopold came to find me. He begged me to tell him where you were."

Leopold. Of course he wouldn't let her go so easily. She should have known that.

"You can't tell him where I am."

"I can do whatever the hell I damn please," Annabelle said, then let out a breath. "What are you doing out here?"

"I'm working," Willow said. It was hard to hold onto her line of thoughts, but she wanted to say this as plainly as she could. "I'm doing something, something useful. I'm living, here. I'm useful here, without being dangerous. Without being deadly."

"You're useful back at the Arcanum," Annabelle said. "You were learning magic. You were learning to control yourself."

"I killed Carl," Willow said. "All of my learning and was it worth it? Carl's life for what? For a freak?"

"Carl knew the risks," Annabelle said. "He knew what it might mean after those idiots in metrology got your capacitance. Nobody works with that kind of power and doesn't know the risks. He'd been prepared for it. Or... he was preparing."

"You can't tell me that he was preparing for his... his imminent demise," Willow slurred. "That he was ready for me to kill him."

"He was always ready to die," Annabelle hissed, pushing Willow up against the wall.

She felt her back bruise, but she pushed back anyway, fueled by alcohol and rage. They wrestled softly in the dim candlelight.

"Listen to me, you child!" Annabelle spat. "We're always ready to die. We don't belong here, Carl and I. We were sent here, and there was always a risk."

"By your mentor," Willow sneered. "Does this all-powerful mythical being even know about Carl?"

Annabelle paused, slackened her grip, then shook her head. "That's what I'm here to ask you about."

She looked to either side down the dim hallway, but they were alone. Then she backed off and unslung the pack from her back. She retrieved a wooden box from the bag and opened its polished brass catch.

Willow wasn't sure what she was looking at.

"Have you ever seen something like this before?" Annabelle stepped closer with the box out-held. "Did Carl ever tell you how it worked?"

Inside was a tangle of thin metal wires, a large cylinder, and what looked like the bell of a trumpet. There also seemed to be a crank, but disconnected from anything else.

Even through the drunken fog, Willow had no difficulty knowing the answer to that question. "I've never seen anything like it," she said. "Did Carl have one?"

"We both did. To receive messages from Asche."

"His would be..."

Annabelle shook her head. "I searched his office, right after he died. It wasn't there. He'd hidden it, and I don't know where."

"Why do you need his?" Willow asked.

"Because mine is broken," Annabelle said. She pulled the crank handle out of the box with a snap and fitted it into a hole Willow hadn't seen before in the side. Annabelle turned the crank a few times, and a light slowly ignited within the box.

It wasn't a light like anything Willow had ever seen. It didn't have the same sheen as a magelight, and it wasn't like sunlight either. It was slightly orange and felt like it was giving off a thin stream of heat. Along with the light came a sound like rain or fingernails running down wool.

"He never showed you this?" Annabelle asked, desperation in her voice. "Never talked about it?"

"No, nothing like this," Willow said, and Annabelle stopped cranking. Immediately the light winked out, followed by the hissing sound. "It's broken?"

Annabelle stuffed the box back into her pack. "I haven't received a transmission in a week."

"That hissing sound, was that—"

Annabelle shook her head. "It's supposed to be silent when it's not picking anything up. This hiss... it either means that my device is broken..."

"Or?" Willow asked.

Annabelle turned towards the door of the dormitory. "Or that something's interfering with the signal."

Chapter 27

Willow didn't let Annabelle's impromptu visit throw her off. The next morning, head pounding from a hangover, she dragged herself to the washbasin and cleaned up as best she could for the day ahead. She heard others moaning in the dormitory and she quickly got dressed in her work clothes and made her way out to the staging yard. The carts were already waiting, attended by the drivers.

She chopped trees, then drank that night, then slept. Woke, and did it all again. Every day, she tried to use her muscles as much as she could, but she tired quickly and had to switch to her unnatural abilities. When she did, she was one of the faster woodsmen on the team.

A week passed this way, then two.

She saw Leopold once out in the staging yard, looking around. Willow hid until he ambled away and then she hooded her face as she helped load the wagons. He hadn't been looking hard for her there. That meant he still didn't know where she was. Neither Annabelle nor Bryan had told him.

Still, Willow didn't look at the wall top as they passed underneath in the mornings and evenings, for fear that she'd see Leopold's familiar silhouette staring down at her. And she didn't look at the Arcanum, standing proud upon the highest hill in the city.

Instead, she kept her eyes down on her hands, which were growing hard and calloused. She continued to drink heavily and soon found she could withstand the first pint without keeling over. And she was grateful that the men who had to carry her back to her rooms never commented about the shape of the body they felt under her woodsman's outfit.

It was... normal. Normal beyond anything she expected. She was just another apprentice, just another woodsman. Chopping and sawing and hauling and drinking and sleeping. The days bled into each other, and she welcomed the abyss into which her old memories fell.

Days, weeks, then a month passed since she'd cast her last spell. She didn't miss magic. She'd found what she had always wanted.

Purpose. Usefulness.

It all seemed to be going so well.

It wasn't until the convoy exited the warded tunnel and approached the stand of trees that Willow felt something was off. Something in the air, almost like rain. Like thunder. But when she scanned the horizon, there were no dark clouds in the chill, bright sky.

Frost crunched under her boots as she once again abandoned her cane by the wagon and followed Tyrone into the tree line. It was getting colder every morning as winter approached, and she'd added a heavy canvas jacket stuffed with chicken feathers atop her uniform. It kept her warm enough for now, but she'd have to do something else by the time winter really settled in. Not using her muscles to move left her susceptible to frostbite if the temperature dropped too low.

Tyrone silently appraised each tree, mentally measuring diameters and sometimes even knocking on the bark. Meanwhile, Willow leaned up against a trunk and watched. These things would be what she'd learn for her journeyman exam, but Tyrone had said that wouldn't be for another few weeks. He was advancing her in the schedule because she was so adept with the ax.

She should be. To her it was like being adept with her fingers or hand. There was no separation between her body and the wood when she took up the handle now. It was a part of her.

A tree sprite peeked out from behind a trunk a few paces away.

"Tyrone," Willow said, nodding over to the sprite. It surveyed the scene, taking them both in for a long while, and then crouched down on its four equatorial legs like it was waiting. For what, she didn't know.

"Mark it," Tyrone said and continued tapping on a trunk.

Willow walked using the ax as a cane until she was alongside the sprite.

"You know the drill," she said to the sprite, and deftly cut an X into the trunk—a symbol meant to represent the sprite's splayed legs. It would warn off woodsmen from selecting this tree and possibly gaining its ire.

To Willow's relief, the sprites—the only magical creatures this close to the warbeast's domain—didn't seem attracted to her the way the deathworm had been. This strengthened her belief that even though she was outside the wall, she wouldn't be drawing any dangerous magical creatures to her woodcutting team.

Willow smiled down at the sprite, then the corners of her mouth dropped as she noticed the thing was shivering. Willow slid down the tree trunk until she was on her knees and bent closer to it.

It gripped the tree with its four identical arms, each terminating in a little hand with three fingers. The central node of the sprite had a single dark hole through which it observed the world. It was quivering against the tree, shaking hard enough to almost lose its grip.

The sight brought unpleasant memories to Willow's mind, and she shoved them down. What could be affecting the creature so much?

"Tyrone—" she said, but a blaring sound interrupted her. It was horn-like but way deeper. It seemed to be coming from the tree line back towards the city.

The blast went on for a handful of seconds, then stopped. She turned towards Tyrone.

"What—" she said but was cut off by the look on his face.

His mouth was open, eyes wide. She turned instinctively towards what he was staring at, but nothing was there. Just the bright light from the near edge of the forest.

"Get back to the caravan!" Tyrone yelled, and Willow heard a clatter. She looked back and saw he'd dropped the ax he'd been holding—unheard of. The axes were precious to the woodsman's guild, and he'd just dropped it in the loam.

He rushed towards her and scooped her over his shoulder. Only the thick jacket saved her from intense pain, and her surprise was so great that she dropped her own ax. It hit the ground, shuffled a little ways towards her as she reached out for it, but fell for good as Tyrone sprinted away.

"What?" Willow managed to gasp between Tyrone's hurtling steps.

"Home Call. Durum's sent up the Home Call."

They burst through the trees, and Tyrone dropped her roughly beside the lead wagon. He immediately went to work with a half-dozen other woodsmen who were unlatching the final two empty wagons.

"Get in the wagon!" Tyrone shouted when he saw Willow was still staring at him as he worked the pin.

"But the tools—"

"Leave them," he yelled. "Just get in the wagon!"

Willow turned and climbed up the stairs to the back of the lead wagon, which had just been unhitched from the other two. The driver and two other woodsmen were quickly gathering the horses from their grazing and ushering them back to the front. Willow slid down the bench until she was pressed up against the canvas.

She was the only one inside for almost a minute before the rest of the woodsmen poured in all at once. They jostled and shouted as they crammed into the wagon, and she saw Tyrone near the end of the tide, just barely grabbing a seat on the bench at the canvas' edge.

The wagon moved with a lurch and headed back towards the city at a much faster clip than they usually used. Willow looked around the wagon and saw fear in the faces of not a few woodsmen.

"What's the Home Call?" she asked a grizzled man with a beard sitting beside her. She remembered that he'd passed her a new mug at her celebration just a month ago.

"The city sends it out to recall everyone outside the walls. It means they're going to shut the gates."

"Shut the gates? But why?"

The man shook his head. "I don't know, but if you're not in by the time the gates shut, you're locked out. We're close enough with the horses that we can make it in the standard period of time."

"And if you're not?" Willow asked.

"Flee in the other direction," the man said. "It means something's coming. Something to threaten the city."

They made the hour-long journey in thirty minutes. When Willow recognized the delta of churned earth she breathed a sigh of relief. They'd made it to the warded tunnel.

"Look!" one of the woodsmen said, pointing out the back of the wagon. Willow was so far forward she couldn't see anything save the low hills in the distance.

"Gods have mercy." A woodsman began feverishly praying, bowing his head above his hands over and over again.

None of the others stopped him.

There was something on the horizon. With enough time focusing, Willow could see it. It was moving and even as she watched, it grew larger. She was reminded of the deathworm and clenched her fists. No, it wasn't like that. Not this time. This time she was with others. This time she'd be within the city walls.

She heard the driver shriek in surprise, and suddenly a shadow blotted the canvas overhang. An enormous beast leaped over the wagon and the warded tunnel both, then skidded in the churned earth as it righted itself to continue its headlong rush. For a second, Willow saw vaguely canine features and strange, slippery tentacles. Then a miasma of rot passed over the wagon and Willow nearly gagged.

Was that Durum's warbeast?

"Gods," several other woodsmen cried out and joined the first in prayer. Willow locked gazes with Tyrone at the front of the wagon and saw real fear in his eyes. He really had never seen anything like this before in all his years.

As they raced down the warded tunnel, the thing in the distance grew closer. It moved in a strange shuffle, almost like it was crawling, and it was surrounded by a purple haze. The warbeast rushed to meet it, little flecks of flesh scattering on the ground behind. In a matchup between such terrifying beasts, she wasn't sure which she wanted to win.

The cart gave a lurch forwards as it slowed abruptly. The wall's shadow passed over them as they trundled through the gate. A thick sea of onlookers parted to either side of the wagon as it came through, just as the two creatures met in furious battle. Durum's warbeast rose up and pounced on the encroaching thing, and the newcomer swatted the warbeast to the side. The dog-thing turned end-over-end before springing to its feet to make another charge.

The onlookers crowded the gate as if they were watching a sporting event. Willow doubted whether she would get that close, even with the walls protecting them. The wagon, now moving at a leisurely pace, rolled through the sea of bodies towards the woodsman guild's staging area, leaving them with a clear view of the churning carnage outside.

One thing was clear: the creature wanted to get closer to Durum, but the warbeast was upsetting its progress with its incessant attacks. Each time the creature flung the warbeast to the side, it rushed towards the warded tunnel as if it knew where the arcane structure was. The warbeast pounced on its back and began to tear at its head.

The creature grabbed Durum's warbeast with its overlong arms and tossed it into the air. For the first time, Willow saw the creature's outline plainly against the bright sky: vaguely humanoid, hairless, with a shortened torso and long legs and arms. The nimbus of purple light brightened around the creature for an instant, and a bolt of lightning caught the warbeast as it flailed in midair.

Willow blinked, not believing what she'd just seen. The warbeast tumbled to the ground and landed in a boneless, smoking heap. The creature didn't even take a moment to relish its victory, turning to scramble towards the warded tunnel.

The home call sounded once more, almost overwhelming so close to the city gates, and the great doors began to close. As they hinged shut, Willow saw enormous bars and chains of bright silver strung across the studded wood.

These doors were meant to protect Durum from threats, both mundane and arcane.

The home call trailed off, leaving a heavy silence. It was Willow's turn to leave the wagon now, and she stepped out onto the step.

"Willow?"

She looked down at the familiar voice. Leopold was there, disbelief in his eyes, like he couldn't fathom seeing her in the staging area. A riot of emotions clashed inside her, from shame and anger to embarrassment. She took the steps slowly to give herself time, and because she'd left her cane back at the wagons near the forest.

"Leo—" Willow managed to choke out before he was upon her, wrapping her in an embrace.

She hesitated for a moment, then wrapped her arms around his back. She pressed her face close to his ear in the chaos of the crowd.

"I'm sorry," she whispered. Leopold shook his head. He broke the embrace and stepped back, but didn't let her hands go. "I'm sorry I ran away," she said.

"No, it's me who should be sorry. I didn't know. Still don't know how much it's affected you. I'm sorry I couldn't give you your space."

"Oh," Willow said, and tears blurred her vision. She dug her fingers into his blouse and pulled him closer.

That's when the world exploded.

CHAPTER 28

Willow came to lying on her side, her body a symphony of pain. It reminded her of days long past when not even a bare inch of skin was spared from the pain of existence. Since then, she'd had her hands and arms cured to some extent.

It didn't seem to help now.

Willow moved her head, and the world blurred. She was surrounded by rubble—crushed stone blocks larger than wagons, splinters of wood, and bright white metal. There was smoke on the air and the tangy smell of roasting meat. It took effort to remember where she was.

"Leopold," she whispered but only heard herself on the left. She'd experienced this before: her right eardrum had blown out. She reached towards a cracked stone block and winced as pain lanced up her arm.

Her arm.

The sleeve of the woodsman's outfit was burned to charcoal and bright red showed through from the wasted bicep beneath. Her hand hadn't fared much better, scored by flame and shrapnel. Her pinky pointed off in an unnatural direction.

Willow groaned, the pain making her nauseous. She retched, and what was left of her triple-breakfast of eggs came up on the rubble. She knew what the smell was now, and wished more than anything that she hadn't recognized it.

"Leopold," she grunted again, pushing herself up with her left arm. Something sticky and hard crackled against the right side of her face and there was a scent of burned hair. She raised herself up just enough to see over the field of rubble and scanned the bodies.

There were over a hundred bodies, or pieces of bodies, in the mixed rubble. Some had been crushed by stone, others burned by whatever had exploded. Shrapnel from the gates laid all around her, including lengths of silver chain and shattered bars. She searched for the face she didn't want to find.

Leopold was there, his legs hidden by a large stone block. He looked like he was sleeping. There was blood seeping down from his hairline and the corner of his mouth.

Willow clenched her teeth and screamed as she pulled herself over the shattered remains of the staging area. There was a roar in the distance, and she spared a look out of the gaping hole that used to be the reinforced gate.

That *thing* was there, at the end of the warded tunnel. It crouched low and strained against an invisible barrier above it. As she watched, the barrier grew red, glowing, and then burst. The creature moved forwards until it encountered the next obstacle.

It was coming through the warded tunnel.

She had to get to Leopold. Willow gained her knees and crawled until she was at his side. It was only then that she saw just how bad the damage was.

The stone block had fallen on Leopold and his legs disappeared beneath it. A small rivulet of blood came from the seam between the stone and the ground, but there was no space for legs to exist there. He didn't have them anymore.

Willow moaned in despair and laid her right ear against his chest. She searched for the strong beat of his heart that she'd heard so many nights as they lay together in bed. She listened for the gentle wheeze of his lungs.

There was nothing.

"Willow!" a familiar voice shouted her name.

Willow was blinded as the tears flowed freely. She ran her fingers through Leopold's hair, touched his lips, and wailed. Annabelle scrambled over the rocks to her left, swept her gaze around, spotted Willow, and went to pull her up.

"Willow, are you alright?"

"It's Leopold," she sobbed. "He..."

Annabelle didn't even look down. She took Willow's face between her hands and stared hard into her eyes, then surveyed her burned arm.

"Stand. You have to stand."

"Why?" Willow whispered. "It's coming. It's coming."

"Stop moping, you child!" Annabelle said, hauling Willow to her feet. Willow screamed at the pain—charred skin cracked on her right arm, and she felt a gout of warmth splash from bicep to elbow. But Annabelle wouldn't let go. She threw Willow's left arm over her shoulder and made for the gate.

Towards the monster making its way into Durum.

"Oh Gods," Willow gasped, seeing it closer now. It looked almost like a man—a man who had been piteously melted. Its face was like candle wax, one eye drooping down to its chin. It crawled and struggled against the tunnel wards like it was possessed to destroy the city. All the while the purple nimbus crackled and snapped at the air.

"Stand tall, Willow," Annabelle ordered, and gestured to the creeping doom which was still taking the warded tunnel apart piece by piece. Willow didn't want to look at it, so she kept her eyes fixed on Annabelle. "This is your test."

"My what?"

"Your test. My mentor, Carl's mentor, he sent you this… beast. To prove yourself to him. I think Carl knew it was coming. Our master is a harsh instructor who doesn't suffer mistakes lightly. He has made this creature your test, Willow, and if you do not defeat it, this city will burn."

"W-Why me?"

"Don't you know?"

Willow looked from Annabelle's stone-serious face and back towards the center of the walled city of Durum. Towards the Arcanum at the pinnacle, which still shone even though the world was ending all around. Across at the men and women pulling survivors and bodies alike from the rubble.

The beast had blasted apart wood, steel, and silver. It was now coming for her. For all of them.

"Willow?" Annabelle pleaded, catching Willow's gaze.

She pointed at the approaching doom, and Willow reluctantly followed her gesture. It was closer now, barely three hundred feet away, and the air had taken on the tang of an approaching storm. She saw a thin bolt of lightning crackle from its back towards the ground as it burst yet another band of the warded tunnel and made its way forwards.

"Because I can," Willow answered and shifted on the unstable rubble until she faced the broken gateway. The creature paused for a moment, locked eyes with her across the great distance, and there was silence.

Then it screamed.

A high scream like a man's but warped as it came through the creature's throat. It clawed at the earth with too-human hands and tried to pull itself under the warded tunnel. Towards her. It was targeting her like the deathworm.

She knew then that *she* had caused this. Her very presence in this city was a clarion call for disaster. Everyone around her died. Carl, Leopold. Even when she'd tried to keep him away, she couldn't help but hurt him. And now the city was doomed as well.

Margaret and Benny! Their faces flashed in her mind, just for a moment. If this beast came through the destroyed gates, they wouldn't stand a chance.

Willow looked at Annabelle, but the woman was gone. She'd abandoned her to face the monstrosity on her own. She faced the encroaching doom again, squared her shoulders, and took a shuddering breath. Even though her arm was charred and bleeding, she visualized the essence swirling within. Bending her mutilated elbow, she took the stance Carl showed her.

"In, then out," he said in her memory, her last memory of him, and she filled her lungs to the brim. As she exhaled, she pushed the essence in her arm through her chest and felt the familiar tremolo in her heart.

When the essence reached her left arm, it had doubled in volume. Her arm felt full to bursting with power, but she mingled the essence there with the essence that had come in from her cycle. Then she took another breath, moving the blob of essence back through her chest.

The pendant around her neck warmed at the passage of the essence, and she felt her heart skip a beat. The essence pooled in her right arm. She blew the air in her lungs out and moved it back to her left.

Every time she cycled, the essence doubled in volume. Had Carl known this would happen? That it wouldn't be just a slight increase, but a massive boost? Her lungs spasmed at the passage of the essence, but she moved the blob back across again.

There was fear. Yes, there was fear—like there had been in the training room. A selfish fear for herself, and fear for those around her. She'd gone from being a burden to being a danger so quickly the emotions were all mixed up in her head. She'd attracted the deathworm, and she'd attracted this warbeast as well. Everyone was dead because of her. She knew she had to destroy the warbeast or die trying.

The creature seemed to realize what she was doing because instead of pushing forwards, it anchored itself on the ground and the purple nimbus on its back brightened. Willow could feel the hair on the left side of her scalp rise as the creature did something with its essence. She knew she didn't have long before it fired.

Willow moved the essence blob back into her right hand. When she raised it to her chest in a spell-form she was surprised to see that her skin was transparent, lit from within. She placed her pointer and middle finger against her chest, right below the pendant. The silver became uncomfortably hot.

She blew out the final breath, swept her fingers towards the creature, and intoned the concept.

"Scouring flame."

Fire essence exploded from her fingers in a line through the gate, catching the smoldering wood aflame. At the same instant, the creature let loose with its attack. A finger-thin bolt of lightning arced from its back through the air and met Willow's beam. They warped as they passed each other, and then the bolt raced along Willow's arc of flame and slammed into her full force.

She fell into darkness.

Dean Weatherby's Interlude

It was Dean Corinth Weatherby who ordered the sounding of the home call—which hadn't blared for over a hundred years—in the observation tower of the Monstruwacans. As the massive copper plates reverberated with their deafening drone, he reflected that all he had worked to be known for prior to this moment was nothing in comparison. From this point on, his tenure as Dean of the Arcanum of Durum would be highlighted by the sounding of the call.

And the approaching warbeast.

The chief Monstruacan stood beside him and watched through a massive crystal plate as the new monstrosity approached the city from the west. They both knew the meaning of such a bearing, although neither would freely admit to the implications. If this wasn't a ploy at subterfuge, then this creature had come from Asche.

War was upon them once more.

For the last few days, he'd been receiving updates from the Monstruacans. Memos that warned of increasing essential gradients to the west and strange movements in the city's own warbeast: the Rotting Hound. He periodically received reports on the Hound—it was, after all, the Monstruacans' duty to catalog and report the movement of all magical creatures and warbeasts which surrounded the city. But these reports had the scent of terror on them. A fear of the unknown.

An hour before, the chief Monstruacan had arrived breathless at his office, sweating through his thick outer robe, and begged the dean to follow him up to the tower. In all their years of sitting side-by-side at faculty events, he'd never seen the chief so shaken. So he swept out from behind his desk and followed the Monstruacan to the small brass cage that whisked them up to the highest point in the Arcanum, and of the city itself.

They'd registered a glow over the horizon in the last few minutes. Once they trained their sensitive instruments on that point, they were able to get essential readings, and those didn't bode well. Essence capacity the like of which they'd never seen before. The air seemed to split and come back together from the passage of the fell beast. What it could be, none knew, but its approach was an ill omen.

He, technically the Mayor of Durum from his post at the Arcanum, made the decision to sound the home call. To close the gates that had been open for a century. To protect his people.

What he didn't expect—what none of the Monstruacans expected—was the reaction of the Rotting Hound. When the approaching warbeast crested the last hill, which had until then mercifully spared the viewing crystals from its visage, the Rotting Hound began a charge from the north of the city. Dean Weatherby had never seen the Hound move so swiftly, although it had been written of in ages past.

"What does it mean?" he'd asked the chief Monstruacan, who only responded by shaking his head.

It had been even longer than a century that two warbeasts were on the field at once, and more than three hundred years since those two were from opposing city-states. What that meant, no one knew. Would they team up, finally stirring the Rotting Hound from its stupor to attack the walls anew?

It didn't take long for them to find out. They watched through the magnified screen as the Hound leaped over the warded tunnel and bounded towards the crawling thing. Its form was truly hideous to behold, and the dean had the sickening impression that this warbeast had been based on a human body. What sickness of the mind could lead man to twist the form of his fellow man?

The Hound and the creature met in brutal combat. Monstruacans around the transparent domed pinnacle of the school shouted readings as each clash produced scrolls of data that would be later analyzed. The creature threw the Hound to the side like a wet bag of mulch and loped towards the warded tunnel—as if it knew where it was!

The Rotting Hound made one last attempt at the creature's life, and the creature threw it in the air, unleashing its true might. Lightning speared down from the heavens and sprayed against the Hound, which hit the ground in a boneless smoking heap. The creature reached the churned delta at the entrance to the tunnel and began burrowing into the wards.

"Gods," Dean Weatherby whispered.

Monstruacans were shouting numbers that made the chief's face pale beside him, but the dean knew there was nothing more they could do. The sounding of the home call would set the wall guard to preparing the ancient cannons. Soon enough, they'd see the creature destroyed by the city's defenses, pummeled by the cannons until it was little more than ash scattered under the warded—

No! The guard wouldn't be able to see the creature, not if it was crawling through the warded tunnel. Even with the Monstruacans' instruments, it was nearly impossible to discern the beast through the interference. Every few seconds, a band of warding popped free to expose a slash of pale flesh, but nothing more came clear to them.

They were being blinded by their own defenses.

Dean Weatherby removed the intricately inscripted device from the inside pocket of his robe. A symbol of those days when the defense of the city rested solely on the power of the Arcanum, he'd received it when he'd been elevated to the position of dean. Many thought the device was purely ceremonial.

Not so. He slid a brass switch, and the cover of the device hinged down. A filigreed plate within began spinning at high speed, and he spoke into the whirling metal.

"This is Dean Corinth Weatherby. All able-bodied mages are ordered to appear at the western gate. A warbeast is approaching."

Short and sweet, an easy-to-follow order. Any mage who'd graduated from the Arcanum would have an inscribed plate that both proved their credentials and also served as a short-range receiver for the dean's broadcast. Soon, at least a hundred mages would arrive at the gate to battle the creature, and they'd see how strong it truly was trapped in that tunnel.

The large crystal screen flashed white, and then a distant boom shook the glass panes of the observatory. The dean looked at the chief Monstruacan, but the man was already shouting orders about tuning and filtering the lens.

Long seconds passed until the image came back. The creature was still there, distorted in the tunnel, but a plume of smoke drifted between it and the observatory. One of the tuners panned the image down to utter devastation. The inner wall just above the gates had been rent and brutalized. The gates were nowhere to be seen. Stone, wood, and silver littered the staging area before the western gate, splashes of red indicating sights best left unseen.

"Gods," it was the chief Monstruacan's turn to mutter. "It blasted the gate."

Dean Weatherby could do nothing but watch as the creature clawed its way through the tunnel. Some of the turrets above let off half-hearted shots where the warded bands had popped and they could see the creature's flesh, but none wanted to damage the tunnel any more than it already was. He couldn't have told them to do otherwise. The tunnel's defenses were such that even their most massive cannons wouldn't be able to penetrate the warded bands.

"Sir," a Monstruacan shouted, and a flurry of hand movements panned the screen down even further and zoomed in.

There were bodies strewn about—things the dean didn't want to see—but among those were two women standing directly before the gate. One, dressed in the white robe of the Sisters of Mercy, supported the other as they gazed out at the oncoming creature. The dean wanted to scream at them to run. Why wasn't this nurse taking the wounded woman away? It was clear she'd been terribly burned on one half of her body. Her hair was melted to the right side of her head.

"Demter, release the sighting glass—" the chief Monstruacan said, but he was interrupted by the observer in question.

"These numbers are off the charts," he yelled, hands flying furiously over his own crystal plate, and an overlay appeared on the large plate. The woman in white had a thin yellow glow suffusing her body, which the dean assumed was a measure of her essence.

The wounded woman, however, was something else altogether.

Purple nodes dotted her legs and back, a countless number, and a white glow shifted back and forth from arm to arm. The nurse had let the woman go, stumbling back into the rubble and fleeing, but the wounded woman held her ground. As he looked longer, he began to recognize the motion.

Cycling? This was the first of his mages come to defend the city from the creature? The colors on the screen meant nothing to him, but when he turned to the chief Monstruacan to inquire, the man's face was ashen.

"That's... impossible," the man said, and the dean looked back at the screen.

The blob of essence moving from arm to arm had intensified to the point that it overwhelmed the lens, leaving only a slowly shifting white-out. The interrupting Monstruacan tapped on the screen, and the overlay disappeared.

The woman was standing on her own—how she could with those injuries, he had no guess—and laid her fingers on her chest. Her right hand, horribly burned from the savage attack, was *glowing*. She swept her fingers out in what the dean recognized as a spell-form.

A thin line of fire exploded from her fingertips and passed instantaneously through the gate. In response, purple lightning arced along the stream of fire, landing directly beside the woman and blowing her off her feet. The screen whited out completely, and the Monstruacans scrambled until the image pulled back, revealing an overview of the carnage, the gate, and the warded tunnel beyond.

It was a maelstrom. Everything west of the city was on fire for a thousand feet. The massive creature was burning and scrabbling at the ground in a localized inferno, then collapsed and exploded in a crackle of lightning. There was fire everywhere, which meant the warded tunnel had been completely destroyed. The devastation was unreal.

"I'm going down there," the dean said to nobody in particular and swept out of the silent observatory.

By the time Dean Weatherby got to the remains of the western staging area, the ruins were crawling with mages and medical personnel. He stumbled across the broken scree, staring dumbfounded at the carnage. Bodies lay covered with bloody sheets, amputated limbs piled in front of cafes and shops. He made his way through the scurry of activity towards the place where the two women had been standing. The fires outside the city were guttering now, but the creature was still burning like magnesium.

A young man screamed in pain as two mages worked to lift a stone block off his legs. The dean glanced back at him, then quickly turned away at the grievous injury. It would be a miracle if the boy ever walked again.

"Willow," he screamed, clawing at shards of stone and silver, attempting to drag himself towards the gate. "Where is Willow? Willow!"

In the fugue state the dean found himself in, the name struck a memory. A thin young woman sat before his desk—he hoped to smooth over a potential litigation nightmare. Not only had students of his used Arcanum resources to perform a near-lethal experiment, but then they'd had the gall to disappear before disciplinary proceedings. The entire episode was extremely embarrassing for both him and the Arcanum. If he could convince her that they would be dealt with if and when they were found, all might be forgiven.

"Willow," the young man sobbed as a nurse held him down while a doctor wove anesthesia over his head. His eyes began to droop, and he murmured. "She was right there."

Dean Weatherby looked where the young man's hand had dropped, pointing towards the gate, and he saw her again. Not seated, but standing. Not whole, but burned.

Could it be? That young woman. That... waif?

He looked out the broken gate to the city, past the field of flames and ash, towards the undulating hills in the distance. Towards the wild. Towards Asche.

Acknowledgements

I'd like to thank my agent, Ed Kim, for always having my back. Also my editor, Kirsten Lund, who worked tirelessly and enthusiastically to bring this world and its characters to life. And I'd like to thank my beta readers: My critique group Sue Quinn, Rebecca Devendra, and Alayna Frankenberry; My sister, Erin Cox; and all of my followers on RoyalRoad who went on this journey with me.

And I would love to thank my wife, Caitlin, not only for her invaluable advice, but also for believing in me. And my son, Malcolm, who keeps me grounded and helps me remember what's really important.

MORE BOOKS YOU MAY LIKE

Blueprints for Tomorrow by M.J. Markgraf

Every upgrade pushes Alexander closer to a power others would kill for.

On a dusty fringe station far from civilized space, Alexander scrapes by repairing the junk no one else will touch. The shop is a dead end, and his memory is fractured, yet each job sharpens instincts he can't explain and reactivates dormant systems with capabilities no civilian machine should possess.

Alexander knows he isn't built like any other robot, and someone has noticed.

A pirate lord has marked him for capture, convinced Alexander can build the war engines he needs to elevate his rag-tag fleet into an empire.

As Alexander unlocks the secrets within his damaged body, he's thrust into a fight to protect the only people who've shown him kindness. He will have to rebuild shattered defenses, restore derelict stations, and reverse-engineer stolen technology to keep his new home alive and lay the first foundations of an enterprise that will one day shape the frontier.

Perfect for fans of *Bobiverse*, *Backyard Starship*, and *Expeditionary Force*.

Available now on Kindle Unlimited, Audible, and in paperback!

***Tiny Dungeon Core* by The Bearded Man**

Discover a dungeon worth rooting for in this exciting LitRPG series for fans of Dungeon Life and The Bee Dungeon.

A new dungeon is born…
and it's unlike anything the world has seen.

In a realm of epic quests and powerful gods, the tiniest dungeon core ever created is about to prove that size isn't everything. Armed with a mysterious system and a handful of fiercely loyal creatures, the Core must grow, adapt, and defend itself against a world that sees it as prey.

But building up a dungeon is no easy task when you're practically pocket-sized. Every upgrade, skill, and creature summoned is a gamble for survival. One misstep could spell destruction.

Don't miss the start of this LitRPG adventure with a non-human protagonist, strategic base-building, and a unique take on dungeon fantasy. Expect a story that blends light progression, loyal monster allies, and slice-of-life with rising stakes.

Available now on Kindle Unlimited, Audible, and in paperback!

Thank you for reading a MoonQuill original novel. More exciting stories can be found on at www.moonquill.com.

We would greatly appreciate it if you could take a moment to leave a review. Each one helps the author and supports their ability to continue writing fantastic books for everyone to enjoy!

Scan the QR code below to subscribe to our mailing list and be notified of new releases. You'll receive a few ebooks for free!